THE MOST HOPELESS CASE

John Pease

The Most
Hopeless Case

John Hearson

Chapter 1

Olivia and I had just switched on the radio for the 7 o'clock news. We caught the tail end of the short programme that preceded it, 'Point of View'.

"...How *could* He?" thundered the speaker. "He's the most mean-minded, fickle-natured, egotistical bully you could ever imagine. The very last person you would ever want to meet. It's a pity he doesn't exist, because if he did, I'd love to ask him why he made a world full of misery from start to end. Why a world full of sickness, hunger, wars, cruelty, earthquakes, typhoons, tsunamis? If he's omnipotent, then why doesn't he put an end to all this carnage? Or if he's powerless to prevent it, then creating a world like this is the very height of recklessness, irresponsibility and gross negligence on a cosmic scale.

"And yet the high priests of religion go on claiming he's a 'loving god'! What god would allow children to die with emaciated, malnourished bodies whilst fat cats sail their luxury yachts? What god would invent wasps that sting caterpillars to paralyse them for a life of slavery as they are eaten alive day after day by the larvae? What god would create Motor Neurone Disease and callously watch people die as, little by little, their bodily systems shut down?

"And worse still, these same high priests turn around and claim that euthanasia is immoral! Having invented a god of cruelty, they tell us there's no escape – no hope for the chronically sick other than to endure day after day of pitiful existence until, having exhausted every last drop of needless suffering, they finally, mercifully, die of 'natural causes'."

Finally the speaker ended his rant. It was almost a relief to hear Big Ben chime. The news was a little less gloomy, although not much so. The pound had once again lost value against all major currencies. Another car bomb had exploded in Baghdad. Islamist extremists had made progress in capturing another Middle Eastern city. Another prominent celebrity was to face historical child abuse claims. And… inevitably, another round of 'cost savings' in the NHS. For that, read job losses, ward closures, extended waiting lists, outsourced services, and more highly paid consultants' fees as 'experts' were engaged to implement the changes. Olivia and I were both 'specialist trainee' surgeons – registrars, as the term used to be - and had grown used to the never-ending cycle of trying to do 'more with less'. This modern virtue has become so praiseworthy in today's topsy-turvy world that flies in the face of all common sense.

It was Friday evening, and Olivia was tired after a full working week. Mine continued into Saturday although I had Wednesday off. We decided to brew coffee then to watch a Star Trek film.

"He had a good point, don't you think?" said Olivia as she came in with two mugs and the cafetiere. "About euthanasia, I mean?"

"I certainly agree there," said I. "I found I got quite angry when I listened to that guy speaking. Particularly after my ordeal in El Fasher. If I'd thought there was a god before I went there, I was pretty well convinced there wasn't when I left."

As Olivia poured the coffee, a further thought occurred to me.

"Anyway, I'm going to throw a challenge to this so-called god. I'm going to pick the most hopeless person I can find, someone who's a perfect case for euthanasia, and issue a challenge to he-she-it to make their life worth living. Then let's see what he-she-it's really made of!"

Olivia laughed at me. She enjoyed poking fun at my little hobby-horses and the random questions I posed for myself to answer. I loved standing at a bus stop betting how long it would take the bus to arrive, and whether two would come at once…

-o-O-o-

My alarm buzzed at 6:45 on Saturday morning. I got up, made myself a quick breakfast then took Olivia a cup of tea. I put on my coat and gloves then grabbed my umbrella. I headed out of the lift into a blustery April shower and strode along the pavement for my fifteen minute walk to the Royal Somershire Infirmary. My ward rounds began at 8:30 a.m. so I had time for a quick cup of coffee in the doctors' mess room before donning my lanyard that held my badge stating my identity as

Mr. James McAlister
Specialist Trainee,
Oral and Maxillofacial Surgery

We worked on weekends because the hospital managers were determined to tackle the backlog of surgical procedures so that we could only fail to meet the infirmary's performance targets by a small, rather than a large, margin. Following my ward rounds, I went to the consulting rooms to begin a series of appointments. I saw a whole spectrum of patients, some awaiting surgical procedures and others in various stages of recovery. Three of those I saw in the morning were new. The first two were to have their impacted wisdom teeth removed. This is a relatively simple procedure once you master the use of the drill employed to cut the tooth so you can take it out in bits.

One of these patients, a young man of 27, was much more interested in his novel than his mouth. He was quite nonchalant about the whole affair. If all went to plan he would be a 'day case', probably on his way home by early evening. The other was a petite student aged 20, who was much more anxious about her fate. Her teeth were more seriously impacted and she was expecting to stay overnight. In my well-honed professional voice I reassured her that her case presented no unusual challenges. Within a week of her 'op' she'd be eating normally again and would probably be free from all the niggles that arise from wisdom teeth. I remarked that these had served our ancestors well but were a left-over relic from our evolutionary past.

But patient Number Three was not a routine case. It was my habit to briefly study each patient's notes immediately before I saw them. Deborah Loveless was in her mid-thirties. She'd been referred to us by her dentist who had diagnosed a serious case of periodontal disease. His notes indicated she needed a dental clearance or, in lay language, the taking out of all her remaining teeth. What was more, she suffered from a severe form of Multiple Sclerosis. The dentist was nervous about performing the extraction himself in view of the complications that her condition may have caused. I sighed. Dental clearances were sometimes necessary. Once in the operating theatre, we just got to work without any thought for the patients' feelings. The technical challenges involved in surgery consumed the whole of our attention. But outside the operating theatre I sometimes had throwbacks to the gruesome things I'd experienced in the El Fasher teaching hospital, Darfur, during my student placement. I didn't like making people toothless. It usually led to an improvement in their general health but I often felt it was taking away a part of their personality.

And so, I called her name. One minute later there was a knock on the door and in she came. A severe lady in her fifties wearing a blue-and-grey uniform wheeled her in. On the uniform was the name:

The Limes
A Carrington Care Home

I gazed at the chair's woeful occupant. What a pathetic sight she was! She couldn't move any part of her body apart from her head. Her fair hair was matted, and she wore cheap pink glasses with thick lenses that made her appear boggle-eyed. It would have been more accurate to describe the glasses as hanging loosely off her nose, as the side-pieces were badly distorted, one lying in a direction that pointed towards the ceiling rather than anywhere near her ear.

The carer added that Miss Loveless had no control over her bladder or bowels and so had to permanently wear incontinence slips. Miss Loveless raised her eyebrows and said,

"It's not quite true…"

"Oh, come on!" interjected the carer. "You're certainly incontinent as far as *we're* concerned."

I let matters rest. This wasn't my concern. But what did bother me as I read her 'medicines' sheet was the cocktail of pills she'd been prescribed, including some to treat a UTI (urinary tract infection) and also antidepressants. I reflected that she certainly had enough to be depressed about…but I made a recommendation in my notes that her medicines should be reviewed when she came into the ward.

"Doctor," she said, "will I really have to lose all my teeth?"

"I'm not actually a doctor," I said, "I'm a dentist who's become a surgeon. But anyway, open up and let me have a look."

Inside her mouth were the most inflamed gums I'd ever seen. I gently touched her lower teeth with my finger and, sure enough, found that they wobbled like candy sticks in jelly. Even had they been firm, they were hardly the prettiest teeth I'd seen…

"Absolutely," I said. "There's no other way your gums are going to recover from the infection that you've caught; it's too advanced. Periodontal disease affects your general health. If it's not checked, it can cause a life-threatening infection and we don't want to take chances. It needs doing straightaway so we've reserved a theatre slot for you on Monday. Never mind," I added with a professional shrug. "Most people in your position feel better for it. They adapt to wearing dentures relatively easily and are usually able to recover most of the function of their natural teeth."

I didn't add that adapting to dentures depended on keeping them clean, soaking them in cleansing agent and visiting the dentist regularly in the early stages so he could make adjustments. Judging by this lady's condition when she'd arrived for her appointment, I very much doubted she'd ever receive the care and support needed for a happy denture experience, if you could ever have one, that is.

"How long will it be before I get them?" she asked.

"Oh – didn't the dentist discuss this with you?" I asked. "Didn't he give you the option of having immediate dentures when you had your last appointment with him? He'd have needed to take impressions so you could have had a set made to bring with you into hospital. Otherwise it'll take three months for your gums to settle before the dentist takes the impressions for your new teeth."

These days, most people have a set of dentures made from impressions taken about a fortnight before their teeth are extracted. These are fitted straight afterwards, so that the patient can go back to work, for example, without the embarrassment of toothlessness. Most people would rather endure the painful process of wearing their dentures whilst their gums are still healing, than have to explain to everyone they meet why they've lost their teeth. Modern dentures can be made to match a patient's natural teeth almost exactly so other than close friends, no-one needs to know. It takes about a month before the patient can eat properly, and during this period they are likely to make several visits to their dentist to have rough edges removed where their gums are chaffing on the plastic in their mouths. However, the patient's gums shrink, rapidly at first, so their dentures become loose. After around three months, their dentist takes fresh impressions and has their permanent dentures made, which normally last for five years. These too need adjustments in the early stages but are usually less troublesome.

"No," said the lady. "He didn't talk to me about impressions or immediate dentures."

The carer interrupted at this point and shook her head. "Let me explain;

we've met this situation before in The Limes. There's no way we can take our residents to have immediate dentures altered every few days. Besides, a normal person can take their teeth out when they get sore. She won't be able to do this, so it'll be much more practical to let her gums heal and shrink over the next three months. Then she can go straight to having a permanent set."

Although the carer's words made sense, they were spoken with cold efficiency and with no hint of sympathy for the lady.

"You mean I've got to manage without teeth for over three months?" she said, her face reflecting the frustration that she hadn't been given any option.

I nodded. It struck me that someone should at least have explained to her what was the usual choice and why the home couldn't support her having immediate dentures. How must it have felt to be considered too disabled to have any say in one's own treatment?

Amidst tears, she gasped, "Are *you* going to do my operation?"

"Probably," I replied. "Or it could be my colleague Martin. He's at work tomorrow so he'll finalise the surgical list for Monday, whilst I'm playing rugby, that is…"

I wondered why I'd added such an irrelevance; on reflection I suppose I thought it would help lighten the lady's despair if I added a human touch.

-o-O-o-

It was 1 o'clock by the time I'd completed my morning consultations. As ever, I'd over-run my schedule and had only a twenty minute break before my first afternoon appointment. Sister Marion Harman normally worked on Ward 17 where our team's patients were accommodated. On this particular morning she had agreed to help with the consultations. Marion enjoyed looking after people, and I was very grateful to find she'd bought me a ham sandwich and a cake. She sat me down in the office she was using, and then made coffee for me.

"Goodness, that lady, Deborah Loveless is a picture, isn't she?" I said. "It's like meeting someone out of a horror movie. How come her mouth got so badly infected before anyone dealt with it?"

"You may well ask," said Marion. "As you saw, she lives in The Limes, just up Wolverstone Road. It's a small care home, mainly residential although it has some dementia patients and just a few disabled people, and she's only recently moved there. The home referred her to their dentist after she complained of toothache all over her mouth. The delay in treating her may have been her fault to some extent. I was talking to the carer who brought her, and they think she isn't 'all there' so it's been difficult to work out what's been wrong."

"Where was she before The Limes?" I asked.

"It's a really sad tale," replied Sister Marion. "She has a family but from what the carer understands, her partner ran off with another woman six months ago because he couldn't cope with her illness. Maybe he couldn't deal with her going wrong in the head, either. He left her with her two sons aged 7 and 10. She tried to cope alone with the help of two carers who visited every day, trying to organise the boys from her bed and electric wheelchair. Before long it became obvious the situation was beyond her so the boys were taken into care and Social Services found her a place at The Limes. It makes you weep, doesn't it?"

"All I know," I said, "is that if I was her and if anyone offered me a way out, a trip to Switzerland perhaps, I'd grasp it with open arms. No way is that lady's life worth living!"

Marion nodded in agreement. I downed the rest of my coffee and headed off to my next set of appointments.

I had certainly found my Euthanasia Case, he-she-it's big challenge. After arriving home, I waxed lyrical to Olivia as we worked together to prepare beef carbonara which we enjoyed with a bottle of Cotes du Rhone.

Chapter 2

On Sundays it was Olivia's turn to make breakfast. We enjoyed a lazy morning in bed, talking together and reading the news before taking an early lunch. My rugby game was at home, which meant I needed to be at the ground for 2 p.m.

Olivia meanwhile went riding with her companion Victoria, another doctor who, likewise, worked in Obs and Gynae. They both owned horses which they loaned out during the week to a riding school. The school provided their 'livery' for a much reduced fee. Besides her Sunday hacks, Olivia took lessons as she entered dressage competitions. Horses weren't my scene but I'd sometimes been to watch her compete. She looked splendid in her smart kit that she kept for such special occasions. I couldn't see the point in going around an arena in circles and loops but I appreciated it took skill to communicate with a horse at the level she'd achieved.

She'd been to watch me play rugby, just occasionally. She didn't understand the rules and didn't easily become impassioned about the game. Once she saw me score a try, and I saw her jumping up and down on the touchline with pleasure at my success. But today was a typical Somershire League Division Two game so there was no particular incentive for her to watch me.

Once into the game, my passions were aroused. I played as a wing three-quarter as I was a fast runner and able to dodge and swerve my way around the opposition. Once I'd had two or three touches of the ball, my adrenaline began to surge and I felt primal instincts kick in – the urge to conquer, to trample the opposition, to reach faster, higher, stronger than our foe. With twenty minutes gone, the ball was passed across from one three-quarter to another following a scrum on the other side of the field. I was last to receive the ball and saw my opposite number baring his teeth just 5 yards ahead. I ran towards him, side-stepped and pretended to pass, then stepped the other way right past him. Now to dart for the line. The opposition had regrouped quickly and I saw I'd have to pass three more players. I lowered the ball to my boot and kicked it along the ground, then sprinted after it for all I was worth. Unluckily for me, it bounced towards the touchline just a little too early and out of play.

Later in the half it was my opposite number's turn to bear down towards me. I realised that only I stood between him and the line. He was stronger and stockier than me, and looked angry and mean in attack. I focussed my attention away from his face and towards his lower body. As he accelerated past me I flung myself towards him, arms outstretched to grasp his waist. Got 'im! My arms lowered down his legs like a noose and he collapsed, sprawled out on the ground. Our full back did his job, falling on the loose ball so that a loose ruck could form around him. He released it to our advantage and we gained possession.

Halfway through the second half, with the Infirmary leading 13-7, we won a scrum on 'my' side of the field. The scrum half pretended to feed it to the stand-off half, but instead decided to dart around the 'blind side' and fed the ball to me. The opposition weren't expecting this. Here was my chance… if I could only dummy my way once more past my opposite number, I'd have a clear run at the line… I went for it, swerved to one side then the other… but this time he didn't buy my dummy. He tackled me and I came crashing down in a heap. To my horror I found I couldn't get up. The opposition full back had the ball, and kicked it miles up field and out of play. My opponent stretched out his hand and helped me to my feet. I could hardly move my right leg. Our coach saw my predicament and straightaway ran onto the pitch. After a brief attempt at a massage he substituted me and asked two other team members who were 'on the bench' to place an ice pack on what seemed to be the damaged area.

We ran out winners, 16-14. I wasn't a winner, however. One advantage of playing for a team of medics is that you receive the very best in the way of diagnosis. They quickly ascertained that I had superficial bruising, and was unlikely to have a fracture. But I could quite possibly have damaged a ligament. I'd have to be checked out tomorrow, Monday. A friend drove me home and I ran myself a hot bath so I could have a good soak before our evening Chinese takeaway.

Olivia arrived home at about 6 p.m. with several delicious-smelling cartons. I dragged myself out of the bath, dressed and stumbled into the dining room ready to enjoy it. Olivia watched my halting progress with amusement.

"You boys and your little games!" she teased.

Olivia had enjoyed her ride, in a matter-of-fact sort of way. She'd been admiring Victoria's new saddle which looked even smarter than hers, so wondered if she should spend out and replace hers for a similar type. It wasn't a cheap hobby, riding.

After a leisurely meal, Olivia kissed me goodbye and set out for her own apartment half a mile away. This was a convenient arrangement that seemed to offer the best of both worlds. At a weekend we were lovers, enjoying relaxing together and sharing my bed or hers, whilst during the week we kept our independent lives. We both liked to arrive home from a day at hospital, shut the door on the world outside, and then spend the remainder of the day recovering without having to speak to another soul. When I wasn't 'on call' I enjoyed nothing better than to crack open a Rioja and drink about two-thirds of it in an evening, watching TV or tackling the Guardian crossword. Exceptions for me were Tuesday night when I went to the gym, and Thursday when I played squash against Martin, my colleague, and two of his mates. For Olivia, Monday was Pilates night and Wednesday was Somershire Symphony Orchestra *evening* (not *night*, she kept reminding me) in which she featured on the oboe.

It was nice to have such a smart girlfriend with whom to go on holiday. I reflected that my injury could have come at a far worse time, as we'd enjoyed our annual ski trip two months previously.

Occasionally one or other set of parents would ask whether we were considering 'settling down and getting married'. No doubt grandchildren were their main motivation for asking. For my part, I fended off the question. Why tie myself down when I was perfectly happy to enjoy life's pleasures with no strings attached? In common with many intelligent post-modern young men, I regarded the compulsion to bear children as Evolution's way of ensuring the survival of my genes. The world is seriously over-populated already and my view was that I had no intention of dancing to this ancient tune and contributing more hungry mouths for 21st century farmers to feed. Perhaps I might alter my view in future, but certainly not yet. And as for marriage? This was an antiquated social convention that underpinned Evolution's purposes, reinforced by that necessary but deceptive evil, religion. Well, did Karl Marx observe that this was the opiate of the people, used by successive generations of elites to suppress their poor subjects and equally so by Evolution to insulate the human population against the harsh realities of a cold, dark, sinister world? Too many of my friends had married with lavish celebrations at great expense, only for their relationships to end in disaster and disillusionment with the inevitable acrimony of their divorce settlement.

Besides, much though I enjoyed Olivia's company, her intelligent conversation and her skilful sex technique, I stopped short of telling myself that I wanted to spend the rest of my life with her. Things seemed just fine the way they were.

-o-O-o-

Sure enough, my leg was stiff the next morning. I wasn't sure I'd be able to perform surgery but decided to go to work and assess the situation. Certainly I'd need to be checked out. I called a taxi to take me in. Martin, my colleague, arrived at the same time. We both had ward rounds, followed by a mixture of consultations and surgery so we decided to rearrange our schedules so that he took over my theatre duties. I called our consultant Mr. Davy who gave his approval, saying it was important to get me 'sorted out'. My revised schedule would also allow me time to visit the sports injury clinic in the afternoon, so I booked myself an appointment.

I wasn't looking forward to seeing Miss Loveless again. I was at the other end of Ward 17 when she arrived. An ambulance man wheeled her into the ward, whereupon Sister Marion and Grace, the Filipino nurse, busied themselves settling her in. I could vaguely hear some sort of animated talk between the two nurses but kept out of the way.

At 3 o'clock I hobbled into the clinic. From a cursory examination they suspected I'd sustained moderate to severe knee ligament damage and this was confirmed by an ultra-sound scan. The ligament was partially, but not completely torn. They gave me a brace to wear and booked me in for physio. I was to exercise my leg gently but was advised that I'd have to take a three month break from rugby and to make sure I built up my strength with an exercise programme before resuming. Oh joy! They gave me a crutch to support myself as I walked until the pain wore off. At least I would now be able to perform my surgical duties and to walk unaided.

It was half past five by the time I finished my consultations. I'd left some belongings in Sister Marion's office so headed back to Ward 17. I couldn't resist asking how Miss Loveless had fared. Marion's eyes rolled, and a pained expression came over her face.

"James, I don't know what's been going on, but our first job was to change her incontinence slip. It wasn't fun, I can tell you…but you should have seen the state of her bum. She's got one of the angriest rashes I've ever seen. To make matters worse, she complained that when she urinated into her pad, she suffered from severe pain. Whatever treatment she's been having, certainly hasn't been working. Poor soul, she needs a lot more than her teeth seeing to. I don't know what the home's been playing at, but they should never have allowed her to get such an awful nappy rash, and someone should have sorted out her UTI ages ago. We've called for an urologist who's coming to see her tomorrow, so she's staying overnight. It's not our ward's job, I know, but we can't let her go home like this. Meanwhile we should be able to make some progress in treating her bum with cream."

I liked Marion's approach very much. She was an old-fashioned nurse who treated the patients, not just their conditions. She was thorough, organised and cheerful, and she instilled this in the junior staff members who worked on our ward.

"So, did her extraction go alright?" I asked.

"Yes, as far as I know it was straightforward," said Marion. "She came back to the ward and went to sleep, so we've just left her in peace."

Just then, Marion looked out of her office window.

"Here, she's just woken up so you can see her if you like?"

This was definitely not what I'd intended. Concerned I may have been, but I didn't want to be reminded of the horror story that her life presented. But it was too late to stop Marion's determined march towards the lady's bed. Marion placed the lady's glasses on her nose, turned around and announced,

"Mr. McAlister's here to see you."

Straightaway the lady turned her head in my direction and those boggle eyes, reminiscent of a toad, watched my reluctant advance. She opened her mouth to reveal the ghastly sight of bloodied gums, the ugly residue of where her teeth had been.

Over the years I had treated many a patient with far worse injuries and had become hardened to the brutal aspects of their treatment. But somehow this lady's condition had reminded me of earlier traumas of my own. I fought to overcome my sense of panic. It brought back such dreadful memories of writhing bodies on stretchers fresh from the front lines of Darfur's civil war, of mangled arms and legs, of the horror of having to steel every nerve in my body whilst using that most awful of implements – the surgical saw…

I approached the bed, trying to look the other way. Like a spectre, she articulated a faint sound which I thought may have been an attempt to address me. It sounded like,

"Daimth – dibuimn."

I remembered Marion's comments that she wasn't all there. Were these the ramblings of a mad woman? However, as I forced my head to turn around towards her she repeated,

"Dibuimn?"

Summoning a superhuman effort to overcome my revulsion, I looked at the stumps of her gums which resembled the battle of The Somme. At least all the poison would soon be gone and she'd have a healthier mouth. I just said,

"Well, all done now. I'll see you tomorrow."

I turned to make my way out of the ward.

"Dibuimn tzwub-bee?"

Help arrived in the form of Grace. I quietly explained that this patient seemed to want to ask me a question but I was getting ready to go home and I hadn't time or patience to find out what it was. I was about to put on my coat, but if she could get some sense out of the ghostly lady, please could she call me back to the bed.

I was all dressed for departure when Grace summoned me. "What she asks you, is- 'James, did you win at rugby?' She can't articulate her words properly, poor soul."

I returned to the bed. I felt quite touched that this pathetic lady had learnt my name from reading my badge on Saturday, and that she'd remembered what I was doing on my day off.

I didn't want a conversation with her so I replied professionally. I thanked her for asking. I explained that yes, indeed, we'd won our game. I walked out of the ward and, with the aid of my crutch, walked home.

Chapter 3

On Tuesday morning, which happened to be my birthday, I limped into work using my crutch. Wearing my brace, I felt relatively comfortable when standing straight up, so I was sure I'd be able to perform my surgical duties as normal. I decided to play safe and use my crutch to walk down the hospital's interminable corridors, leaving it at the nurses' stations whilst doing my rounds.

Oh God, I thought as I entered Ward 17, *I'm about to meet The Toothless Wonder again.* Like the previous afternoon, my approach didn't escape her notice. She seemed to have recovered a little from her latest ordeal, and was less reminiscent of a wartime casualty. Instead I was reminded of a woodland walk I'd once done in the North Downs after it had been decimated by gale-force winds. Many trees had been ripped out of the soil, and there had been no choice but to chop off all but the stumps. These were left to rot, leaving gaping holes where they'd previously been anchored in the ground.

In a slightly louder whisper than previously, she said,

"Heyo Daimth. Why you yimpim'?"

I rolled my eyes and summoned Grace, who was busy taking blood pressures three beds away. Grace laughed.

"Come on, James!" she teased. "You'd never make an interpreter, would you? It's obvious – she says, 'Hello, James, why are you limping?'"

"Tell her I got injured playing rugby," I said.

Grace looked into my eyes with a serious expression. "No, James," she said, "it was you that she asked, not me. You need to answer her question."

Seeing there was no escape, I looked vaguely in the toothless woman's direction and explained that I'd got injured in a rugby tackle.

"How bab ith ip?" came the immediate reply.

"Look here, I'm the medic!" I answered, becoming increasingly impatient.

"Well if you must know, I've sustained a moderate-to-severe knee ligament injury and I have to miss rugby for three months. Now open your mouth, let's have a look."

Her gums certainly appeared less of a bloody mess than yesterday so I added the words, '*Satisfactory progress with healing gums*' to her notes, and prepared to move on. But I hadn't escaped yet.

"Daimth, cam I pway for you? Cam I pyathe my hamb on your mee?"

I looked at her with consternation. Was she asking what I thought she was? Once again I summoned Grace, whose long patience was wearing thin. The spectre repeated her words, and Grace said,

"She wants to lay her hand on your knee and pray for you. I think she must be a Christian of some sort."

"For God's sake, Grace, it's her that needs healing, not me!" I said taking notice of Grace's anxiety that I'd raised my voice. "She's hardly an advert for what she's offering to do, is she? Now I can understand what Marion and the people from her home mean when they say she isn't all there!"

Grace replied, "Go on, James, humour her. She'll be out soon, after the urologist's been to see her." She, like many Filipinos, was a Catholic and had some limited sympathies with the lady's request.

By this time I was seriously rattled but agreed that we'd draw the curtains around her bed, and then I'd sit on her visitor's chair whilst Grace placed her hand on my knee.

I felt irritated, made to look stupid and felt highly embarrassed by the whole affair. So with her limp hand on my skin, she said,

"Hoyee thpiwip, foryer om Daimth now. Fiyer hith bobby with you yove. In Dethuth mame, Mee, be heayedz!"

Once again I had to ask Grace to interpret. She asked the lady to repeat what she'd said. With great effort the lady contorted her mouth to better articulate her words.

"She says, 'Holy Spirit, fall on James now. Fill his body with your love. In Jesus, name, knee, be healed!'"

I looked at the lady and said,

"Okay, thanks, I don't believe there's anything in this healing business at all, but I appreciate the thought. *Now goodbye!*"

And I opened the curtains, turned away very deliberately, and moved on. Tomorrow was my day off. With any luck she'd have gone back to the home by the time I came around on Thursday.

I enjoyed my Wednesday lie-in. I hobbled out of bed, put on my brace, then made a pot of leaf tea and warmed up a croissant which I ate with a little butter and lashings of marmalade. I opened my birthday cards, all six of them, enjoyed a few giggles at the fond comments that my family and Olivia had made, and placed them on the window sill.

I reflected that I'd enjoyed a particularly good night's sleep. I often had nightmares and it wasn't unusual for me to wake early with a particular sense of gloom that only dissipated once I'd become absorbed in my work, been out shopping or chatted to Olivia. She talked me through my feelings one morning and we worked out that I was probably still suffering from delayed reactions to the trauma I'd witnessed in El Fasher. This was during my student placement eight years previously which I'd taken up just as the war in Darfur had started to escalate.

I had gone into medicine with a strong sense of vocation. I'd been a passionate, caring young man. Perhaps this made it all the harder when I could feel the heartbreak and hopelessness of families who had lost everything; children who had lost parents, brothers and sisters; and of those who had lost limbs and become disfigured. As the carnage worsened day by day my mental anguish only grew greater and after my return to England I had to take counselling for Post-Traumatic Stress Disorder. I converted to dentistry which provided a good alternative career. But over time I began to miss the world of the operating theatre where I'd shown a lot of promise, and eventually found a route back by specialising in oral and maxillofacial surgery.

-o-O-o-

It was a lovely spring morning and I thought I'd head out across the park then do a bit of shopping. Should I bother with my crutch? Yes, okay, it would be best to play safe. I walked out of the lift, and then headed across the road. The trees were just bursting into leaf. Somehow I noticed the interplay of the sunlight on the infant leaves as never before. It was as if the world was coming to life in a whole symphony of shapes and colours. I walked past an elderly couple who pleasantly said, "Good morning." Funny, I didn't usually greet anyone on my walks. It occurred to me that for some reason I hadn't bothered to don my regulation headphones to listen to music on my mobile.

The busy High Street lay on the other side of the park. A rather rough-hewn man sporting military medals and an official-looking badge, wearing a beret, was holding a collection tub and asked me for a contribution to 'Soldiers Off the Streets'. The cocooned world of my phone normally provided immunity from such requests. I plopped a £2 coin into his tub and said, "Keep up the good work."

I walked along the High Street then turned onto the road that would take me back home along the side of the park. Waitrose was about 250 yards from home, so I went in with a list of about ten items to purchase. At the checkout was a sight I normally dreaded. I'd forgotten the schools were still on holiday and a group of girl guides were bag-packing. My standard approach was to say I didn't need help and ask them to stand aside, and then toss a few 10 and 20 pence coins into the bucket. I looked into the face of the girl at the end of the aisle, wearing her smart blue uniform. Mine was only a small shop, but I thought how it would actually give her pleasure to pack my bag, so I let her help then tossed a pound into the bucket.

The guide leader saw my crutch and asked, "Sir, have you far to walk with your shopping?"

I replied that I should be okay thank you. It was only three minutes up the road. The lady smiled and said,

"Please let us help you. It'll be a pleasure."

I looked into the lady's eyes. She meant what she'd said. Reluctantly, I surrendered my detached self-reliance and allowed two girl guides to walk home with my bags. On the way they told me how excited they were about going camping and kayaking off the north Wales coast in June, for which they were doing the bag pack. As we approached my block of flats, I reached into my wallet for a fiver but the girls pre-empted me, smiled, and simply said,

"No, sir. We've really enjoyed carrying your bags."

-o-O-o-

Thursday dawned. I got up as usual and set out for the hospital. I reflected with a smile on the fact that my knee hadn't miraculously healed, not that I'd ever expected it to. It felt a little better just as I'd anticipated, in tune with the course of nature. Following my usual routine I downed a coffee then set out for the wards. I arrived at the nurses' station on Ward 17. Surely Miss Euthanasia wouldn't still be in residence?

Well, yes, she was. The urologist had indeed been to see her on Tuesday and had organised bacterial culture tests. Meanwhile she was to be treated with a different broad spectrum antibiotic that he hoped would prevent her infection becoming worse. He had been sufficiently concerned about her to recommend that she stay in hospital for an extra day or two, under observation. Marion commented that she seemed more comfortable today. The urologist would be visiting shortly. Marion thought he'd be discharging her, and proudly told me how much less sore the lady's bottom was. She'd make sure several bottles of cream accompanied her on her return to The Limes.

It was then that I realised that I wasn't dreading meeting the lady again. I was, in fact, quite looking forward to demonstrating my non-healing. But also, I wondered what surprise she'd come up with today. The point was she'd made life interesting. A picture of misery she may have presented, deluded she may be, but she was a 'somebody'.

I looked into the ward to where she lay in bed. But she wasn't alone. A tall gentleman dressed in a dark overcoat was talking to her. As I approached, I noticed his dog collar. My colleague Martin, who'd done her extraction on Monday, was also by her bedside and said,

"Ah, good morning, James. Can I introduce you to the Reverend Gilbert McPherson?"

It turned out that the goodly reverend was the minister of Patterdale Road Baptist Church. The hospital chaplain had been doing his rounds and it seems the lady had explained that she now lived in a care home and wished to find a church. The chaplain had contacted Rev. McPherson as Patterdale Road was the closest place of worship to The Limes. This was his first encounter with her, and I wondered if he knew what he was letting himself in for. They'd been discussing how to get her there on Sundays. Rev. McPherson, in his pleasant Scottish accent, said that normally this should be no problem but that this particular Sunday, most of the people he'd ask were away.

Martin loved to tease, and had found my rugby injury quite a source of amusement. He said,

"You should ask James here. He's not doing anything on Sunday for the next three months…"

I could have crowned him! Quickly I made out as to run away, then said,

"*No way on God's earth!* Sorry, Reverend, but I won't be darkening the doors of any church this Sunday!"

Grace had appeared by this time in response to the mock commotion, and, with great delight, said,

"Come on, James! This is just the job for you. You'll find it easier to push a wheelchair than to walk with a crutch!"

Then came the voice I dreaded. "Pleath, Daimth. I'b like you der tzake me."

I noticed that she was regaining her ability to pronounce some of her vowels.

I made the mistake of looking into her boggled eyes. As a result, I said, "Yes."

Note on The War in Darfur:-

The genocide in Darfur has been one of the bitterest conflicts in recent history outside the Middle East with an estimated half a million people killed and three million displaced. It began as a dispute over grazing rights when population growth outstripped the capacity of Western Sudan to sustain the eight million people who live there. Tensions escalated after oil was discovered in the region, after which the Sudanese government headed by Omar al Bashir adopted policies that discriminated against the non-Arab population. Protests broke out, headed by the Justice and Equality Movement, who rightly claimed that the Darfur region was being neglected in providing funds to develop its infrastructure. They also accused the government of arming an Arab militia called the Janjaweed, and in self-defence an armed resistance movement was formed. The flashpoint that the government sought occurred when rebels attacked a Sudanese air force base at El Fasher. In a totally disproportionate show of force the Sudanese air force then bombarded villages sympathetic to the rebels, then the Janjaweed (meaning 'devils on horseback') unleashed their full fury, invading like swarms of locusts, burning the houses, killing the men, raping the women and enslaving the children. They'd even cast the dead bodies into the wells to contaminate them lest anyone should think about returning home.

The government cynically stood by and watched the Janjaweed carry out its dirty work. The UN stood by impotently as China, who wanted Sudan's oil and had sold it much military hardware, and Russia opposed UN resolutions that would have provided peacekeepers. Eventually in 2008, a joint UN and African Union initiative tried to raise an army of 26,000 but was only able to secure 9,000 troops with limited equipment – not enough to contain the Janjaweed. Various peace treaties have been signed with some limited success, but the Sudanese government has no reason to change its ways. The sufferings of the people of Darfur continue to the present day although it's no longer considered newsworthy.

Chapter 4

"Oh, come on, James. This gets more and more hilarious by the hour!" teased Olivia as I explained to her how I'd been press-ganged into such an unlikely good deed. "It's not quite a week since you were joining in that radio speaker's tirade against God. Now you're going to church on Sunday! And if that isn't funny enough, you've made the best ever choice of candidate for euthanasia. Her life's so much not worth living that she's recruited you as her informal carer! Then you end up being invalided out of the rugby squad for three months. Are you sure it shouldn't be *you* who challenges the Almighty to make *your own* life worth living?" By this time she was bent over with laughter, and even I myself could see the funny side.

"Tell you what," she continued, "I don't believe in God any more than you, James, but if he's actually there after all, he's got one terrific sense of humour!"

And this time we both enjoyed laughing at the irony of my predicament. My question back to Olivia, however, took the wind out of her sails.

"How d'you fancy coming along on Sunday morning to lend some moral support then?"

Olivia thought for a bit, and then stated, "No, James, I just don't fancy doing a good deed on my Sunday morning. I do my caring Monday to Friday. My weekend's for me – well, let's say, us. Sorry, James, you got yourself into this situation so I'll leave you to deal with it." And then she smiled in the rueful way a shopkeeper apologises for not stocking the item you wanted.

I was disappointed that I'd have to fend for myself. I'd have enjoyed sharing my experience of the toothless boggle-eyed mad woman with Olivia. She'd enjoyed my descriptions of the lady especially the 'healing' scene around her bedside. I was beginning to do quite a good impression of her voice, and Olivia herself had begun to join in, calling

"Daimth! Daimth! Thupper'th weddy!"

I'd have liked her to meet the lady herself so that we could have enjoyed further merriment at her expense, *not* about her condition but about her strange ideas and her dogged persistence. I expected the church service might also provide fuel for the fires of mockery and cynicism about religion. But I appreciated Olivia's assertive reply. She was a proper upper middle class Miss, well-honed in the school of knowing her own mind. I knew where I was with her.

-o-O-o-

On Saturday evening we sat in a comfortable restaurant in the old part of town where Olivia treated me to a sumptuous meal to celebrate my birthday earlier in the week. It was the first time I'd eaten roast pheasant.

On Sunday morning Olivia and I woke up an hour earlier than usual. Olivia made tea and toast, brought it up to the bedroom, then we enjoyed being together to the accompaniment of Mozart's oboe concerto and clarinet quintet. I washed, shaved, and put on my best imitation of a Sunday best ready to worship the Almighty. Olivia finally decided to offer some sympathy, drove me the mile to The Limes, then beat a hasty retreat. At 10 o'clock prompt, bearing my crutch, I rang the bell.

The door was opened by a lady in a similar blue and grey-coloured uniform to the one I'd seen previously, aged about 40 with her hair tied up to fit under her carer's hat. She asked who I'd come to see, and I replied that I'd arranged to take Miss Loveless to church. The lady rolled her eyes.

"Oh, *her*," she said.

"Yes, her!" I replied. Obviously Madam had made her presence felt at The Limes. Madam... now that seemed an appropriate name, didn't it? Mad Dame!

The lady, whose badge named her as Penny, took me into the well-decorated lounge where my rather fraught patient was sitting in her wheelchair in her dressing gown. About fifteen elderly folk were sitting around the room in a variety of poses, some attempting to hold teetering coffee cups in their hands, others looking as if they'd already done a day's work and gone to sleep. It was a clean, generally orderly scene although a faint smell of urine hung in the air. One or two folk were attempting conversation, one gentleman having to shout to the lady next to him, another lady struggling to understand her neighbour through her whistling hearing aid. I couldn't imagine Madam finding it easy to make herself understood when she even needed an interpreter to talk to someone like me!

She looked up with her toad-like eyes and said, with a great deal of relief, "Heyo, Daimth. Oh, I'm *tho* pyeathed to thee you!"

I replied, "How come you aren't ready?"

"I tzwieb an' tzwieb to tzey dem. Bup I cou'mp ma'e them lithen…"

It was obvious that as she'd become worked up, she hadn't been able to pronounce her consonants. I just about got her gist, turned to Penny and asked,

"Can we get her ready to go to church, please? I believe the Rev. McPherson arranged it with you when she came home on Thursday."

Penny looked irritated and flustered. "Well, it would have been nice for somebody to tell us!" she said. "We're at minimum staffing levels this morning and we're busy enough as things are." She shrugged. "Seeing as you've come specially, I'll see what I can do."

The voice from the chair piped up, "Peath – you meed to chamze my thamitzwawy pab before we go."

I looked blankly at Penny who obviously understood this latest pronouncement. Her reaction was to screw up her face, wring her hands and reply,

"Who are you then, the Queen of Sheba? We don't just have you to look after, you know!" She looked at me with frustration. "She means her nappy. Both bathrooms are occupied, so we'll have to use her bedroom. It'll take several minutes to find the nearest hoist. Without one, it'll be a two man job to change her. How the hell are we going to do that?"

"Look, I'm a surgeon," I said, and I showed her my hospital ID card from my wallet. "I'll help."

Penny summoned a younger carer called Amanda, who pushed Miss Loveless' wheelchair back to her room and gathered a large plastic sheet and a paper mat, together with a bag for the waste from the copious wipes we'd be using. Our patient was slightly built so working together we had little trouble transferring her to the hospital type bed in her room. Before lifting Madam onto her bed, Amanda placed a pillow to support the middle of her back. Then another problem became apparent. Because Madam had no movement in her legs, it needed one carer to hold them out of the way and another to change the nappy. Then I saw a trolley table that would normally have been positioned across the bed. I placed a pillow on it, and then rested Madam's legs on top.

"Is that comfortable enough?" I asked her. She nodded and smiled.

Amanda removed the nappy to unleash an unbearable stench that sent me scurrying to open the window. She eventually cleaned the offending bottom with copious antiseptic wipes. I could see there was a danger that all our nurses' good work in hospital could go to waste unless this unpleasant job was carried out more often. Amanda picked up a fresh nappy from a large package labelled, 'All-in-One Slips' and prepared to apply it to Madam's red bottom.

"Hold on!" I said. "What about her cream?" Amanda looked blank. I was becoming irritated myself. Surely the home would have been given the antiseptic soothing cream Marion had provided, and been told to use it to fight her nappy rash?

"Tzwy my cupboarbth," came Madam's voice, and sure enough I found the cream. I asked Amanda if it was okay for me to apply it, and did so.

I hadn't anticipated the effect this would have. As the cool cream was massaged into her sore skin, the unlovely lady's face relaxed in pure pleasure. And I, too, felt tenderness in bringing comfort to this part of her body that had had so little to soothe it. I last remembered such a feeling when I was applying cream to the sores on the body of a small boy shortly after arriving in El Fasher hospital.

Working together, Amanda and I had her dressed and ready to go by 10:30 and we set out for church.

"Thank you, Daimth!" she said again. "I'm *tho* glab you've come."

When I'd first arrived and seen Penny's shrug at the mention of Miss Loveless, I had thoroughly sympathised with the home's experience of her as a challenging resident. I had to admit that my opinions had changed just a little.

My plan had been to wheel her into church, make sure she had been introduced to some folk, then go for a walk until the service finished. Unfortunately, as we arrived, they were just finishing the first hymn. There was nowhere to dock a wheelchair so we were ushered right to the front where there was space, in full view of the whole fifty or so worshippers. I was trapped. Rev. McPherson noticed us straightaway, and said,

"Well hellooooo! Welcome to our service!" but didn't introduce us for which I was profoundly grateful.

I looked around the neat little building with its pews, preaching stand, a fine-looking organ, wooden rails and stained glass windows. It had a gallery, and I wondered how long it had been since there was enough of a crowd for this to be used.

The service measured fully up to my expectations. We were the youngest worshippers by almost a generation. There were about five more hymns, prayers, a couple of scripture readings, and Rev. McPherson's sermon. He based this on a scripture passage in Luke's Gospel where Jesus was summoned to an important guy's house because his daughter was dying. On the way a lady in the crowd touched his cloak because she wanted to be cured of a continual vaginal discharge. Hey presto, she was instantly healed. Jesus knew something had happened and he stopped to talk to the lady. All this delayed his progress towards the sick girl's house, and she apparently died. This didn't bother him; he told everyone she was "not dead but sleeping" and raised her to life and, one presumes, good health.

Rev. McPherson's sermon was about how we shouldn't ignore people who need our help. Jesus could easily have ignored the lady with the discharge. But – I thought – if that's all these good folk have come to hear, why do they need a church, a service, and a minister to tell them? There are lots of columnists in today's Sunday Observer for example, saying pretty much the same thing. Wasn't this whole story about miracles? Why didn't the reverend dare to address the question that screamed at me; that if Jesus performed miracles and these people were meant to be his followers, why was the church such an impotent organisation today?

The notices were about the women's guild, a sponsored knit and coffee morning for work in Malawi, somebody being in hospital for an unspecified operation, and the fact that there wouldn't be drinks afterwards because the boiler had broken, "but do stay and chat". A few people came up after the service and said a rather stiff "Good morning," or "Hello" to us, but the only semi-meaningful conversation we had was with the reverend's wife who asked if I was "this lady's carer." I explained that I was just here today, a hospital surgeon who happened to have some time available. Madam tried to make conversation but it was obvious Mrs. McPherson was rather disconcerted by her boggle-eyed appearance and toothless lisping which she struggled to understand. Nevertheless, much to my relief, Mrs. McPherson said she'd make sure someone was available to "do" next Sunday.

"So there you are," I said, as we arrived back at The Limes, "I hope you're satisfied with your weekly dose of religion. He certainly does you a lot of good, your god, doesn't he?" As soon as I'd made this rather callous remark, I regretted it, but I didn't expect the reply. Now she was calmer, she had recovered her ability to pronounce the consonant, 'L'.

"Daimth," (which came at the start of every sentence), "*I* wath dithappointzeb, becoth I know Gob'th gop *mutz, mutz more* der give uth than wha' we hearb thith mormin'. Bup he loveth me vewy dearly, an' he loveth you tzoo! One day you'll know!"

It was difficult not to be moved by this wretched woman's blind faith. Anyway, I'd done my duty. I could consign her to my list of interesting encounters and move on. As none of the staff was around I wheeled her to her room. At that moment an unfortunate urge got the better of me. I'd got fed up of her silly glasses and decided to try to bend the distorted side pieces back into position. It wasn't as easy as I thought. I should have given in there and then, but applied yet more pressure. One of the sidepieces snapped off. *Damn!*

And then I realised the implications of what I'd done. I'd get an Elastoplast from the staff to fix her specs temporarily but I'd have to come back on Wednesday and take her to the optician. I was under no obligation but from what I'd seen today, I knew there was fat chance of anyone else sorting her out.

I arranged with Penny that I'd pick her up at 10 a.m. Wednesday, made a comment to her about Madam's sore bottom and the cream, then grabbed my crutch and set off home. On the way, I wondered how I'd have coped in her place. Could I ever have asked my visitor to change my filthy nappy? What was amazing was that this silly woman had about her a dignity that refused to be destroyed by what I considered the most humiliating and degrading of circumstances. Perhaps there were worse people with whom to spend Wednesday morning.

As Olivia and I ate our coq au vin, I poked plenty of fun at the service, as expected, but mixed this with a rant about the poor quality of care provided by the home. Then I explained to Olivia that I'd given myself another assignment, this time at the opticians. She couldn't stop laughing! "Yet another good deed for Daimth!" she hooted.

Chapter 5

Wednesday morning dawned, a fresh spring day. I decided on a cafetiere to accompany my midweek breakfast treat of a pain au chocolat, and then read the paper till 9:45. It was time to set out to fulfil my extra 'Good Deed'.

Once again I felt irritated to find Madam in the lounge bedecked in her dressing gown although this time I was less surprised. Once again she sighed and said,

"I tzwieb der tzell dem," and smiled ruefully.

Once again the staff hadn't been told she was due to go out at 10 a.m. Once again she needed her nappy changing. And once more they told me the bathrooms were occupied and that they'd have to search for a hoist or use two people. I'd made sure I had my full hospital ID which was just as well. The senior care worker, the same lady who had brought Madam to her first appointment with me, was very reluctant to let me help and would have had me waiting around until God-knows-when for a member of her own staff to become available. Eventually she relented and I was allowed to participate in this odorous activity. I was very pleased to see that her bottom was now being treated with cream more regularly and that this part of her anatomy was now a bright pink rather than a blotchy scarlet shade.

Finally we set out to town and arrived at Specs-R-Us on the High Street. The receptionist took one look at the taped up, pink boggle-eyed spectacles and declared that it would be hopeless to try to repair them. In a sudden moment of financial recklessness I offered to buy her a new pair. They sat me down near a machine that served dreadful free coffee and wheeled Madam in to have an eye test. Twenty minutes later, she emerged having thoroughly enjoyed the experience of being the centre of attention, and the optician announced that she was handing us over to one Oliver, a dashing young man in his early 20's, who would help select a frame.

The problem was that Madam's eyesight was too bad for her to see herself in the mirror, so we placed her broken pair back on her nose and held the various candidates by the side of her face. She and Oliver liked two heavy, modern, dark coloured frames whilst I thought a lightweight, gold frame would suit her complexion. Oliver teased her by placing them around her existing glasses, then on her forehead. She began to giggle.

"Daimth, will *you* pup dem on?" she asked.

I shrugged, and placed the various candidates on my face in turn. Oliver had already begun to address her as Debbie, and discovered her sense of fun. In the end, each of us wore a pair and she insisted we take a 'thelfie' with Oliver and I on either side of her. Even I had to see the funny side and finally let my hair down, joining in the merriment. I found her schoolgirl giggle infectious and just couldn't contain my own laughter. Oliver capped it off by placing all three pairs on her face at once and taking a photo, which she loved!

Oliver became aware of the manager's curious glances and that decision time had arrived. He took a picture of Madam in all three pairs separately, and then let her view them one at a time whilst wearing her broken pair. As expected she chose a dark brown frame with which she was thoroughly delighted. Back we headed to The Limes where I actually found a member of staff able to take her off my hands. We parted company and agreed to repeat the experience next Wednesday as arranged with Specs-R-Us. I spoke to the severe senior carer lady and pleaded with her to put the details into whatever system they used, so that we could get away promptly at 10 a.m. She said she'd make sure it went into the appointments' log but couldn't make promises as sometimes emergencies cropped up.

I walked home reflecting that it hadn't been at all an unpleasant morning. It had done me good to enjoy a belly-laugh, which normally I only experienced after three pints or so in the clubhouse after a game. And regarding my Euthanasia candidate, I was in no doubt about how much she'd appreciated my involuntary Good Deed.

-o-O-o-

It felt nice to enjoy our usual Sunday morning lie-in once again, with no church to think about. The Infirmary's rugby team was playing at home in the afternoon, so I thought it would be good to go and watch. Olivia had committed herself to spending £1,200 on her new saddle and was due to try it out. I wasn't particularly interested; we kept our own finances strictly separate so it was up to her to decide how to spend her hard-earned cash. Anyway, it had proved to be excellent ammunition when Olivia had expressed surprise at the £138 that I'd forked out for this past week's Good Deed visit to the optician.

I wished it had been me playing wing three-quarter. I spent my energy playing the game vicariously, yelling at the top of my voice whenever we had possession and screaming as we raced down the line for our two tries. We played a good, tight game but a couple of silly infringements in the scrum cost us penalties we could ill afford. Both resulted in the opposition kicker scoring three points from his boot. With five minutes to play we were trailing by four points. We were awarded a penalty in our own half, following which our full back kicked gloriously into touch just in front of the opposing goal line. We won the line-out, from which our stand-off fed the ball along the line of three-quarters. My stand-in received the ball and decided to kick, failing to notice our full back Ken had placed himself perfectly for a pass and was unmarked. I knew for sure that I'd have been aware of Ken's presence as we had a great understanding as players. Unfortunately the opportunity went begging. The opposition safely fielded the ball and closed out the match. Had we scored a try instead, we'd have gained a one point lead and probably would have won.

My mates were pleased to see me cheering for them and asked me to join them in the bar afterwards. I replied that I'd just stay for a 'quick one' as I wanted to be home when Olivia arrived with our takeaway at 6 p.m. It was marvellous to enjoy the lads' company again. It was my first contact with them since my accident a fortnight ago.

Olivia had enjoyed her ride and was quietly satisfied with her new saddle, which she was convinced had been worth the money. She'd look smarter on her horse at her next dressage competition, she thought. This week we'd chosen an Indian takeaway which was spicy but very tasty. As we neared the last few mouthfuls, we talked about the week ahead.

"James," she said, "just be very careful about your Madam lady when you see her on Wednesday. I just suspect she's got a way of wrapping people round her little finger and she seems to have her eye on you as easy prey. Promise me you won't let her draw you into seeing her again, will you? You've done your job and been a Good Samaritan. I think you need to leave it there."

"Olivia," I said, "I've *no intention* of having any further contact with Madam after she's got her new glasses on Wednesday. Don't worry – goodbye will mean goodbye!"

-o-O-o-

Once again, Wednesday dawned. This time I decided I fancied a bacon sandwich at Brunch Bakery on the High Street, and sat reading my paper as I gradually munched away to the accompaniment of a large Americano with an extra shot of espresso. Suitably energised, I headed to The Limes for what was to be my final visit.

She was still in her dressing gown but, amazingly, they'd changed her nappy that morning. Once I'd found a carer to dress her, it only took ten minutes to prepare to go out. The sun was shining and all seemed well with the world. Once at the opticians, Oliver greeted us with a beaming smile and reached into a drawer to find the glasses. He placed them on her nose, and then carefully adjusted the drop around her ears using a small heated chamber. At long last the ridiculous pink ones were laid to rest, and my patient looked into the mirror at herself through her brand new, dark frames. She was absolutely thrilled with what she saw. I had to admit I wouldn't have believed how much nicer she looked, as she turned to me with a smile that reached from her blue eyes around her entire face. Gone was her toad-like appearance, as if my generosity had handed her back an element of dignity.

Unfortunately the weather didn't smile in sympathy. Dark clouds had overshadowed the sun, and we'd no sooner emerged into the High Street when large drops of rain began to fall. Nothing could dampen her spirits, however. She loved the feel of the rain on her head, just to be outside in the open air and away from The Limes Penitentiary. I wasn't so free and easy and diverted the wheelchair into an arcade.

"Daimth," she said, "I'd like to tzweap you to coffee in thith bar here. Come on – letth have a cake, tzoo!" I noticed for the first time that she was wearing a small pouch around her waist, which contained a purse.

This was her 'Thank You' to me and I couldn't refuse. I ordered another Americano whilst she went for a Latte. She asked for "a thtzwaw to dwink thwough". By this time I had become a little more familiar with her pronunciation difficulties. I felt quite proud to be able to interpret this to the puzzled bar staff as, "a straw to drink through". She also asked for a little cold milk, which I explained was to add to the latte to prevent her scalding her mouth.

"Come on, Daimth! Wha' abou' a Thponze cake?"

She had her eyes on a fat, succulent slice of Victoria Sponge which I admitted looked most appetising. We agreed it would do for both of us. I asked for two plates and two forks.

Our next challenge was finding space in the café, which had filled up with other customers who'd decided to take a snack during the cloudburst. It seemed to take every waiter and waitress to move the tables and chairs to make sufficient room for the wheelchair, but they did it gladly. I hated making a scene or creating trouble although it didn't worry Madam. Nothing was spoiling her special day, it seemed. I did make a mental note of how much the staff at The Limes could do with taking a leaf out this coffee shop's employees' book.

A smiling young man brought our drinks, and I divided the cake between us. Then I realised that I'd have to feed hers into her mouth. How I'd have hated to be fed, to be so helpless that I depended on others for almost every aspect of daily living! Yet she revelled in the pure enjoyment of every mouthful, closing her eyes with a smile as she tasted and swallowed it. How I'd have hated to drink through a straw, always needing someone to check my drink was lukewarm rather than piping hot! Yet again, you'd have thought she was drinking champagne. She couldn't swallow as easily as me so, despite my having to feed two of us, I easily finished my cake first. It made sense for me to talk rather than her. She said,

"Daimth, pleath tzell me abou' you. Are you mawwieb, an' do you have a family?"

I explained that I had a partner but that we hadn't talked seriously about marriage. Some day in the future, maybe we'd have kids.

"I think you' be sutz a goo' dab," she said.

I couldn't help saying a bit more than I'd intended. My mind flashed back to the children's ward in the hospital in Darfur and those little boys and girls looking totally lost without their parents. I'd wept for them but with no-one to comfort me. Then I'd felt so horribly guilty... why should I weep when I knew I'd be going home to my own family, to a secure future back in a wealthy country...?

"Tho, d'you like bein' a thurgeon, Daimth?"

I said that I felt very satisfied when I'd been able to cure someone, to make their lives better by what I did. I tried to do my best for every patient but it was hard to see people suffer. What I didn't tell her was that I'd originally planned for a career in A & E as a doctor but had never got over the traumas of El Fasher...

Whenever I talked, I instinctively knew that my words had registered. I wanted to say more, because I knew she was interested. More than that, my story mattered to her.

I asked her if she'd enjoyed church on Sunday. She replied, "Yeth, thanth. Ip wath a lo' bether. Thith week they gop me weddy on tzime, tho we were in churtz early. An' we hab coffee aftzerwarth. Thevewal people came up to tzalk."

Finally it was time to go. She insisted I used her money to pay, and that we placed a pound coin in the 'Thank You' cup.

And so, back at The Limes, my assignment had ended. Miss Deborah Loveless had a nice new pair of glasses. They were putting cream on her bottom. And I was now excused.

"Daimth," she said as I made to leave, "pleath will *you* tzake me to churtz on Thunday?"

"Look, it's been nice knowing you, but *no*, I shan't be doing that. The reverend will have organised someone, surely?"

"He thaib he'b gep back to me abouth ip. Bup – it'th no' juth thap... I like theein' you!"

"Sorry, *no!!*" I said. "My job's done now. It's time to say goodbye!"

"Bup, Daimth," she replied tearfully, "arenp' we fwienth?"

"Not exactly," I said. "I've enjoyed sorting out your glasses but no – I've got my life, you've got yours. *Goodbye!*" and I turned around to leave.

I could hear sobs from her wheelchair as I walked out of The Limes.

-o-O-o-

I fought battles with myself all afternoon. I scolded myself for being too soft. In my mind's eye I saw Olivia nodding and heard her approval of my taking a firm line. But something seemed wrong. No matter how much I tried to distract myself with TV, a film downloaded from NetFlix, or a detective novel, I couldn't escape. I wondered if Olivia was free, then alas, remembered she was at orchestra.

At around half past ten I switched out my bedside light. I suspected I wasn't going to sleep. I was wrong. But in between, something happened. Believe it or not, I recalled the Rev. McPherson's talk about Jesus and the woman with the vaginal discharge. It was a watered down sermon but I remembered his point, that Jesus could so easily have ignored this lady. By making her feel special, he revealed treasure that everybody else would have missed.

I had a strong sense that I could rest my brain, that my thoughts would become clearer in the morning, and that I needn't try to solve any more dilemmas that night.

My Thursday morning rounds took me into the children's ward where I saw Billy, a 9-year-old boy on whose mouth I'd performed a routine but delicate procedure. His permanent teeth had been coming up in the most unusual places and he clearly needed his milk teeth removing, then a little corrective work. The tricky part was to wrap a tiny gold chain around his buried 'eye teeth' in preparation for the orthodontist to finish the work by fitting a brace. His dentist wasn't confident of getting it right, so referred his case to us. The operation had been – for me – straightforward and Billy gave me a toothy smile as I entered the ward. He gave me a picture he'd drawn of myself portrayed as Superman although pointed out that in my case the capital S referred to Surgeon. I was touched, and drew a picture of a knight on a horse.

"There's you, Billy," I said. "You've been a really brave boy!"

Once again, encounters like this were not my normal style. Mine was the aloof, professional manner, a style I adopted to protect myself from the deeper sort of emotional involvement of which I'd had enough for a lifetime whilst in Darfur.

And then it began to dawn on me. I was beginning to change, to regain my compassionate heart. As I realised why, I saw with horror that I'd just cut off the source of this new dynamic in my life. I hated to admit the truth, but it had all begun that day in Ward 17 when the most pathetic woman I'd ever met had laid her hand on my knee.

I took my full lunch hour and walked around the hospital grounds. I reflected on the word 'Friendship'. My relationships were all based on 'transactions'. My rugby mates had been pleased to see me on Sunday, but none of them had thought to contact me after my accident once I'd let them know I had to take a break. Our relationship was based around my contribution to the team. My colleagues at work respected me as a professional and enjoyed my company and I theirs. Yet the relationship was based primarily on the job. And Olivia? No, surely, that couldn't just be transactional? I must admit I wondered if she'd ever promise to love me "For richer, for poorer, in sickness and in health." For my part, I'd cynically dismissed such lofty promises as outdated, impractical, and a vestige of evolutionary necessity. But had I ever understood what 'love' actually meant?

Deborah Loveless had nothing to offer me. There was no transaction she could offer to balance my good deed. Yet in that café she had listened to me, taken a genuine interest, and drawn me out, in a way few other people had ever done. It was time I admitted the truth. I liked her; in fact I liked her a lot. But did I like her sufficiently to be her friend? Could I put up with all the inconveniences of her smelly bottom, her cumbersome wheelchair, her gruesome toothless mouth, her having to repeat much of what she said, her quaint ideas and her blind faith?

As I reflected further, I remembered seeing her face at the optician's. It was a joy to watch the way she took pleasure in simple kindnesses. I liked the way she expressed such gratitude and I respected her enormously because of her extraordinary spirit that refused to be humiliated by the many indignities that life had imposed on her. And, deluded she may be, but she stuck steadfastly to her religious crutch. It was a heck of a good crutch, and no way could anyone level against her the usual companions of the word 'religion' – stuffy, judgmental, hypocritical, a killjoy... Indeed 'joy' described her rather well. It was time I admitted the improbable fact that my visits to the optician had been among the highlights of the last fortnight.

There and then I made my decision.

-o-O-o-

After work, I called around at The Limes, expecting to be delivering good news to a broken woman. Instead, she was propped up in bed looking peaceful, listening to Radio 2. Her eyes lit up as I walked in. I'd forgotten I'd be meeting her in her new glasses, which enabled her to fix a gaze on me and look directly into my eyes.

"Debbie," I began, "I'm so sorry about the way I left you yesterday. I'm not taking you to church on Sunday, but I'd like to come on Wednesdays – if that's okay, of course? And – yes, we're officially fwienth!"

She was over the moon, and shrieked with laughter as she realised I'd taken off her toothless pronunciation of 'friends'.

"Were you very upset yesterday?" I asked. I knew the answer, but not the whole of it.

"Yeth, Daimth, I wath," she said. "Bup then, ath I wath lyin' in beb here latze in the evenin, ip theemeb like Gob wappeb himthelf awoun' me like a blankip. He thaib, 'I'm with you, Debbie. I haven' forgotzen you'."

My own eyes filled with tears. I suddenly remembered how, lying in my own bed at what must have been approximately the same time, I'd called to mind the reverend's sermon. How strange was that? As if the two were connected…

Chapter 6

It was as well that I had anticipated Olivia's reaction, and prepared a reply.

"James, I just can't believe this!" she said. "What sort of hold does that woman have over you? You can't live your life feeling sorry for people, surely? This'll come back to bite you!"

"Olivia, I know you feel disappointed that, as you see it, I haven't been firm. But you haven't even met Debbie…"

"Oh, so she's got a name now, I see!" interrupted Olivia. "She isn't just 'Madam' or 'that woman' anymore!"

"You've said it!" I replied. "I've admitted to myself that I really like Debbie. Yes, I do feel very sorry for her, and I agree with you that that's no basis for a friendship. But I've made a choice. Both of us want to be each other's friend because we like and respect each other. And I don't see why you can't include yourself in this. Why can't both of us take her out for lunch at a café on Sunday, for example? She's great company and she has a wonderful sense of fun."

Olivia gazed at me with a 'Come on, James, get a grip!' look. It was similar to Mr. Davy's in one of those mentorship moments when he thought I ought to get a hold and pull my ideas together. "Where's this going to lead to?" she said.

"Olivia, aren't there times in our lives when we have to go with our human instincts and allow ourselves to be drawn into situations we can't control? I can't tell you where it'll lead – but goodness, she's not asking for my money, my hand in marriage, anything apart from enjoying my company. And I'm a better person for spending time with her. I feel happier because of seeing her this week. If we became lifelong friends, what would be wrong with that?"

"James," said Olivia with a finality that indicated this was the last word on the subject, "I have spent forty-five hours this week caring for sick patients. If you want to involve yourself with this lady, I can't stop you but I am not going to spend my leisure time wheeling anyone else around town, wiping their bottoms or feeding them through straws. I think you're being naïve and hope you don't fall flat on your face in the process. Subject closed!"

So this would be a part of my life that Olivia would not be sharing.

And I must admit, I found Sunday afternoon rather boring. The rugby match was 'away' this week. Olivia was riding again in her smart, comfortable new saddle. I satisfied myself with a walk in the park followed by a visit to the botanical gardens, then watched a Sunday League football game on one of the adjacent pitches. Then it was home to jasmine tea and the Observer crossword. I imagined what would have happened if Olivia had agreed to my proposal. We'd have taken Debbie to church where we'd have had to suffer the reverend's scintillating sermon. Then we'd have taken her to a café for a sumptuous Sunday lunch, after which we'd have wheeled her home to The Limes. It wouldn't have been our first choice of weekend entertainment but it would have been far better than the empty Sunday I was now experiencing. At least it would have brought someone else some enjoyment. And Olivia would still have been able enjoy her ride.

-o-O-o-

I wasn't quite sure how I'd occupy my first non-Good Deed meeting with Debbie on Wednesday. However, when I arrived at The Limes at 2 p.m. I was in for a surprise. Debbie was in her room and had been entertaining three visitors, ladies whom I guessed were in their sixties. I vaguely recognised them from church. They were preparing to leave, but it became obvious there'd been an upset as Debbie was distraught. On seeing me, the ladies walked out with a "Goodbye, dear", but no affectionate kiss.

"What on earth's up, Debbie?" I asked. "What have they said to you?"

"Daimth," began Debbie as always, "theyer gweevin' him! Theyer gweevin' him *tho mutz!*"

"Debbie, you'll have to help me understand. Something about grieving, is it?"

Debbie's gasps and tears eventually subsided sufficiently for her to explain.

"Theyer bweakin' Godth hearp. I can' bear der hear people gweevin' the holy thpiwip!"

Despite my progress in mastering her toothless language I was no clearer. From my previous excursions with Debbie she'd seemed to be perfectly 'all there', but was I now discovering the part that was slightly mad? An idea occurred to me. I took my smart phone and asked her to repeat what she'd said. I began an internet search for, 'Grieving the holy spirit'. And then it started to make sense. I found these words:-

'Let no unwholesome talk come out of your mouths, but only what is helpful for building up the one in need and bringing grace to those who listen. And do not grieve the Holy Spirit of God, in whom you were sealed for the day of redemption. Get rid of all bitterness, rage and anger, brawling and slander, along with every form of malice. Be kind and compassionate to one another, forgiving each other, just as in Christ God forgave you.'

It was from Ephesians Chapter 4 which I now realised was in the Bible.

It took about twenty minutes to piece it together. Whilst the ladies were with her, they'd been gossiping together about two other members of the church congregation. One was a single man who sat on his own, looking dishevelled. Even from my one visit to church I thought I knew who they meant. Anyway, this gentleman had devoured a whole plate of biscuits at coffee time although he'd only placed 10 pence in the cup. The ladies were discussing the reasons for his greed but were, in Debbie's words, "pullin' him aparp!" The second victim of their gossip was Rev. McPherson's wife. She had offended one of the three ladies who happened to be the head of the Flower Committee. They'd been planning the flowers for Pentecost Sunday and had resented Mrs. McPherson sticking her oar in to suggest using some plant or other to represent the "holy thpirip" in "tzongueth of fire". From their visits to the minister's manse, it was evident that these ladies held a dim view of Mrs. McPherson's abilities as a flower arranger, and this extended to her capabilities as a home maker.

Debbie had become increasingly agitated throughout the ladies' visit and had tried to tell them how their talk was upsetting not just her, but – as she perceived it – God. I was in absolutely no doubt that she herself would now be the subject of gossiping tongues for several days to come.

Now I had the story straight, I looked at the helpless figure propped up in her bed and then it occurred to me that never in the three weeks I'd known her had I ever heard her speak badly of anyone she'd met. She had so much reason to grumble and complain about the staff, but she didn't. Yes, she became deeply frustrated with their poor standard of service but she never spoke about them with any bitterness. She cared deeply about this 'holy spirit' that to me meant absolutely nothing, but obviously had to do with God. It seemed she was distraught because she hated the destructive effect these ladies were having on the church community. Or rather, the lack of it. Like a tiny shaft of light, it was as if a window opened in my mind and I had a brief glimpse inside a secret chamber. I was looking at a very beautiful person. I was very glad I'd chosen to see her again, as a friend.

The staff and their failings became a further topic as the afternoon progressed. We decided to go for a walk through the park but once again, Debbie needed her dreaded nappy changing. I was not pleased by the resentful attitude of the staff. However, I was even more displeased when I saw the state of her bottom which had again become sore. It was obvious that they weren't changing her often enough. She herself had to remind them to apply her cream.

Eventually we made it out into the sunshine, and I spent about an hour wheeling her around the park. It was as if this was her first time, as her well-focussed eyes feasted on the greenery, the lake, the ducks, the children on their scooters and bicycles. I'd had ideas of repeating the coffee house experience but she just seemed to want to drink in the outdoors that she had so sorely missed. We spoke very little, but sat by the lake, she in her wheelchair and me alongside her on a bench. All she said was, "Daimth, thith ith *tho, tho lovely!*" In a way I couldn't describe, her peace became mine, too.

It was obvious she was becoming tired so we headed back to The Limes. Once I'd settled her in bed, I marched off to the office to see whoever was in charge.

-o-O-o-

On the door was the name Nathan Cooper, Day Manager. As I knocked, a busy-sounding man's voice called, "Come in." Nathan Cooper was an ordinary-looking young man aged about 35 with closely cropped dark hair and keen brown eyes. Without smiling, he gestured towards a chair and asked what he could do for me. I explained that I was Mr. James McAlister; that Miss Debbie Loveless had been on my ward at the Royal Infirmary, and that I'd been visiting her.

"Yes?" came the rather terse response.

"I've come to see you because Miss Loveless has some particular needs that I feel deserve special attention at the moment," I said.

"Such as?"

I explained how, on Ward 17, the nurses had worked hard to cure her of a Urinary Tract Infection and a very sore bottom. I was concerned that unless she was changed regularly and her bottom treated with cream, we'd need to admit her again.

Nathan Cooper's eyes rolled. "From the day she came in here, Miss Loveless has been a more demanding resident than anyone else," he explained. "Some of this isn't her fault because she is so severely disabled. You wouldn't believe how much time it takes to feed her her meals, what with her having swallowing difficulties even before she lost her teeth. But it's things like demanding that we take her to her room, and then put on particular radio programmes that take time. Everyone else is content to be sociable or to take their place in the lounge in front of the telly. As for her toileting, it's a long job for one person to take her to the bathroom or to find a hoist to bring to her room. Otherwise, even if she's in bed, it takes two members of staff to change her, and – I'm sorry – we often don't have two available."

"But if she's in bed it can be done quite easily by one person!" I said. "You can use the bedside trolley to keep her legs out of the way…"

"Excuse me!" said the affronted Mr. Cooper. "Are you trying to tell us our job? Our Care Home management would certainly not allow that!"

"Which is better?" I asked. "To keep your own rules and risk her re-admission to hospital, or to adopt an unorthodox but perfectly safe procedure that you could easily risk assess yourselves to keep her much more healthy and comfortable?"

"We are *not* compromising on our Health and Safety principles!" said Mr. Cooper, standing up behind his desk. I wondered what sort of 'health' he was promoting.

"Besides all this," he continued, "no other resident asks to be dressed up to go outside more frequently than your friend here. And it's all very well but when she says she wants to go out, the carers have to listen to her several times over before they can understand what she's saying. She speaks quietly and she can hardly pronounce her words."

It was my turn to become irate. "Look here!" I protested. "She's in this home because she's disabled, right? I'd have thought understanding what Debbie was saying was part of caring for her. In my opinion one of the best things she can do for herself is to try and have a life. I can't believe you aren't glad she wants to get out and about. And let's be clear, Mr. Cooper – we've sometimes made arrangements with your staff and found the messages haven't been passed on."

This had the potential to generate into a real dingdong. The stakes were raised even higher as Mr. Cooper played his trump card. "Mr. McAlister," he said, "in my opinion and that of my staff, we believe Miss Loveless isn't mentally stable. We hear her talking to herself in her room, often loudly. She seems to suffer from a strange type of religious mania. And you, as a medical professional, ought to have recognised the fact."

I tried to restrain my desire to throttle him, and responded, "Mr. Cooper, I don't know where this myth has come from. I thought Miss Loveless had very strange ideas when I first met her. Now I'm getting to know her, I believe she's very sane indeed. I haven't heard her talking to herself but I know she prays. I believe she copes remarkably with an awful disability that would have left most people despondent and miserable. Instead, she has a remarkable love of life, a bubbly humour and a compassion for others. I'm amazed you don't credit her with any of that."

Nathan Cooper stood up, opened his door and motioned for me to leave.

"On that note, my friend," he concluded, "we shall agree to differ."

I had *not* made a friend that afternoon. With an ironic grin I realised that Cooper was an apt surname for the Day Manager – that's what he did for a living. Now I appreciated the extent of Debbie's battle to live any sort of life other than to be cooped up like a battery hen. I was now even gladder that I'd defied Olivia's disapproving caution. Debbie Loveless needed friends, and what was more, she deserved them.

Chapter 7

What distracted me remains a mystery. My final patient on Friday afternoon was a perfectly routine case to deal with, a young man about my age with impacted wisdom teeth. Several months ago his dentist had removed one of them, but then realised the remainder were going to pose a greater challenge. I easily removed the two wisdom teeth from his lower jaw, and then moved to the remaining top one. I can't remember what was preoccupying me but I suddenly realised with horror that I'd just extracted an adjacent tooth by mistake, forgetting that the wisdom tooth had already gone. I cursed under my surgeon's mask, and then fought to regain my grip before successfully removing the correct one.

Nowadays many people are prepared to go to far greater lengths than previously to avoid losing their teeth, and it isn't uncommon for them to spend large sums of money on preserving them. Dreadful forebodings of investigations, a compensation claim and disciplinary action leapt into my mind.

Martin happened to be at work and, as we changed to go home, I discussed the case with him. He didn't see it as the serious issue that I did. He asked me to bring up the man's X-Rays and when we looked closely we could see signs of decay in the tooth I'd wrongly removed.

"There's your answer, James!" he said. "It's simple. You looked into his mouth and saw the tooth had become infected, so you took it out... surely!"

"Not so easy as that, Martin," I said. "I'd have been wrong to extract a tooth without his permission. And anyway, I feel uneasy lying about it."

Olivia and I had arranged to visit the theatre that evening so there wasn't time to have a long discussion. I thought to myself that this was as well. Sometimes it didn't help to dwell on one's misfortunes. One of our favourite pleasures was to have a meal in the foyer of the theatre and whilst we were enjoying our lasagne I mentioned my mistake. She totally disagreed with Martin's suggestion of covering it up. But she had two comments to make, one more helpful than the other. Firstly, she said she believed it was much better to spend one's mental energy avoiding making mistakes than to deal with them afterwards. This I found less helpful as it didn't deal with today's incident. Secondly, she reminded me that I couldn't undo my mistake, so my best course of action would be to work out how to prevent this ever happening again. I recognised this as a train of thought likely to appeal to Mr. Davy. So, altogether, I found Olivia's second comment helpful and very practical.

The play, a comical tragedy set in the East End of London, provided some hearty laughter. It took my mind off surgery and we enjoyed our evening. Saturday followed a normal pattern with my being at work during the day and Olivia and I watching a film in the evening.

Sunday morning began with a leisurely breakfast, followed by enjoying each other. Over morning coffee we talked about our forthcoming holiday in June. We'd planned to go to Majorca where the wild, mountainous countryside would have been ideal for a walking holiday. My leg wouldn't be better in time unfortunately so we decided instead to consider central Italy where we could enjoy Florence then hire a car and explore the charming villages of Tuscany. We made a plan, and then worked together on a bacon and cashew nut stir-fry for our lunch. Olivia gathered up her riding gear and set off for the stable yard.

The Infirmary team were playing away so, after lunch, I was at a loose end. Alone with my own thoughts, I was aware that the 'wrong tooth' issue was still worrying me. Martin had given me what I considered bad advice; Olivia had talked common sense, delivered in a kind and practical manner; but I still couldn't put the incident to bed. How I'd have loved to be racing around a rugby pitch on a bright, showery afternoon such as today! I decided to repeat last Sunday's pattern and to walk across the park. I crossed the road from my apartment and had just bought an ice cream when an odd thought popped into my head. I went back across the Zebra and headed in the opposite direction towards Wolverstone Road. Somehow I sensed I'd find comfort in the one place that three weeks ago, I'd have dreaded setting foot - The Limes.

Debbie was in her room watching TV. She was delighted to see me, and asked me to switch off her programme. She opened with,

"Well, Daimth, thith ith unecthpetzeb! Tho, how can I help you?"

By now I could understand her better. We looked at each other, grinned, and burst out laughing at the irony of her being a help to me!

The words, "This is an unexpected," posed particular challenges for her pronunciation but I'd noticed that she took pleasure in speaking sentences in which she became tongue-tied. She found herself very funny, a fact about her that I enjoyed.

I explained, and she listened. As I talked, I could sense a deep empathy on her part. I felt a freedom not just to describe what had taken place, but how I felt about it – my dented professional pride, my sense of frustration and shame, and my fears at being brought to book. I think Olivia implicitly understood all these things but it helped to spell them out, to share what it was like to be in my shoes. After about ten minutes, I began to run out of words. Debbie spoke,

"Youwer a goob thurgeon, Daimth," she said. "You denuinely wantzer make people well." She paused for a short time, then said,

"Letz pway, shall we?"

I realised that I'd let myself in for this. It seemed churlish to refuse after I'd sought Debbie out specially.

"Cam you fin' my Bible in the cupboar', Daimth, and fin' Philippianth tzaptzer four?"

I searched in the cupboard and found a well-thumbed Bible within a soft brown cover with a sticker on the front showing a shepherd holding a lamb. As she saw me admiring the lamb, Debbie smiled and said, "Datz me!"

About right, I thought.

With some further guidance I found Philippians 4 verses 6 and 7. It said,

'Do not be anxious about anything, but in every situation, by prayer and petition, with thanksgiving, present your requests to God. And the peace of God, which transcends all understanding, will guard your hearts and your minds in Christ Jesus.'

"Thap'th whap we're gointher do, Daimth. We're gointher pwethenp your wequethz to Gob."

"That's all very well," I said, "but I don't believe this stuff so surely it doesn't apply to me?" However, as I suspected, I couldn't escape that lightly. No way was I now in any doubt that Debbie Loveless was 'all there', as she said,

"Daimth, if I thaib I wath gointher poke you with a thworb, wha' would happen if you didn' believe in thworbth? Ip would thtzill hurp, woulbn' ip?"

The thought of Debbie Loveless poking me with a sword was so incongruous that I had to laugh. She saw the funny side too, and soon we couldn't help enjoying another infectious giggle. I gave in. Once again I placed her limp hand on me, this time on my arm. She prayed,

"Lor' Dethuth, come an' fill Daimth with your love." Jesus was an unfortunate choice of deity to worship when you were toothless, I reflected. "Tzake away hith fear of getzin' intzer tzwouble. Lep him know, deep in hith hearp, thap you're in contzwol. Bleth him, Lor'! Amen."

She looked into my eyes fondly, and yet it wasn't just her shining gaze alone that drew me. I felt as if I was being magnetised by something way beyond Debbie. It felt as if a weight was being lifted off me; I wanted to cry, but I didn't want to give in to my feelings.

She said she had another verse for me to look up on my smart phone. It was where "Dethuth" said that the truth would set me free. I found it in John's Gospel, Chapter 8. It was set in the context of Jesus having a rather tense discussion with people who doubted who he was, but Debbie explained that she believed truthfulness was always the way to freedom.

"Debbie," I said, "it's all very well reading this God stuff, and I know what I have to do about it tomorrow. But what's God-if-he's-there going to do about it?"

She smiled. "Daimth, thath why itth an abventzure followin' Dethuth. You never know whap'th gointher happennetz. Waip an' thee wha' Gob doeth!" She winked!

Three weeks ago the words 'Deborah Loveless' and 'Adventure' would have seemed light years apart.

I was disappointed to hear that she hadn't been to church. The person who should have taken her had been called away at short notice to visit his sick brother and hadn't arranged a replacement. It crossed my mind that I wouldn't mind taking her in future if all else failed, rather than seeing her miss out.

I walked home with a spring in my step, called at the Indian takeaway and at M&S, and then surprised Olivia by making her a trifle to accompany our meal. Following her comments I'd worked out how I was going to avoid repeating my mistake or others like it. But that wasn't the main reason why I slept well. I awoke feeling a sense of innocence that was totally new to me, as if I no longer had any need to defend myself from the consequences of my folly. So – was this 'the peace that transcended all understanding'?

-o-O-o-

On Monday morning I arrived at work and made myself an appointment to see Mr. Davy. It would not have been true to say that my confession lifted his spirits, nor was it the case that I lifted myself up in his estimation. In the same way as Olivia, he reminded me of how much better it was to put my efforts into avoiding mistakes rather than damage limitation once I'd messed up. However, he did thank me for coming clean immediately. At least he could make plans to deal with the inevitable fall out. We had a good relationship due to having worked together for four years. He always talked tough to my face, but once the flak came, I knew he would back me up solidly. The patient, Mr. Paul Glynn, had been discharged on Saturday morning, so we agreed I would contact him straightaway. I walked out of Mr. Davy's office chastened but not humiliated. Those words, "Youwer a goob thurgeon, Daimth," still rang in my ears.

Mr. Glynn's phone went onto Voicemail so I left a message asking him to contact me.

-o-O-o-

I'd arranged to call at The Limes at 2:30 p.m. on Wednesday afternoon. By this time I was known to the staff, who just nodded to indicate that Debbie was in her room. As I reached the door I heard tears. I knocked on the door, and found not one, but two women sobbing their heart out. The other was the younger carer, Amanda, who hastily tried to compose herself and said, "I'll be going now." I knew Debbie's face well enough to read her feelings and to see that this wasn't what she wanted.

"Amanda," I said, "please stay. Don't go because of me. Do you two want more time together?"

"Daimth, pleath come in. Amanba, can I eztplain?"

Amanda nodded, and offered to tell me herself. She had found out last night that her husband was having an affair, and when she confronted him, he announced that he was considering walking out on her, leaving her with their two small children. Debbie, whom she'd been dressing and toileting earlier in her shift, had noticed that she seemed upset, so after she'd completed her shift at 2 p.m., Amanda had called on Debbie to unburden herself. She supposed that I wanted to take Debbie out as usual.

"Tzell you wha', Amanba," said Debbie, "why don' Daimth an' I tzweap you tzo coffee an' a cake? Ith thap okay, Daimth?"

"Are you sure?" said Amanda.

By now I was used to my encounters with Debbie turning out in all sorts of unpredictable ways, of which this was yet another. We went back to the coffee house near the opticians where once again we ordered a large slice of Victoria Sponge cake and also a toffee and walnut cake. As before, it took considerable time to feed Debbie her share, a task that I appreciated sharing with Amanda. And equally similarly, Debbie refused to let her swallowing difficulties spoil her enjoyment of the treat. Amanda and I exchanged small talk in between bites; I realised with alarm that I had forgotten to behave like Mr. James McAlister and that I'd taken an interest in her family life. It was a far cry from the men's world of the rugby clubhouse and the doctors' mess which the lady staff members largely avoided. For my part I opened up about my frustrations at being injured and unable to take part in sport. Amanda's face expressed genuine sympathy.

Debbie at last finished her cake and we presented her with her drink that was now lukewarm. The staff had enjoyed making a fuss of her and had created a special Teddy Bear shape within the foam on her latte. She disturbed the pattern and sucked half the drink up her straw with great delight. Unfortunately, she swallowed it a little too quickly and began to hiccup, and accidentally blew instead of sucking. The foam spilled out onto her clothes. I grabbed the almost-empty cup and placed it on the edge of the table, then had to slap her between the shoulder blades to stop her hiccups. Unfortunately, in so doing, I knocked the cup onto the floor where it shattered into a thousand pieces. I have never been able to believe how a tiny residue of liquid could cover so much floor space when it's spilled. Oh, how humiliating, I thought. I looked around at the glances of the other customers who'd witnessed this scene although afterwards admitted that their curious looks had reflected sympathy rather than annoyance.

"Come on, Debbie; let's get out of the way. Time to go!" I said, standing up to leave as two members of staff appeared, one with a pan and brush, the other with a bag and also a mop. But Debbie shook her head.

"Nop yep, Daimth. We haven' finithed. Amanba, can we pway for you?"

Amanda said that was okay, although in five minutes' time she'd need to be off to meet her children out of school. She opened her handbag to look for her purse. Debbie shook her head. It was Daimth' and her "tzweap".

Had I been able, I'd have fled out into the street. Unfortunately there was no escape as I was trapped in between the busy staff members, the wheelchair and the other tables. In one final attempt to avoid the impending act of prayer, I called out,

"*Not here, Debbie*! Surely not in front of all these people?"

"Why nop, Daimth? Dethuth ith here!"

Oh my god, thought I…

"Daimth, pup my hanb an' your hanb on Amanba's thoulder," she said.

I was white with a mixture of panic and rage. I wanted to scream at Debbie at the top of my voice. But having been the subject of one scene, I felt I couldn't cause another. As Debbie began to pray I wished with all my heart that a trapdoor in the floor would open up and carry me down out of this present humiliating scene to the bowels of the earth. But it didn't. The music had to be faced.

"Lor' Dethuth, come now an' fill Amanba with your peath. Pup your armth aroun' her an' make her thtrong. Sthzow her how mutz you love her. Amen!"

Unlike me, Amanda seemed to have appreciated the prayer. She got up to leave, whereupon I paid the bill and finally dragged myself, Debbie and her infernal wheelchair out of the café of shame. I felt like returning her to The Limes at a forced march and just dumping her inside the door. However, I wanted to sound off at her first. I crossed the road, pushed her into the park, found a bench, parked the wheelchair with an almighty jerk, and plonked myself down.

"Debbie, don't you *ever, ever* embarrass me again like that!" I stormed. "I'm not taking you anywhere if you're going to make such a fool of me. You're welcome to your own silly beliefs but you can keep your pious prayers to yourself. You know as well as I do that God never does anything useful when you pray. I'm a professional person and I'm not here to be made to look like an idiot!"

"Daimth…"

"And for God's sake stop calling me Daimth at the start of every sentence, will you? I know my own name well enough!"

"Bu' it'th no' my faulp tha' Dethuth ith weal!" protested the impossible Debbie. "An' I knew I hab to pway for Amanba before she lef'. Thowwie, Daimth, bu' I hab to pup Dethuth firth."

Oh my god! Now I could understand why Nathan Cooper found her so exasperating and thought she wasn't all there. Common sense had to be waived to one side as her imaginary Dethuth commanded her to do all these eccentric things, to the great embarrassment of her carers and the annoyance of the general public. I just sat for two minutes, quivering with a mixture of frustration and fury.

"Daimth," she piped up, clearly oblivious to my request not to address me that way, "whap happened abou' the man whothe tzooth you tzook oup by mithtzake?"

"Look, don't b****y well call me Daimth every time, will you?" I yelled. "How the heck do I know? He hasn't returned my call!"

I stood up and released the brake on her chair. Perhaps a walk around the park would do both of us good. I needed to calm down after my Vesuvius moment and she needed her dose of fresh air. Maybe it would restore her sense of normality?

We arrived at the pond and I sat at the same bench as previously. I felt so confused, a mixture of every imaginable emotion swirling about my head. Neither of us said anything. Debbie had at last got the message that another "Daimth" might not be welcome.

My mobile chirped into life.

"Hello, James McAlister speaking."

"Doctor, my name's Paul Glynn and I'm returning your call."

The voice sounded a bit terse, as if the speaker was having difficulty opening his mouth fully. Of course! The wisdom teeth man! I suppose I should have stood up and walked around the lake out of Debbie's hearing, but for some reason it was as if my bottom was glued to the bench.

I didn't bother explaining that I was not, technically speaking, a doctor. I did explain very professionally that the procedure to remove his three remaining wisdom teeth had gone to plan, then about my mistake in removing the extra tooth.

"You mean you took out the tooth next to the one the dentist removed?" he asked.

"Yes, exactly," I said. I added that I had no excuses. It was a simple error and that I expected he would want a complaint form sent to him along with details of how to claim compensation.

"Well, actually, Doctor," he said, "I'm not that bothered about it. That tooth had been niggling me quite a lot lately as it happened, so perhaps I'm well to be rid of it. Look, occasionally I make mistakes in my job, too. You've been honest with me about your mistake and I recognise that. Don't worry about it."

"Mr. Glynn, I really appreciate what you say," I replied, "but I think I should arrange for you to receive the forms in the post in case you change your mind."

"No, Doctor," he said, "forget it. I've made up my mind. I've enough forms of other sorts to deal with already. I don't want more for something I'm not going to fill in." And with that, he said goodbye and rang off.

"Phew!" I said, letting all the air out of my tightened chest. I'd almost forgotten about Debbie by my side, who was smiling.

"Daimth," she said, "whap were you thayin' abou' Gob no' doin' anythin' utheful when we pway? Pleathe do tzell me more!"

I looked at her and saw the corners of her mouth creasing up. I knew what was coming. The dreaded Debbie giggle was about to descend... and as I looked at her I knew that I, too, was about to be enveloped in the experience. I giggled with relief at the outcome of my medical incident, with amusement at the ironic timing of the call, but also I was bathing in the infectious joy of this infuriating woman whom I so admired.

Ten minutes later I dried both our eyes and headed the wheelchair back towards The Limes. An ice cream van was sitting in our path and Debbie decided we should celebrate. She was paying, she said, and we'd have a Cadbury 99 cone. Unlike me she couldn't have a chocolate flake, "no' tzill I've go' my dentzureth."

She was beginning to look forward to her new teeth. I was, too, on her behalf.

It took her a quarter of an hour to eat her ice cream. I didn't begrudge her a minute of it. As I held her cone in front of her face, I watched her tongue come out of her mouth and lovingly embrace her prize. Tenderly, I broke pieces off the bottom of her cone and placed them around the ball of ice cream so she could enjoy it to the full. By this time it was late afternoon and I looked at her peaceful face silhouetted against the sun. I reflected on what I'd observed in the café but refused at the time to acknowledge; that Amanda had been deeply moved by Debbie's prayer. Peace, strength, a sense of Jesus' love... it all seemed so alien to me but I could see why it had helped Amanda. This was the woof and warp of Debbie's soul, the fabric around which her whole life was built.

I looked at the profile of her face as she sucked and licked, oblivious to my gaze, contentedly enjoying the moment. I remembered unkindly comparing her to a toad, with her boggle-eyed misshapen spectacles which gave her a stare that a comedian would have been hard pushed to imitate. Now I saw her differently; her hair had recently been washed and blow-dried, her cheeks were no longer sunken in despair, and the lines on her face had softened through giggling and smiling. In her new glasses she wasn't at all bad looking.

Indeed, as we began our journey back to The Limes, I looked at her face. It shone.

I could have paid good money to enjoy an activity less enriching than that afternoon's, with its range of emotional highs and lows, pathos, hilarity and happy outcome. I could have gone to the theatre, taken a helicopter ride, climbed a mountain, gone white water rafting, or many other things. But it wouldn't have rivalled The Debbie Loveless Experience.

-o-O-o-

The afternoon wasn't over yet. We were making our way along Wolverstone Road when once again my mobile chirped into life. It was The Limes to ask how long we'd be, because Debbie had visitors. I replied that we were almost back at the front door. On arrival, we were ushered into a little-used lounge at the side of the reception area.

Debbie's visitors appeared to be a family, a man and his wife aged around 50 with two boys. She burst into tears as she saw the boys, and urged them to come close to her. The couple hastily made their way outside the room and left Debbie to have some 'alone time' with them. As she spoke, I could see their faces recoil in horror. The older one said,

"Mummy, where've all your teeth gone?"

As I saw Debbie's forlorn look, I realised it was time to play my part.

"I'm James. I'm a surgeon who's looked after your mum. She's had an illness in her mouth, and to help her get better we've had to take her teeth out. I know she looks strange at the moment but don't worry, we'll be making her some plastic teeth soon, and she'll look just as beautiful as you remember her, and even prettier. We'll make a beauty queen of your mummy yet, you'll see!"

"Will she be able to eat with her plastic teeth?" asked the younger boy.

"Yes," I said, "and I hope she'll be able to eat even better than before because all her teeth will be matched up and none of them will be missing."

This was definitely looking on the bright side of Debbie's future experiences with dentures. But as we talked, I realised I was making a commitment to her. If there was one thing I wanted to do, it was make sure her dentures were well fitted and comfortable. Indeed, not only that, but beautiful, an outward reflection of the person I was coming to know.

I asked the boys their names, which turned out to be Jonathan and Ethan. I searched Debbie's face to find out if she wanted me to leave her with them. I decided I'd better stay as she was struggling to 'hold it together'. It was as well I did. She needed my interpretative skills as she tried to talk toothlessly through her tears.

She asked if they were happy in their foster home. I had the impression that the couple were trying their best to provide a loving environment but that the boys were missing Debbie terribly.

She asked what their house was like. Jonathan showed us pictures of it on his phone; it seemed pleasant and spacious.

She asked how they were doing at school, and urged them to work hard.

She asked Jonathan about his football and Ethan about cubs.

Did they go to church? No.

Had Dad been in touch? No.

This upset Debbie and caused another round of tears to well up.

She urged them to be brave. She told them to come close and place their arms around her. She looked into their eyes. "Gob'll tzake care of you, boyth," she said, somehow summoning the faith that lay at the very core of her being. A faith that she must have needed to summon many times over in the latest sad chapter of her life.

I hated seeing Debbie cry but even more so her boys. Now it was my turn to speak words to encourage them.

"Boys," I said, "last week something bad happened to me when I made a mistake at work. Let me tell you what your mum read to me."

Quickly I took out my phone and searched for 'transcends all understanding'. I read out the same passage.

'Do not be anxious about anything, but in every situation, by prayer and petition, with thanksgiving, present your requests to God. And the peace of God, which transcends all understanding, will guard your hearts and your minds in Christ Jesus.'

I reckoned the boys might be too young to understand, but at least it would convey something to support Debbie.

"And, Jonathan and Ethan, I felt much, much better afterwards. Your mum believes Jesus really does care about you just like she tells me he cares for me. And guess what – nothing bad has happened after my mistake. I haven't got into trouble at all. So be brave!"

Had I been able to, I'd have prayed for Debbie and the boys like she had for me and Amanda. But being religious wasn't something I could play at. I'd done my best.

At this point it seemed right to finish the rendezvous and to invite the couple back into the room. Debbie suppressed her tears enough to thank them gratefully for looking after the boys. Then the little party left, declining the offer of tea, and Debbie and I retired to her room. I had never seen her cry like she did then. It seemed that oceans and oceans of tears just cascaded out of her eyes. Being separated from her boys was her deepest grief. I'd long exceeded the time I'd planned for my afternoon visit, but I wanted to stay with her until she felt less distraught.

As her tears gradually subsided, a carer arrived with Debbie's evening meal. I took my cue to leave. There and then I made another decision. I was taking her to church on Sunday. Not out of duty, but because she was worth it.

Chapter 8

My decision was not greeted with joy by Olivia, who pointed out that I should have consulted her before making a change that would affect our weekend together.

"James, I just don't know what's come over you," she said. "It's not like you to become so emotionally involved with a disabled person. I'm concerned for you about where it's all going to lead. She's obviously very strong minded and seems to have some sort of a hold on you. If she was getting you to take her somewhere that you'd enjoy going, I'd understand but as we both know, you and church are at opposite ends of the spectrum. I honestly wish you'd get yourself out of her orbit as soon as you can, before you're drawn in any deeper. We both do a great deal of good for all the people we treat whilst we're at work. Being good doctors really does change their lives for the better. We owe it to ourselves to have time away from caring, doing what we enjoy."

"Olivia, you're right in saying you don't know what's come over me," I replied. "That's why I really wish you'd meet Debbie. I don't feel any longer that I'm doing her good. I know I am, of course, but she enriches my life, too. It's a long time since I've met anyone with so much sheer courage and nerve, and I love seeing the way she laps up every little bit of pleasure that life offers. She's got a sweet, tender heart, but an inner strength that I enormously admire." I recounted the incident in the café, starting from my entrance into Debbie's room when she was weeping in sympathy with Amanda.

I noticed an expression on Olivia's face that I hadn't seen before. It was as if she felt slightly threatened. Was I implying that Debbie had qualities to which I was attracted, that she lacked? Instinctively I knew I couldn't share with Olivia the sequel to the café story. Of course, I'd told her straightaway about the phone call from Paul Glynn, and she'd been delighted for me that I'd avoided a complaint with the inevitable investigation. But to explain to Olivia about Debbie's prayer, the Bible verses and the timing of the call that came during our fracas in the park would have had an effect similar to pouring water into a boiling chip pan.

Neither did I feel I could talk about the tragic meeting with Debbie's boys, and how I had been drawn into this pathetic scene. I couldn't explain how, with every fibre of my being, I'd wanted to bring hope to this sad family. I'd been profoundly grateful for the one trump card I possessed; that I could use my professional connections to help fix up my friend with a new set of teeth that fitted comfortably and looked good, so that her boys could enjoy their mother's smile again.

Perhaps it was good timing that Olivia and I would be spending most of our time together that weekend planning our trip to Italy. She sensibly decided to call Victoria and they agreed to ride earlier on Sunday so that we could spend the afternoon together.

-o-O-o-

I'd called Rev. McPherson who seemed very relieved that I was offering to bring Debbie on Sunday. I anticipated that not all would go to plan and so arrived at The Limes at 9:45. Predictably, Debbie was not dressed. And, just as predictably, she needed her pad changing. I gave the home approximately 6 out of 10 for the state of her bottom. It wasn't angry red, but neither did it look a picture of health. Once outside in the fresh air, Debbie livened up, tuning in to the joys of the birdsong, the smells and sights of May blossom and the sunshine peeping through the clouds. We arrived on the stroke of 10:30 and were able to secure a space at the back where a coat stand and a rack holding hymn books were moved aside to accommodate Debbie and her chair.

I sat on the back pew across the gangway from her, alongside an elderly couple with whom I exchanged the obligatory 'Good morning. Nice day isn't it.' The service followed a similar pattern to the previous time I'd been. I had chance to observe Debbie and wondered if it meant more to her than it did to me. We sang familiar hymns and I could see her becoming absorbed in them, singing her heart out with whatever volume she could muster.

A little later in the service, a gentleman stood up to sing a solo, to the accompaniment of the organ. I recognised the hymn as a golden oldie that I remembered from my childhood. It went:-

'O love that will not let me go,
I rest my weary soul in thee...'

The words to the third verse were:-
> *'O Joy that seekest me through pain*
> *I cannot close my heart to thee;*
> *I trace the rainbow through the rain,*
> *And feel the promise is not vain,*
> *That morn shall tearless be.'*

I looked across at Debbie. I saw the tears streaming down her face as she identified so strongly with the words. She loved this person she called God, and though she didn't understand why she had ended up in such a wretched condition, he-she-it was still there for her. And it was her love for he-she-it that made her the warm-blooded, compassionate, brave soul that I was coming to appreciate.

In fact the theme of suffering ran all the way through the service. There was a prayer for sick people, poor people, and for those affected by the most recent civil war in the Middle East. The lady leading the prayers had a good appreciation of the causes of conflict. Then the reverend preached on one of the Scripture passages where Jesus was introduced to a blind man. Everyone else wanted to know whose fault it was that the guy was blind. Had he sinned, or had his parents? Jesus said that neither had sinned, but that his situation had been allowed to happen so that he (Jesus) could demonstrate the works of God. What was the conclusion? The reverend's main point was that suffering is usually not a form of punishment for the wrongdoing of the victim. If we look hard enough, we may perhaps see something of God in it.

I was becoming impatient again. What a monumental cop-out! Jesus' main point was so much more than that! Why weren't these people expecting to see 'the works of God'? If the church was truly the People of Jesus, why did they not expect to see Debbie get up from her wheelchair and walk?

The opportunity to sound off about my frustrations didn't come immediately. After about ten minutes of stiff hellos and telling people my name, that *No, I wasn't a carer but a friend*, and insisting people ask Debbie her name rather than me, I wheeled her into the adjoining hall and sat down at a table where coffee was being served to go with bourbon and digestive biscuits at various tables. They didn't have straws but suggested I used a child cup for

Debbie. I knew her well enough to predict that she wouldn't see this as the insult that many disabled people might. I arrived back at the table to find we'd been joined by a rather rough-looking man aged around 35 which was right at the younger end of the church's age range. He could have done with a haircut, a razor and some deodorant. Clearly he was alone. And he loved biscuits! Now I remembered what Debbie had told me about the three gossipy ladies who had visited her at The Limes, who had few kind words to say about a man whose description and behaviour matched our 'friend'.

My companion took the initiative.

"Pleathetzer meep you, I'm Debbie," and nodded to me.

"And I'm James. Who are you?"

Perhaps it was Debbie's helplessness that seemed to draw people out of themselves, although I suspected that a 'fit and well' Debbie would have had a gift of empathy.

He explained that he was Bill. He lived in a hostel in the town centre and was on a Zero Hours Contract delivering engineering parts to garages. He'd once been married but that had fallen apart and he'd left home with nowhere to stay. At one time he'd worked as a haulier and had delivered all over Europe... and he expanded on his travelogue.

"Bill, whap bwindz you to churtze?" asked Debbie.

"Well, it's somewhere to go where at least everybody'll say 'ello to you," he said. "Anyway, I always went to church as a lad."

"Tho, are you lonely?" she asked.

"Yeah, I am a bit," was the reply, "an' I really do get hungry!" Bill excused himself to grab another cup of coffee.

"Daimth," said Debbie, "could we invipe him for coffee on Wenthzday?"

I now knew her well enough to judge that any such arrangement would not be boring. I nodded. Bill said he'd like to come and we arranged to meet at 'our' coffee house. He passed me his mobile number just in case he had to be at work all day.

The hall began to empty at around the time when our conversation with Bill had reached its natural end point. I excused myself to visit the Men's. On the way, two ladies caught me. I recognised them from The Limes. They asked with very concerned, supposedly compassionate faces how Debbie was. I replied that life was tough for her but that I admired her spirit.

"You know, it's a terrible shame for her, isn't it?" said one. "She got quite upset the day we went to see her."

"Ahh, it's sad to see," said the other, "but… well, you know, it looks like she isn't all there, doesn't it? That's what the home say about her…"

Blood rushed to my temples. "I'm sorry, but that's not what I see," I said. "Debbie's all there all right, in fact very much all there. She told me about your conversation in her room. She explained to me afterwards that you were speaking about people here in a way that grieved the Holy Spirit. We looked it up afterwards in the Bible and what Debbie said made perfect sense. If you hold on I'll find it for you. I'm not a believer myself, but it stands to reason that if the Church is ever to achieve anything you have to work together rather than pulling each other apart!"

The ladies' eyes expanded to five times their normal size. Their faces went as white as sheets. Their mouths opened wide as they looked around in disbelief. I whipped out my smartphone, typed in "grieve Holy Spirit", and showed them the passage. Then I said, "I'll tell you straight that I'd never come to this church in a month of Sundays if I knew you people were going to slag me off behind my back!"

There were about twenty people in the room. About ten were in earshot. I caught a very subtle exchange of glances between the reverend and Mrs. McPherson that said, "Three cheers for someone who's said in plain language what we've wished we could say for years!"

Debbie was still sitting at our table out of earshot. She was talking to the soloist and telling him how much she'd loved the way he'd sung the hymn, and how, through his beautiful voice that reflected God as a father, "Gob yuthed itzer comforp me." The man's face went a soft pink colour.

And so, back to The Limes we went. Life with Debbie Loveless was never boring.

-o-O-o-

Wednesday afternoon was café time. As I approached The Limes, I passed Amanda on her way home. The James of several weeks ago would probably have been oblivious to a care home worker other than to acknowledge her with a nod. But as we approached, our eyes lit up and we smiled. Amanda spoke first.

"James, thank you *so much* for sharing your coffee shop time with me last week. I don't know how I'd have faced life without spending that time with you and Debbie."

I listened as she told me rather painfully that her husband had left. She'd given him the choice – be faithful and stay with her, or leave. It had taken a lot of strength to spell out what she would no longer tolerate; the daily torment of having him pretend to be her husband whilst carrying on with another woman, making her feel like dirt. She'd have rather he'd chosen to stay with her but at least she knew where she stood. Having made an assertive move had helped her seek out legal and financial advice. She added that our prayer had helped her stay strong when she was confronting her husband, which she'd always previously shied away from. I felt pleased for her. We said a pleasant "goodbye" and I walked on to The Limes. Amanda had changed Debbie's 'All-in-One' slip, creamed her, and dressed her ready to come out. Debbie was thrilled to have been treated kindly for a change. It took so little to make her feel grateful. Sometimes, the way she talked, you'd have thought Debbie was the queen being adorned for a state occasion rather than a severely disabled person needing a high level of personal care, being cleaned up ready to visit a coffee shop.

We took our time on the way to the coffee shop, arriving nicely before half two just as Bill was walking across the road. Once again the friendly staff made space for Debbie, last week's debacle making no difference to their welcome.

I had a hunch that we'd need three cakes between us and I was right! We added a scone with jam and cream to our now-traditional "Thponze cake" and our recent addition the toffee and walnut cake. We cut them all in half. Debbie ate half the Victoria sponge, I ate half the toffee and walnut and half the scone; and Bill ate a half of each of them, and could have eaten much more! Bill wolfed down his share in about five minutes, and then kindly offered to feed Debbie whilst I enjoyed my share and supped my coffee. He couldn't quite coordinate himself with Debbie's painfully slow progress in swallowing her cake, but we laughed about our relative rates of food consumption.

"I'm the tzortzoithe, you're the hare!" she said.

I reflected on the amazing way that Debbie's helplessness so often acted as a bridge to build trust and to create bonds with others.

Bill and I had finished our coffees whilst we still had to negotiate Debbie's without incident. She started the conversation rolling by asking him,

"Pleathe tzell uth all abou' your family, Bill. Do you thtill thee dem?"

Bill's reply took about ten minutes, by which time Debbie's drink had finally disappeared safely down her throat. It was a sad tale. Bill didn't seem to have had the best start in life, and left school early to find whatever work he could in car body shops and small engineering firms. He met his wife when they were 19, and within three months she was expecting. A hastily arranged marriage followed but neither was prepared for parenthood and the challenges of a long term relationship. Bill's only hope of earning decent money was to become a long-distance lorry driver, but this only added to the difficulties at home. Finally, two years ago, he lost his job. His wife, deciding she had no further use for him, kicked him out. It was a year since he'd seen his children.

When Debbie shared her own sadness, Bill was shocked to hear that her partner had abandoned her because she was disabled without taking on the challenge of looking after her boys. A tear rolled down her cheek, but she stayed strong. She asked me to pull out my Smartphone and look up two Bible verses, where she knew the references by heart. The first was in Romans Chapter 8 verse 28, which read,

'And we know that in all things God works for the good of those who love him, who have been called according to his purpose.'

She said, "Bill, it'th been thutz a challentze to believe (and she used all her facial muscles to emphasise) *'all* thinth" when I'm like thith. Bup the more I've tzold Gob thap I twutht him, the more I feel hith love for me."

The other reference was in Hebrews Chapter 13 verse 5, which read,

'Keep your lives free from the love of money and be content with what you have, because God has said, "Never will I leave you; never will I forsake you."'

"an', Bill, he'th *never, ever* forthaken me!"

As Bill looked at the helpless lady in her wheelchair with no teeth, who had to drink through a straw and ate so painfully slowly, he began to see what I saw. Both of us couldn't hold back our tears. It just seemed to follow very naturally when Debbie asked me to lay her hand and mine on Bill's shoulder so she could pray for him. She prayed for him to become in every way the man that God designed him to be. She prayed for his relationship with his family to be restored. Finally, she prayed that he'd come to know her beloved "Dethuth". Then she smiled a Debbie smile, the sort where her eyes lit up the room.

This time I looked around the cafe. Several other customers had noticed that we were praying. It was as if they, too, had become part of a very special event, as if the 'Debbie effect' was influencing them, too. The whole café seemed to have an atmosphere of well-being about it. The staff didn't just smile as we walked out. On their faces was a fondness, a sense of privilege at hosting our gathering.

Debbie and I paid, but we invited Bill to contribute the tip. He placed £2 in the 'Thank You' cup.

She and I said goodbye to a hugely grateful Bill and crossed into the park for a few minutes of 'alone' time. There were two things I wanted to ask her.

"How is it, Debbie, that you pray for me, for Amanda, for Bill, whilst you're the person with the greatest need?"

"I don' know, Daimth," she replied. "Bup whap I do know ith thap I feel a vewy thpethal doy when I share Dethuth' love with other people."

I had to ask Debbie to repeat herself. What was that word Doy?

"Doy – thath Day-Oh-Why."

"Oh, you mean joy? What's that really mean?"

"It'th a vewy deep feelin' thap'th like happineth bup it cometh fwom knowin' how mutz Gob loveth me," was her reply. Then her face relaxed, and she added with a glint in her eye,

"Daimth, you'll thoon know whathip feelth like!"

With a slight sense of panic, I noted that Debbie's track record at predicting outcomes was uncannily good.

"My other question is, how come you pray for all of us, but God doesn't heal you, or do something about your circumstances?"

"Again, I don' know, Daimth. Bup if you look on your phome again, you cam wead a verthe thap dethribeth how I feel. It'th in 2 Cowinthianth Tzwelve verthe nine."

I entered 2 Corinthians 12 verse 9 and read,

'But he said to me, "My grace is sufficient for you, for my power is made perfect in weakness." Therefore I will boast all the more gladly about my weaknesses, so that Christ's power may rest on me.'

"Daimth, I'b love der be healeb. Bup I believe Gob cam yuthe me now, jutht ath I am. And I love him enough to be contzenp with how I am, for now."

All my intellect railed against this lady's blind faith. Somehow 'Big

E(volution)' was distorting her perspective in a way that shielded her from the full awfulness of her existence. But my emotions were in overdrive. As I wheeled her back to The Limes, I experienced a feeling I couldn't believe. I didn't just admire Debbie. I *actually envied* her for her faith, her peace, her mysterious 'Doy' that probably I'd never experienced.

Once again I said I'd take her on Sunday. I didn't want to miss out.

-o-O-o-

Debbie had something to tell me when I arrived on Sunday. It gave us plenty to talk about during the inevitable wait for a carer to toilet and dress her. She'd had an unexpected visit from Mavis, a widow, one of the three ladies who'd gossiped at her bedside. Mavis was heartbroken to think that through her tittle-tattling, the church was being destroyed. She explained to Debbie how, following my tirade on Sunday morning, she'd gone home, opened her Bible and found the passage in Ephesians Chapter 4. She'd sat on her bed and wept.

As Debbie described the scene, I could just imagine a middle-aged lady blushing as she entered the room and, in a highly embarrassed small voice, saying sorry to her. Debbie had told Mavis she wished "Daimth" was there with his smartphone, but she'd have a go at remembering another favourite Bible verse. She guided Mavis to look in her Bible and to find the tiny first letter of John, 1 John Chapter 2. They didn't have to look far – it was plainly written in the first two verses which read:-

'My dear children, I write this to you so that you will not sin. But if anybody does sin, we have an advocate with the Father—Jesus Christ, the Righteous One. He is the atoning sacrifice for our sins, and not only for ours but also for the sins of the whole world.'

Debbie thanked Mavis for coming, and said she forgave her. But more importantly, she wanted Mavis to know that God had forgiven her because of what Jesus had accomplished when he died. I knew that Debbie would have struggled to pronounce many of the words she spoke, and Mavis would have had to be patient as she repeated herself. But however stumbling it would have been, Debbie would have been speaking from her heart. That was the best language of communication.

It seemed as if this was new to Mavis. It was new to me, too!

I noticed that our arrival at church, just before the stroke of 10:30, provoked more of a reaction than previously. Several members of the congregation said a warm, 'Good morning, Debbie', a few adding 'Good morning, James'. The three gossipy ladies were sitting together and I noticed a definite sense of discomfort as I turned towards them. I could immediately tell which one was Mavis, as she didn't avert her eyes.

The reverend's sermon was on a different topic this week, about using your talents. It arose from a story Jesus told about a rich man who went off on a long journey. He entrusted three of his servants with different amounts of his wealth. The two 'star pupils' to whom he entrusted a lot, went out and put the wealth to use, so that when the master returned it had doubled in value. But the third servant, who'd only been entrusted with a single portion of wealth, had no confidence in his abilities and so he buried it in the ground! The master wasn't impressed at all; even if the servant had simply put the wealth in a bank account, it would have increased in value. He was flung out on his ear to what obviously referred to hell. The application of this strange story was that God had entrusted each of us with talents, both natural ones to benefit society, and less obvious ones to bless the church. We had to make sure we used these talents to the full.

I was especially impressed with his example of blessing the church; "Debbie, here, who always has a warm greeting and an encouraging word for people she meets." I was pleased that he saw what I saw.

After the service we went for coffee where I found I no longer needed to sit with Debbie. Bill was more than happy to organise her drink and feed biscuits to her. Mavis came for a chat with her and Bill and I talked to the reverend. He was very interested to know about my professional life and how I'd become involved with Debbie. I shared with him how at one point I had said a final goodbye to her, but that the words of his sermon had helped to change my mind. I said I was very, very grateful I'd reconsidered. He seemed very pleased that his sermon had impacted me, as if he rarely had such feedback.

He broke off for a while to spend time with other church members, but then reconnected with me to ask me how long I'd been a believer. When I said I wasn't, he asked why. I chose to tackle him over the way the Church seemed to cop out of the miracle question. In his sermons he talked about Jesus' miracles as if they were examples for us to follow, but where were the miracles of today? He rolled his eyes and said it was a big, big question. Basically miracles were used to kick-start the Church, but then God decided we didn't need them anymore especially as we had modern medicine and "people like you, James, to look after us."

Mrs. McPherson was in earshot, and walked up to us. "Gilbert, have you read that wee book about miracles in Mozambique that we were lent last month, 'Always Enough'?" No, he hadn't. I made a mental note of the title.

Debbie was singing to herself as we arrived back at The Limes. Our coffee party on Wednesday would now be expanding to include Mavis and she was also inviting Amanda!

-o-O-o-

Olivia was becoming less and less happy with the turn that events were taking despite the fact that she was actually seeing more of me at a weekend than before my rugby injury. I think what galled her most was that I was obviously enjoying what initially I had done purely under sufferance. She felt it was a world she couldn't share. I urged her one more time to come and experience it for herself. But her boundaries were her boundaries. She believed that Debbie had cast some spell upon me that was distorting my taking a common sense view of my responsibilities. She was very pleased that our trip to Italy was now only two weeks away and that, as she put it, a good holiday would help restore my perspective on life. When I questioned why she was so sure I was out of kilter, she simply said,

"I don't want to discuss that. I think you're still suffering the after-effects of El Fasher."

I felt sorry that Olivia had such an inflexible view on the world. I wondered whether assertiveness, that much-praised modern virtue, could sometimes be taken a step too far. I sympathised with her in that life had been "just fine the way things were" before my new adventures with the unfortunate Debbie. Olivia was just as she had been; it was I who was upsetting the proverbial apple cart.

-o-O-o-

There were five of us for coffee on Wednesday. Amanda had prepared Debbie to come before going off shift at 2 p.m. She said she'd see us at 2:30, but that she'd a bit of shopping to do and would join us separately.

She showed up just after 2:30, clearly upset. It wasn't about her family problems. Nathan Cooper had called her into his office and said he'd noticed she was spending too much time talking to Debbie when she was on shift. This was all very well, said Amanda, but the only time she spent alone with Debbie was when she was caring for her. Nathan said he wasn't having Debbie given VIP attention. If she needed to wait her turn, she must. Amanda told us she didn't feel she was giving Debbie VIP attention but simply the care she needed, done properly.

I felt my hackles rising very quickly but Debbie's answer was:-

"Don' wowwy, Amanba. I don' wan' you to give me betzer tzweapmen' than anybody elthe. Bu' thometzimeth we have to accepz tha' people don' like ip when we do whatz wight. They hatzeb Dethuth, dibn' dey?"

My reply to Amanda was not in the same vein. Maybe it was complimentary to Debbie's.

"Yes, Amanda, carry on doing what's right," I said. "It's getting close to the time when I'm going to sort this Nathan out!" I had already made a note of the Carrington Care Company's head office number.

It was a merry party, in which we all talked to each other naturally and freely. Mavis let slip that she'd worried over the reverend's sermon. She felt as if she could be the servant with the single talent, and that God might judge her as somebody who'd wasted her life.

"I just hope God'll think I've done enough good deeds to get me to heaven," she said.

It was clear Mavis thought that God weighed up your good and your bad deeds and decided you were going to heaven if you ended up on the credit side. Debbie smiled and shook her head.

"But, Debbie; isn't that how it works?" I asked. Surely that was the role of religion in achieving social cohesion; didn't people need to be held in check and persuaded to behave decently by the prospect of pie-in-the-sky as opposed to the fires of hell?

"Daimth," she grinned, "you wouldn' thtanb a chantz!"

I was affronted. "You mean it's just holy people like you who get to heaven? Just because I'm not religious doesn't mean I'm not a good person!"

"You don' underthtzand!" she continued. "*You* don' thtanb a chantz, *I* don' thtanb a chantz, nor do Bill or Amanba. Neither the wevewend nor Mithith McPherthon thtanb a chantz …"

"Then who *does* stand a chance? Who *does* go to heaven?" I asked in sheer exasperation. "Just the Pope, the Archbishop of Canterbury and St. Francis, I suppose?"

Debbie was giggling. She was thoroughly enjoying my struggle to understand the rules governing God's apportioning of a place in heaven. Oh my, what a sense of mischief she had!

"Nobody! Nobody eczep' people who've athed Dethuth to forgive dem thwough hith death on the Cwoth," she said. "Wonthe you've done tha', you don' have to wowwy abou' gointhzer heaven, becoth you belon' to Him!"

I had to admit that Debbie acted completely differently to someone who was worried about heaven and hell. She belonged to, and felt loved by God and by her mythical Dethuth.

She turned to Mavis. "Mavith, why don' you thank Dethuth tzoday for dyin' on the Cwoth for you? We cam pway now."

And in a simple, moving prayer led by Debbie, Mavis thanked Jesus for dying for her. Debbie assured her that now she belonged to Jesus, and that no-one could take her away from him. Mavis placed her hands on Debbie's cheeks and planted a huge kiss on her forehead, then made her way home. I noticed as she left how tears of relief were pouring down her own cheeks.

And the following week yet another person joined the coffee party. The staff suggested that if the weather was fine, we could go out the back onto the terrace. They loved having us. It was consuming more of my Wednesdays than previously but I didn't mind at all. I always made sure I had my own 'alone time' with Debbie. One more week at church saw us get to know another two or three people. It was as well that we now had a little group going, as they'd need to organise Debbie for the fortnight I was on holiday.

I would miss them whilst I was away. What would have happened in my absence?

Chapter 9

Olivia and I exchanged contented smiles. We'd caught the train to London at the crack of dawn, boarded the Heathrow Express, and then, after an easy passage through customs, had spent an hour in the coffee lounge. Each of us had brought a newspaper but we'd sat together thumbing our way through the must-see pages of our Lonely Planet book on Italy. Now the plane was cruising at 32,000 feet above the English Channel, and both of us had chosen red wine to enliven the first part of our journey. We were both glad to take a break from ward rounds and theatre duties and were looking forward to being looked after for ten days and to seeing some of the most wonderful art and architecture ever created. We squeezed each other's hand in eager anticipation.

Florence did not disappoint. We'd booked five nights in a 3-star hotel with a classical façade, in the foyer of which sat a bust of the type found in museums, a taster of what was to come. The renaissance picture on the wall above our beds helped set the tone, and we snuggled under the covers for an hour's fun before venturing out to find ourselves a café in the corner of one of Florence's many piazzas. As the afternoon turned into dusk we found our way to the Ponte Vecchio with its tiny shops built onto the sides of the ancient bridge over the River Arno. We walked across and back again, taking in all the sights and sounds of this city steeped in its long, colourful history. We spent a good half hour altogether taking photographs, trying to capture the atmosphere of the dusk, the floodlights, the elegant street lights and the stonework. Olivia and I had a shared distaste for modern mass photography with its selfie sticks. Our rather sophisticated Canon camera was the one item of property that we co-owned. We finished by finding our way to a delightful restaurant with a marble floor where we feasted on lasagne dishes, mine with fish and Olivia's the classic one with meat, helped down with a delightful bottle of Chianti. Olivia followed this with gelati (multiple scoops of ice cream), I with tiramisu.

We agreed we'd read at bedtime but after five minutes I fell fast asleep, dreaming very contentedly as had been my pattern recently.

The following morning we ate a leisurely continental breakfast with fruit juice, croissants and plenty of coffee. We found ourselves sitting with Geoff and Susan, a couple from Guildford who were celebrating their tenth wedding anniversary. Susan's parents had very kindly offered to look after their three children for a long weekend. We compared notes, and swapped recommendations for good restaurants and bars.

In the morning we visited the Uffizi gallery and marvelled at the many classical portraits. I loved the way the artists had captured their subjects' features in such beautiful detail, but nothing could match the sculpture corridor and particularly the work of Baccio Bandinelli and his recreation of a Greek sculpture called, 'Laocoon and his sons'. The bodies were intertwined in an amazing montage of human shapes.

It took the whole morning to view the gallery. It totally absorbed our attention, and by lunchtime we felt as if we'd entered a completely different world. We bought ourselves bread, salami, salad items and a patisserie each then sat down to enjoy them in a park.

We allocated the afternoon to exploring Florence's famous historic Duomo with its pink, white and green marble exterior. It was deliciously cool inside, away from the fierce early afternoon sun. We admired the amazing frescos of The Last Judgment on the rounded ceiling before climbing up the Cupola, a rounded tower from which we could view the whole of the city in all its splendour.

At breakfast the following morning we were sitting talking to Geoff and Susan when the chief waiter came to the table to say that there was a call for Susan. She hurried over to the reception desk, returning looking anxious and flushed. Issy, their 5-year-old, had fallen off a wall and was in hospital with a broken arm. Should they return home straightaway? Both Olivia and I felt so sorry for them. Having jumped through many hoops to extricate themselves for their much-deserved holiday, they were about to have it snatched away. Clearly they felt guilty about the idea of staying in Florence, whether or not Susan's parents could cope at home.

At the far side of the restaurant I saw a girl with cerebral palsy in a wheelchair. It reminded me of the one wheelchair I wished was at our table. That of a peaceful woman whose faith would have made such a difference here in this moment of crisis. Debbie's prayers wouldn't have changed the fact that

Issy was in hospital with a broken arm. But they would have reassured Geoff and Susan and sucked away all the anxiety so that they could be free to make the best decision. I could imagine the scene:-

"Can I pway for you? Daimth, pup my hanb on Thuthan'th thyolder," and I bet she'd have added, "an' your hanb on Deoff's thyolder... Lor' Dethuth..."

The very thing I had previously cringed about the most was the thing I now wished could happen so that we could reach out to this couple. But Debbie wasn't here. I was having a fabulous, luxurious holiday in the cultural capital of Europe. She was incarcerated in The Limes, not that she would ever complain. I decided to send her a postcard.

We never found out what happened to Geoff and Susan although I suspect they caught a plane home. We carried on with our own holiday, exploring Florence for a further three days before picking up the hire car in which we were to explore Tuscany. We'd bought, written, and stamped ten cards between us and took them to the hotel reception at the time we checked out. The receptionist agreed to post them for us and Olivia handed them in. She noticed Debbie's name and address, turned, and looked straight at me.

"James, what's this? You're sending a card to that girl at The Limes? Haven't you forgotten about her whilst we're here in Italy?"

"Olivia, she's part of my life," I said. "I may be away on holiday but she's a good friend. I can't forget her. But that doesn't take away from the time you and I are enjoying together, surely?"

Olivia just went quiet.

We buried the issue and set our stall out to enjoy the luscious countryside with its rolling valleys, pretty vineyards, traditional stone-built hamlets and Etruscan villages mounted on top of rounded hills. In particular we loved the ancient village of San Gimagnano, and were grateful that we'd booked two nights at a farmhouse just 5 miles away within the wooded countryside. Our hosts spoke sufficient English to explain from a map they lent us, how to walk into San Gimagnano along country tracks. My injured leg had recovered sufficiently to cope with this gentle challenge.

It was a beautiful morning and our camera worked overtime photographing the ever lovelier views as we approached the top of the hill on which lay the village. We were glad to have made it by 11 a.m. before the midday sun gathered strength. The modern art museum provided welcome refuge as did one of the village's pleasant bars where we sat, drank beer and read our novels.

We set out again at 4 p.m., returning home via a different set of tracks to complete a circular walk…

All in all, we both felt very well rested as we returned to England ready to resume work and play. As the plane was touching down Olivia asked me,

"So, now you've helped Debbie find a group of friends, d'you think your work's done? You've played your part; is it time to let the church take over?"

My reply was, "It's not 'work' anymore, Olivia. No more than coming on holiday together has been 'work' for us. I *like* her. You would, too."

It was as if Olivia hadn't heard. She couldn't cope with any further discussion.

-o-O-o-

I looked forward to my first Wednesday back at home. I wasn't disappointed. The coffee house staff had placed a canopy above two tables on their terrace, which was as well since it turned out to be a showery afternoon. In total there were eleven of us, now including the man who'd so moved Debbie with his solo in church, his wife, and Amanda's older colleague Penny. It was the nature of the conversations that struck me as interesting. When people asked each other how they were, they meant it. And when they replied, they always began with a reason to be thankful. As ever, Debbie wanted to pray for somebody and we laid hands on the two care workers, Penny and Amanda, and asked the "Holy Thpiwip" to bless their efforts to care for the residents and staff alike.

I was delighted when Penny told me that a letter had arrived from the home's dentist to say that Debbie had been referred for her impressions to be taken. They'd hoped I would pick up the baton and arrange an appointment, then take her myself. I was very pleased to be signed up for this particular duty. I rang the dentist, explained the circumstances and they kindly fitted us in for 1:15 p.m. the following week.

Church, on Sunday, followed the same pattern as previously, and I noticed that Debbie had made more new friends. Bill sat talking to the soloist and his wife, whilst Mavis, with a new curly hairdo, appeared to have detached herself from her two judgmental friends and was making conversation elsewhere.

It struck me that there were two people who would greatly appreciate being with us at Wednesday coffee time, whom people would find it difficult to include. That's why I invited the reverend and his wife. They were very pleased to be asked.

-o-O-o-

It was a good thing I had allowed plenty of time to get Debbie ready on Wednesday. The staff had to cope with an emergency as an old man needed to be taken to hospital in an ambulance with a suspected heart attack. I did my best to cope alone making sure the door of Debbie's room was wide open lest anyone suspected foul play. As I was busy wiping her bottom, she said,

"Daimth, how I *withz* I coulb gep tzo the tzoilep when I neeb ip. How I *withz* you dibn' havtzer do thith for me! Bup never minb. I'm vewy, vewy gwapeful."

I was intrigued. Did she mean she *could* control her bowels and bladder for a limited period?

I never found out. We were interrupted by a non-too-friendly voice which asked,

"Excuse me; I wasn't aware you were a member of staff here?"

It was, of course, the admirable Nathan Cooper.

"Indeed I'm not," I said, "but since The Limes has delegated to me the task of taking Miss Loveless to her dental appointment, I deem it reasonable to do what is needed to get her there on time."

"Do we have any record of a Criminal Record Bureau check on you?" asked Nathan.

I thought carefully; I'd have liked to say all sorts of things but I had to remember my first priority was to meet Debbie's appointment which, to dear Mr. Cooper, was of lesser importance.

"Look, Nathan," I said, "you know as well as I do that your staff have been at full stretch. I understand your concerns. Can you just stand and watch me finish this job off please, so I can get Debbie away?"

I had never before exercised so much restraint when faced with such obnoxious pedantry, but my words achieved their objective. Debbie's wheels raced down the High Street like a chair possessed, and we arrived for her appointment just as the nurse called her name. Debbie was very excited as the dentist and his assistant prepared their green goo and placed the upper, then lower moulds into her mouth. "Oooh, it'th tho cool!" she enthused. It seemed to provide an opportunity for a gentle giggle. They had to tell her to calm down whilst they removed the lower impression from her mouth…

The dentist used a technician's lab that I was familiar with, so we agreed that I'd take responsibility for helping Debbie choose the colour and style she wanted. We'd call there after our coffee party.

"So, you're looking forward to getting your new dentures, are you?" asked the dentist.

"You bep!" replied Debbie. "Then I'm goin ther compepe for Mith Worl'!"

As I wheeled her out, Debbie was giggling. I was giggling. The dentist and his technician were giggling. The other patients in the waiting room smiled good-naturedly. One could pay good money to be entertained like this.

Our coffee party once again turned out to be a highlight. The reverend and Mrs. McPherson circulated around and enjoyed talking to Debbie's carers. It was especially moving that Debbie wanted us to pray for the McPhersons, that they'd be anointed to lead the church. The reverend, in turn, prayed for Debbie herself, thanking God for bringing her onto the scene. His was a rather formal prayer but I knew he meant every word.

Southgate Dental Laboratories was situated half a mile away. I rang the bell and Joshua Gibbons came to the door. He and I shook hands, then he addressed himself to Debbie.

"So, my lady, I'm here to give you a happy smile," he said.

"Eczuthe me," said Debbie with a glint in her eye, "my thmile's a vewwy happy one alweaby! You duth' have der make ip pwettzy for me!"

Joshua didn't know what to make of this, but he looked at me and saw my affection for Debbie. He took his cue and said, "Mmmm… we've got a right 'un here, James. Only the best will do, I can see!"

And I added, "Tell you what, Josh. This lady here has been through all sorts. If anyone ever deserves the best, it's her." Joshua could tell I was serious.

Joshua showed us a range of colours for her palate and gums. We persuaded Debbie that a gentle pink colour rather than a deep red would suit her complexion best. Then we looked at the colour of her teeth. We all agreed that she'd suit a pearl colour with a delicate sheen, definitely not the old-style gleaming, glossy white teeth of previous generations. Where we had a lot of discussion was on the shape. Joshua showed us several designs that looked smart and were entitled, 'for that natural look'. You really couldn't have told they were dentures, not at all. Various teeth had been tastefully twisted, shortened or elongated and you could even have molars that looked like they'd been filled.

"Wow, Debbie, I can just see you in this set…" I said, looking at an example.

"No, no, no, Daimth!" she said. "I don' wan' dem der look cwooked. If I'm havin' dentzureth, I wan' dem der look nithe an' thtwaigh'."

"But, Debbie," we chorused, "if you just have them straight, everybody will be able to tell you're wearing dentures."

"Bup, Daimth," she said, "evewyboby I know'th thee' me withoup tzeeth. They all know alweady!"

"Yes, but what about people you're going to meet in future?" we asked.

"If dey can thee I'm wearin' denzureth, I don' minb," she insisted. "I've waitzeb thwee monthth for dem, tho why should'n I be pwou' der wear dem?"

Joshua looked at Debbie, then at me. "Proud to wear her dentures, eh! That's what I like to hear. Well, I s'pose you can't fault her logic!" he said.

"Debbie," I asked, "were you by any chance a bit of an exhibitionist in your past life?"

"I thtill am!" she said, occasioning another round of giggles.

Joshua had some denture designs up on his computer. I looked at a 'straight set', inputted the colour we'd chosen, and made a few careful tweaks so that the dentures looked slightly more natural. Debbie saw it and gasped with delight.

I felt so pleased for her. She deserved to look good.

The dentist had asked me how the dentures were to be paid for. So after taking Debbie back to The Limes, I knocked on Nathan Cooper's door. I reported that Debbie's dentures would be ready at the end of next week, and brought up the issue of payment. Nathan had no answer. They received Debbie's disability pension each week as part of her care home fees but he had never been provided with any other funds relating to a bank account that she had. It was not, he said, his problem. Once again my hackles were rising.

"But surely when a resident comes to live here, you have to establish what funds they have, don't you?" I asked. "I mean, how's she going to pay for her dentures?"

He shrugged cynically. I saw I wasn't making any progress and decided it would be better to phone the number for the Carrington Care Homes although I was also fairly certain Nathan would have made sure of his position.

He had enjoyed watching me struggle. Then he volunteered that the residents all arrived with a bank account to their name. Debbie had arrived with plenty of cash but, because she'd left home in a hurry, no-one had ever sorted out her financial affairs. He didn't know if she had an account with money in it. Had she been '"all there" as he put it, she'd have been aware of the fact that her affairs weren't in order. I could see where this was leading. I'd ask her of course, but I suspected I was going to have to pay for her dentures and hopefully reclaim the money later. I decided I'd ask the reverend for somebody's help to resolve her finances. It could have been worse. At least my finances and Olivia's weren't linked. This was not one of those occasions when I'd have wanted to be open with her about the use of my money.

-o-O-o-

Whilst I was at work on Saturday, Olivia was at the car showrooms choosing a brand new cream-coloured sports car, for which she'd saved up. I had to admit a thrill went through me as I thought of myself driving it. I was a named driver on her car, having chosen not to own one myself. In Olivia's quiet way I knew she was delighted with her afternoon's purchase.

For my part I was more excited about the pearl-coloured items I had helped to purchase this week. At that moment I decided I wouldn't pay for Debbie's dentures out of sufferance. They would be my gift to her. Nathan had questioned her sanity over money, but she'd always paid her share in the coffee shop including that of our first-time guests. Every week before we set out from The Limes, she asked me to top up her purse from a little wallet in her cupboard to make sure she had £20 in it.

She wouldn't expect this of me, but it would give me such pleasure to see her beautiful smile. I'd gathered, too, that her birthday was coming up in a fortnight. Why not do what I'd said we'd do and make her a 'beauty queen' by taking her to a salon, leaving her dentures to complete the picture? I surmised she'd never been 'made up' and made to feel special for many years.

On Monday I phoned The Limes and asked to speak to Penny. I explained what I proposed, and asked Penny which beauty salon she'd recommend. She agreed to sound Debbie out in that delicate female way that doesn't give the game away. I gave her my mobile number and received a text saying,

"Great idea shell like it. Recommend Julies on Hi st"

It took me a few moments to work out that there was an apostrophe missing in 'shell', then found the number of Julie's on my smart phone. We arranged to be there at midday on Wednesday. The dentist also called me to say that the dentures would be ready on Friday and that he'd left a message at The Limes.

-o-O-o-

Both Penny and Amanda were on shift on Wednesday morning and were almost as excited as I was about Debbie's appointment. There she sat in her wheelchair, all smiles, trying to guess where I was about to take her. When we arrived at Julie's, her eyes lit up even more brightly and she said,

"Oooh, lucky me! Now I'll no' dutht *feel* I'm thpetzel, I'll *look* thpetzel!"

Not many people in her situation would have described themselves as lucky or special. That was exactly what made her special…

We were offered a drink whilst we waited, Debbie drinking hers through one of the straws we kept in her handbag for when we were out. Then the beautician went to work, and I left for some 'alone time' in the park, reading a medical magazine then, when I got bored, my novel. I popped into the salon at intervals to make sure all was okay. It was. Debbie was thoroughly enjoying herself.

At 2 p.m. I proudly collected our beauty queen. They'd made her up with sensitivity to her light complexion. Her hair was washed, shiny, and had a slight wave to it. Her eyes looked lovely and soft with an ever-so-gentle glow of blue shadow. Her lips were peach-coloured. Her cheeks, normally all too pale because of being indoors most of the time, had a rosy glow. Her fingernails were glossy and peach-coloured to match her lips. As I pulled out my wallet, I asked myself how we were going to keep her looking like this. I voiced the question, and the salon girls organised a little bag of items for the purpose, for which I paid a few extra pounds. I'd hope Amanda and Penny could help in applying her make-up when needed.

Debbie was so excited at what she'd seen of herself in the mirror that she came out in goose bumps. Over and over again, she repeated,

"Daimth! I can' believe I look tho beautziful! Thank you *tho mutz!*"

We were five minutes late arriving at the cafe. As I pushed the wheelchair onto the terrace, the assembled group stood up, applauded and cheered! Her new looks were very much admired, which she lapped up with great enjoyment. As I looked around the group, I reflected on how such a vulnerable person had acted as a focal point to church members and care workers alike, bringing them together in honest relationships with no regard for social standing in an atmosphere of caring friendship.

As the last of our group left the café, I prepared to take Debbie over the road into the park for the time we normally shared alone. But I could see she was tired out. I gave her the choice and sure enough, she said she needed to rest. No staff members were around as we came through the door. Signing myself in, I wheeled Debbie to her room. By this time she'd dropped off to sleep so, taking her in my arms, I placed her on her bed, discreetly removing her outdoor clothes then placing a cover on her. I looked fondly at this woman who had changed me inside. At last the world could see outwardly the beauty that I, and her friends, could see inwardly. I bent over the bed and kissed her on the lips, ever so lightly. I felt her tongue move to meet mine. Debbie was still asleep; for her it was an automatic response.

It was as if an electric shock passed between two sets of lips.

I was aware of movement behind me, on the other side of the half-open door. I looked around and, through the glass panel in the top of the door, saw a figure disappearing.

-o-O-o-

The following morning I was just completing my rounds when a man in a suit and tie appeared in the ward, looking for me. I vaguely recognised Mr. Hardcastle as one of the hospital's senior administrators. He said he needed to see me in his office at 10:30 a.m. When I asked how long this would take, and what it was about, he said he'd explain at the time. Sister Marion was concerned. So was I; had someone 'snitched' on me over my mistake with Mr. Glynn's dental extraction?

After a five-minute walk I arrived at his office to find Mr. Davy and two other staff members inside, all wearing serious expressions. Mr. Hardcastle came straight to the point.

"Mr. McAlister, you are suspended from your duties with immediate effect whilst we investigate an allegation of serious professional misconduct. We shall hold a preliminary meeting on Monday at 11 a.m.; that is, for the investigation team, not yourself. Until further notice you must not set foot on site. Is that clear?"

To say I was gobsmacked would have totally underestimated my reaction. I began to tremble. All I could muster was,

"Whwhwhat f-for? I'm not aware of anything wrong."

"We can't say anything more at this stage," said Hardcastle. He stood up, gathered his few belongings into his briefcase, and walked out. I looked at Mr. Davy who simply shook his head, as if to say, "Will you never learn?"

One of the two unknown staff members had the job of escorting me off site so I gathered my belongings and handed him my lanyard, wondering when I'd wear it again. I went home to consider my position. I made a cup of tea with difficulty, my hand shaking like a leaf in the wind.

As my mental mist cleared, my next thought was that since I wouldn't be at work, I could now take Debbie for her denture fitting appointment. That would be the silver lining on this dreadful unexpected cloud. I needed to let the home know, and also that I was paying for them. As I was signing in, the older carer who was on duty spoke sharply to me.

"Just a minute please, Mr. McAlister."

I didn't have to wait long before Nathan appeared.

"Mr. McAlister, I have to insist that you don't set foot in The Limes pending an allegation into your conduct. Yesterday afternoon I caught you committing a sexual assault on a vulnerable resident who had been a patient of yours in hospital. Now if you please…" and he motioned towards the door.

"Assault? *What* assault?" I protested as I stood outside on the steps. "Look, you know as well as I do that Debbie's my good friend, and that to be honest, I've helped her get a life!"

"Assault is assault," said Nathan. "Goodbye, Mr. McAlister."

He couldn't contain his glee. It was as if he'd sprung the trap on me. At least I now knew what I was fighting against.

I wandered back along Wolverstone Road towards the High Street. I crossed into the park and walked to the pond, sitting where Debbie and I usually sat. I was utterly stunned, but at the same time livid at the unfairness. Nathan and I had despised each other from the moment we'd met. He had it in for Debbie that was for sure. What was so infuriating was that he knew so well what he could get away with, and I was pretty sure he'd be able to justify himself to his superiors even if I complained about his neglectful, degrading treatment of her. He'd be able to justify his vindictiveness towards Amanda and this ridiculous allegation against me. Technically it was an assault, but every shred of natural justice would tell anyone that no harm had been done. I'd just over-expressed my feelings.

So – where should I turn for help and support? I was pretty sure that Olivia wouldn't be my best hope. Into my mind came the reverend and his wife. When I rang their number, Mrs. McPherson, whom I now addressed as Elspeth, came to the phone. I haltingly began to explain what had happened, but she interrupted,

"James, come and see us at the manse. You know where we live, don't you? Number 68 Patterdale Road. Gilbert's out this afternoon but we'll clear this evening for you. In fact," said she, thinking aloud, "come at 6 o'clock and you can have dinner with us." I reflected that my initial impressions of the McPhersons as a rather stuffy couple had been wrong, but that it was Debbie's influence that had made visible their hidden warmth.

Dinner was a simple but delicious lamb hot pot served with Brussels sprouts, for which, having hated them as a child, I now had a taste. We finished our meal with fruit and homemade flapjack which went down very well with our coffee. Over dinner we filled each other in on our life histories. Gilbert and Elspeth had both originated from rural Scotland but had met at a Baptist Bible College in Glasgow. They'd moved to England many years ago, believing there was more of a need in this the most secular part of the U.K. They had two grown-up daughters and a son, and were proud of their children and three grandchildren although none had continued their childhood faith into adulthood.

Both of them seemed to look back to their Bible College days as a golden era. On one occasion each student had been given £5, then sent out to 'live by faith' for a week. They had to trust God to meet their needs, other than that they could return to the college at night if they hadn't found accommodation. The twenty students in their year embraced this as a faith challenge in a way Debbie would have enjoyed. They preached the Gospel on the streets. They prayed for the sick. They shared their meals with down-and-outs. And, as Gilbert and Elspeth put it, God provided! Not one of the students went without a meal. Strangers placed money into their hands. One student found a £20 note on the pavement and handed it to the police, who gave it back to him three days later when no-one had reported it missing. The students who'd fared the best helped those who struggled. They all put ten percent of the money they received into a special gift box that was later given to a charity for the homeless that the college supported.

We began to talk about my predicament. I told them my whole story starting from my crazy challenge to 'he-she-it'. I told them I had a steady girlfriend in Olivia who had steered clear of involvement with Debbie. When I explained about Nathan they, too, said they'd noticed his animosity towards Debbie and what almost seemed resentment that she had friends and company.

They both said how much they valued Debbie and spoke about what they called her 'charismatic effect' on the church membership. They were excited that the church was now much more of a family. They also spoke of their appreciation of me, and in particular the way I'd spoken out over the gossiping issue. They were delighted to see the transformation in Mavis. They admired the way I'd looked after Debbie and taken her to heart. And they commented that both she and I had something in common – we expressed our thanks and appreciation of others when we'd found their contribution helpful. *Without our even intending it, Debbie and I had already acted as a couple.*

They both expressed their feelings about the injustice of my suspension and added that they were determined to help me. It would be wise for me to stay away on Sunday but they would interview Debbie and, if as expected, she did not feel violated, they would write a letter of support and make sure it was available to the inquiry on Monday. Their argument would be that whilst I may have breached the principles of professional conduct, there was a higher law – that of kindness, esteeming and supporting others, gentleness, faithfulness – that had characterised my conduct around Debbie. She was a far, far happier person because of my influence.

But then this brought them to what they described as a sensitive matter. They had noticed how fond of each other we'd become. They weren't surprised that I'd wanted to kiss Debbie. They said,

"Perhaps, James, this has come at the right time. You see, we think she's falling in love with you, and sooner or later you're going to have to break this lassie's heart. You can't carry on forever visiting her in The Limes. We think you've done everything you could ever do for her, and we're ready to take over where you leave off. She's got enough good friends, and we think we can take care of her. She'll be very upset of course, but with God's grace we can manage that. We love her too."

My face fell. I could understand the impeccable logic, but also the compassion, behind their stance. They could tell straightaway what I was thinking.

"That is, unless you're one of those very rare people who can sacrifice their whole life to looking after a severely disabled person. But, James, please don't consider it. We've seen people try before and in most cases it ends in tears."

The McPhersons both prayed for me, asking God to help me stay strong. They prayed that the inquiry panel would exercise discretion and recognise the goodness of my intentions. They prayed for Debbie and how she'd cope with the forthcoming bad news that I couldn't continue to see her regularly, and also about the way she was treated by most staff members in the home. Finally, Gilbert asked me for Mr. Davy's number.

I walked home feeling deeply affirmed and loyally supported on the one hand, yet greatly saddened on the other. The McPhersons were right. I had to face the situation, take a large step back from Debbie, and trust they could help her face the heartbreak. At least I could resume my relationship with Olivia without a cloud hanging over our heads.

It was 9:30 p.m. when I arrived home. Most Thursday evenings I phoned my parents who lived in Durham, and I decided to do so even though it was late. I'd told them various parts of the tale about Debbie, more so the episodes when I'd first met her and regarded her as a gruesome symbol of misfortune. They'd met Olivia several times and liked her very much, saying what a good match we were and what intelligent, well-bred children we'd have if, as they frequently hinted, we'd tie the knot and settle down.

I thought I'd better give them an edited version of what had happened before they found out from other sources. There was a stunned silence.

"James," they said, "don't ever forget that we, and you, invested a great deal of time and money so that you could build your career. You *are* going to close this chapter with the disabled lady, aren't you? Please don't throw away everything you've worked for out of sympathy for this unfortunate woman. That's what homes are for."

It would have been pointless to try to explain how my own mind set had changed over the last three months.

Friday dawned. I couldn't concentrate on anything at all, not even my novel. I wandered down the High Street and into 'our' cafe where, over coffee and cake, I thought about Debbie. I'd have to take time to grieve over one of the most precious friendships I'd ever known. The staff noticed I was sad.

"Where is she today?" they asked.

I shook my head in a way that said, "Please don't ask."

It was my turn to go to Olivia's that weekend. I waited until we'd placed our fish pie in the oven then I told her my tale of woe. She looked at me pityingly, and gently said,

"James, this is exactly what I feared would happen. Sooner or later I knew you'd find you'd pitched in too deeply. We'll just have to hope you can extricate yourself without damaging your career. Anyway, it sounds as if you've two very good friends in the reverend and his wife. Get out now, James, whilst you can. I'm sure Mr. Davy'll work behind the scenes to get you reinstated. You're too good a surgeon for him to lose."

In bed that night my efforts were half-hearted and, afterwards, I didn't sleep, hardly at all. Something seemed very, very wrong. As the morning light shone through the curtains, I knew what I was going to do. I got up with Olivia then explained that I was making my way to the railway station. I would be catching a train up to Edinburgh, a four hour journey. I was going to see Granny McAlister and I'd be back the next day, Sunday.

Olivia looked at me with consternation. "You're going *where*, James? Are you out of your mind?"

"Yes, I am," I ventured. "But I think Granny may help me get back into it again."

Quite simply I had to admit that I couldn't live without Debbie Loveless. I was deeply, passionately in love with her. I'd never felt anything like this before.

Chapter 10

It was 2 p.m. by the time I boarded a local train at Edinburgh Waverley station and took the service to Curriehill. Granny, who was 82, lived alone in a traditional stone-built Scottish style bungalow with two front rooms both of which had large bay windows. The décor was neat, clean but dated, and the bungalow hadn't been modernised since the 1980's when Granddad was fit and active. The garden had once been a picture but had deteriorated somewhat since its care now relied on a gardener who came for two hours a week during the summer. Nevertheless, it still had plenty of colour and would have qualified for the description of a semi-wild cottage garden.

Granny slowly came to the door pushing her frame. She always had a twinkling smile and her home was one of the most peaceful places I'd ever known. She'd boiled the kettle and, refusing my offer of help, made us both a cuppa and toasted teacakes. Then we sat down and I talked, talked and talked.

I told Granny that I felt like I was on a hike and had seen a beautiful pathway heading through trees. I didn't know what would be along the path but I wanted to explore. Everybody else said "Don't!" But if I walked past and kept to the main track, I'd spend my entire life wondering what lay up the mystery path.

"James, tell me what you love so much about Debbie," said Granny.

I replied that I found her an inspiration. I loved her for her faith, her humour, her empathy, her strength of character, her sweet nature, the way she brought other people to life, and now increasingly her looks. I was now aware how conscious I was of her beautiful face. I loved gazing into her eyes through her brown glasses, her gently rounded cheeks, her fair locks of hair, and if I ever saw her again, I'd enjoy her lovely teeth. Yes, they would be plastic but they'd perfectly express her inner beauty.

"Now tell me why you aren't going to see her again," said Granny.

All the reasons were pragmatic. I had my career to think of. It wouldn't be good for me to be tied down for ever to a helpless partner who had to be fed, toileted, bathed, dressed, and taken everywhere. Sooner or later I'd end up screaming. Gone would be delightful skiing holidays and summer breaks like we'd had in Italy. I wouldn't be playing rugby – not unless we had an army of carers to look after her. We couldn't have children, not that this had been a priority for me.

"James," said Granny, "what if you could look back on your life after you die? D'you feel you'd have been more pleased with your life if you'd gone with Debbie? Or would you have been best to make the so-called sensible choice and say goodbye to her now?"

I thought aloud about the obituary of Mr. James McAlister, distinguished Consultant Surgeon. Gaining the recognition I sought would be a lot harder if I was heading home each evening to a severely disabled partner. On the other hand I thought of how much I'd loved the coffee parties that Debbie and I had pioneered, and been excited at the way the Baptist Church was becoming a community. We had already made a difference to a number of people's lives. And, unconsciously, we'd acted like a couple in welcoming our guests. Which course of action was really the more valuable?

"Does she love you too, James?" said Granny.

I'd thought about this and now knew the answer. Increasingly both she and I had found it very pleasant whenever we touched, such as when I placed on her coat or lifted her out of her chair. It seemed remarkable but that day we had to rush to the dental surgery, I'd enjoyed creaming her bottom, and knew she'd enjoyed it too. Also, I had been used to her gentle, radiant smile being there for everyone but now appreciated how in recent days she had looked ever so deeply and tenderly into my eyes. Her skin had looked soft and radiant. The McPhersons were right. She was deeply in love with me, too.

Granny decided we needed to eat, pulled two Wiltshire Farm meals out of her freezer and asked me to heat them up in the microwave.

"James," she said. It was odd to think that was how Debbie would be addressing me in future if I went against everyone's advice. I'd quite miss 'Daimth'. "I think you know what you're going to do, don't you?"

Granny had been right to talk about how I'd feel when I looked back over my life. Up until now, I'd been used to defining myself by my achievements. Since I'd known Debbie, I had discovered that there was a deeper 'me' that was far more precious. And that 'me' believed there was something incredibly beautiful about falling in love so deeply, and being true to that love through the most challenging of circumstances. Somehow I felt as if I'd been chosen and very specially privileged to receive a challenge that few others would face, as if my choice that day would have a significance that rang out across the cosmos. Although my intellect railed against my feelings, something very deep inside me told me I wasn't mistaken.

Granny had been a Scottish Presbyterian all her life and knew her Bible. "I believe the Lord wants me to share this with you," she said. She pulled her well-thumbed Bible out of the drawer to the side of her padded chair and found the letter of 1 John, which I remembered Debbie had used to great effect with Mavis. 1 John Chapter 4 verse 18 read,

'There is no fear in love. But perfect love drives out fear, because fear has to do with punishment. The one who fears is not made perfect in love.'

Granny explained that to the first readers of the letter, it was written about love between God and us, not about romantic love. But the same principle applied. She asked what struck me about the verse. It was obvious. All my 'reasons why not' were to do with fear – of not fulfilling my career goals, of being stuck at home whilst others were away having fun, of what everybody would think including my parents, Mr. Davy, Olivia... The words, 'love drives out fear' reverberated through my mind.

Olivia, there's a point. It was now obvious to me that she and I had been good friends with compatible interests and cultural backgrounds. On a physical level we'd been good, well-matched partners. But there'd never been any element of sacrifice about our relationship. It was based on mutual self-interest. I had never felt anything of the passion, the desire to give my all to her like I did to Debbie. I wasn't sorry for Debbie, I just loved everything about her, even her infuriating ways of embarrassing me which she giggled her way out of. I longed to have her alongside me.

Granny smiled. She prayed for me very simply, then asked me,

"Do you believe in Jesus yet, James?" I replied that officially I didn't but that I was finding myself increasingly challenged. If only I could see God do something concrete, I'd start to believe in him.

Granny went to warm up her bedtime milk and made me a cup of tea. I went into her tiny spare room to find the bed neatly made up, two towels awaiting my use and a chocolate bar, the sort she knew I liked, on my pillow.

As I lay down under the covers I suddenly started shaking as a thunderbolt struck me.

God was indeed doing something concrete and I was right in the middle of it.

I had challenged 'he-she-it' to make the life of the most hopeless person I met, worth living. In declaring my love for Debbie Loveless and becoming her partner, I was about to become the means of meeting my own challenge! Game, Set and Match. Olivia had said it in fun, but now I believed it. God was real, and what was more, he had the greatest sense of mischief in the universe! I was going to have to confess to my friends and family not just that I loved Debbie but that I couldn't be an atheist any longer and that I had begun to find God.

-o-O-o-

Morning dawned bright and clear. I awoke early due to the birdsong. A whole cauldron of mixed emotions whirled around my head. Whereas last night I had felt a sense of being dragged, kicking and screaming, towards heaven's gates, this morning I sensed a new adventure beginning. I'd left the obvious track going up the hillside and was instead taking the beautiful pathway through the trees. If I was to embrace religion, perhaps there were worse things. And if it was Debbie's type, well… she thoroughly enjoyed being a woman of faith, and she certainly had answers for most things we'd encountered. And as for embracing Debbie herself, I couldn't wait. I so dearly longed to tell her how much I loved her, to kiss her again, to wrap my arms around her and hold her tight.

As for my suspension from work, I had a sense that I was being held close by Debbie's god, embraced by him. I whipped out my smart phone and looked up again those words in Philippians Chapter 4 with which she'd encouraged me over Mr. Glynn's tooth:-

'Do not be anxious about anything, but in every situation, by prayer and petition, with thanksgiving, present your requests to God. And the peace of God, which transcends all understanding, will guard your hearts and your minds in Christ Jesus.'

I was going to make my start on a life of faith. I was going to believe this could be true for me, this time standing on my own infant faith rather than relying on Debbie's. Over breakfast, I explained this to Granny and she beamed at me. "James," she said, "I'm standing with you, too. God won't let you down. Let me know what happens, won't you?"

It was time to catch the first train back to Edinburgh. As I waited on the platform, I called the manse and spoke to Elspeth. I explained my decision and waited for her response.

"To tell you the truth, James, Gilbert and I aren't surprised. We talked about you and Debbie all through yesterday. We can tell how much you love her, but we felt we had to try to put you off by warning you what you'll be letting yourself in for if you partner up with her. But if you still want to go ahead, we'll support you in every way we can. Debbie's coming to church today. She knows why you aren't bringing her and she's very upset about it. But we'll have a good chat with her, then let's all get together later in the day."

The long journey home took until mid-afternoon. I dipped in and out of my novel, barely concentrating. I couldn't wait to be back in Somershire. I went straight to the McPhersons' house to hear how they'd got on with Debbie. I asked how she'd fared with her teeth, and it appeared matters hadn't been straightforward as I had half suspected. Now, about my proposal. Debbie hadn't been able to believe it when Elspeth took her aside and explained my decision. Straightaway she'd admitted that she loved me, but she'd told herself that she could never realistically expect that I'd want to commit to her. So now that I had done just that, would she be my girlfriend? Cautiously, she said she had two concerns. But provided we could answer them, then *wow, yes!* Belonging to me, and me to her, had been beyond her wildest dreams!

Her first concern was that to her, and clearly to the McPhersons, our 'partnership' had to lead to marriage. Debbie strongly believed sex was for married people, and she'd heard me waxing on about my views that marriage was an evolutionary necessity that had now lost its relevance except for ensuring children grew up in a stable home. As I replied to the McPhersons, I found myself reflecting aloud that with Olivia, making a decision to be together for life seemed utterly unnecessary. But with Debbie it was different. With her it would be a delight to make such a commitment! I was ready to give myself to her with joyful abandon. Broad smiles lit up Gilbert's and Elspeth's faces.

The obvious question was that, if Debbie believed sex was for married people, why hadn't she been married herself? The McPhersons had discovered that she and her partner had come to faith about four years previously, just after she'd been diagnosed with MS. But whereas her faith had grown by leaps and bounds, her partner's had been short-lived. He'd been reluctant to commit to marriage despite their having a family. Debbie had very much wanted to marry but he wouldn't; he couldn't believe God would sustain them both whatever happened in the future. Sadly he abandoned her to face her difficult life alone.

For my part I did have one concern. I was anxious to make sure her ex-partner hadn't saddled her with a mountain of unpaid bills and debts when he left.

Debbie's second concern was that she felt she could only marry a believer. At this point I told Gilbert and Elspeth how I'd just had to accept that God had met my challenge and that therefore my position had changed. I still had many questions but believed I was 'on the way' to faith.

They smiled encouragingly. My answers had assured them that it was 'Game on'!

Later that afternoon, Elspeth walked over to The Limes and brought Debbie to their house. I noticed that she was wearing her new upper denture but not the lower one. Rather sadly she said that it just didn't fit. The dentist had taken fresh impressions and they said they'd have a new lower set ready within the week. I still wonder if the lower impression had been pulled out of shape because Debbie had been giggling so much when the dentist removed the plate of goo from her mouth!

On the positive side she could now pronounce almost everything except the letter S! It no longer felt as if we were communicating in different languages. She sat in her wheelchair, with me holding her limp hand. Both of us looked fondly at each other. We were now on the threshold of the world's most unlikely romance. But would I have a job? And would we have to forcibly remove Debbie from The Limes? Firstly, however, we needed to tackle Debbie's and my issues.

Gilbert brought up the question of marriage. Debbie was delighted to hear that I'd changed my tune. I tried telling her that my intellectual position hadn't changed, but saw how ridiculous this appeared when threatened with the onset of one of Debbie's giggling fits. Gilbert encouraged us to go ahead as soon as possible with a very simple wedding without the modern trappings of made-to-measure suits and dresses, an expensive reception, stag and hen parties, a present list at a large department store, and a honeymoon in Mauritius. He and Elspeth said they'd enlist the help of the church membership to make it a very special occasion.

Regarding her finances, it turned out that Albert, the baritone soloist whose singing Debbie had found so moving, was a semi-retired bank manager. Gilbert said he'd ask Albert to sort out her financial affairs.

Then Gilbert said, "Let's exercise our faith! Let's trust God to smooth your path so you can be married." The four of us held hands whilst the McPhersons and Debbie prayed. Finally, in very halting words, I said,

"God, I didn't think you were there. I think I'm about to change my mind. Please help me to understand you."

Gilbert smiled at Debbie. "Leading on from James' prayer, he has something to explain to you about a certain challenge he issued to the Almighty..."

I told Debbie about my challenge to 'he-she-it' and how God had met it. For the second time that afternoon, she started to giggle... and giggle... and giggle... After two or three minutes, Gilbert and Elspeth discreetly left the room, leaving us on our own.

"Jameth," she said, "I shtill can't believe whatsh happened today. Are you sure you're sherioush? I'm so utterly helplesh and I've got nothing at all to offer you exshept myshelf."

"Debbie," I said, "it's yourself that I love. To me, you're the dearest, sweetest, bravest, most strong-minded, and now the prettiest girl I've ever met. Your body's in a wheelchair but your soul soars as free as a bird. I want to soar with you. I want us to have adventures together. The happiest times of the last three months have been those when I've been with you. I want so desperately to be with you, to look at you, to touch you, to hold you. I can't wait to bring you home as my wife!"

I saw tears of joy trickling down her face.

"But what about Olivia?" she asked.

"I like Olivia very much," I said, "but she doesn't have your lovely heart. I've never loved her passionately like I know I love you. I'm afraid my next port of call after I leave here will be to say goodbye to her."

Once again I leant over to kiss her. This time we were both awake. It was a long, lingering kiss, full of soft flesh and tongues. And no-one spied on us.

The early evening sun was by this time sinking in the sky. Gilbert and Elspeth set out to take Debbie back whilst I set off for Olivia's. I rang the bell.

Olivia stood in the doorway. "Where on earth have you been?" she said frostily.

"There's no easy way to say this," I said. "I've fallen in love with someone else."

Olivia recoiled in horror. "Oh no!" she said. Then it clicked. "It's not *her*, is it?"

"I'm afraid it is," I said.

"James, you're absolutely out of your mind!" she yelled. "You'll end up wrecked – personally, professionally, and socially. You're a b****y fool! Come in and get your belongings."

She picked up my bedclothes and slung them into my overnight case. I walked towards the door. Bitterly she called out,

"Get out of my sight, you stupid man!"

We have never spoken to each other since that day.

-o-O-o-

I woke up on Monday morning amidst a maelstrom of emotions. I had lost my long-term girlfriend but was madly in love with the girl I adored and planned to marry. I was facing the loss of my job but had gained new friends. And I was on the verge of discovering what faith in Jesus was all about. Despite the uncertainties I remembered that I'd decided I was going to 'not be anxious about anything', and was looking to experience 'the peace that passes all understanding'.

There was nothing I could do to influence the inquiry, but at 10:30 a.m. I was thrown a lifeline of hope as Gilbert McPherson called me to say that he was to be allowed to attend. I guessed, rightly as it later emerged, that Mr. Davy had used his influence to allow this unusual break with protocol.

Gilbert later talked me through what happened.

Chapter 11

Gilbert's Chapter

I feel very privileged to have played a part in defending two wonderful people, James and Deborah; James from losing his career, both of them from losing the love of their lives.

I have the strong impression that James' consultant was determined to use every influence he could bring to bear to keep him. He had to lobby hard to allow me to attend the hearing. In the room were Mr. Hardcastle, the Senior Administrator; Mr. Davy; two police officers; the hospital's HR Manager and his assistant.

The senior police officer started by reading out the allegation following the complaint to himself by Mr. Nathan Cooper, Day Manager at The Limes. It seemed pretty damning in that James had kissed Deborah, who was a vulnerable person, on the lips without her permission. At least the account generally squared up with James'. What wasn't pleasant to hear was the way Cooper insinuated that he'd suspected James had been looking for an opportunity to commit an assault during several previous visits and that he'd found James performing personal tasks in her bedroom the previous week without a staff member being present. Fortunately James had mentioned this incident and I knew about the circumstances – that he was hurrying to keep a dentist's appointment.

Eventually I had my opportunity to speak. I'd typed it all out so that I could leave copies with the team. I said:-

"I am the minister of Patterdale Road Baptist Church which Miss Loveless has been attending for three months. Mr. McAlister has often brought her to church, initially purely in the role of an informal carer but more recently as a part of the church family. My wife and I have come to know them well. Together they have launched a successful informal fellowship group at the Trefoil coffee shop on the High Street.

"I first met Miss Loveless in hospital during April where she had had all her teeth removed. I can honestly describe her as the most pitiful person I had met for a long time. We have since come to appreciate her as a very special person whose joyful, caring nature has influenced my whole church. This would never have happened without Mr. McAlister's enabling. He has patiently befriended her and cared for her during the time they have been with us. My wife and I have watched their relationship develop to the point where they are now discussing marriage. They are a delightful couple and we feel very happy for them."

There was a hush about the room. Mr. Davy looked perplexed. In a later, private conversation I realised he couldn't square what he'd heard with his understanding that James already had a steady girlfriend.

"I would therefore submit to the inquiry that Mr. McAlister's kissing of Miss Loveless was in no way an assault but an expression of his love for the woman he intends to marry."

Mr. Hardcastle's eyes narrowed. He cleared his throat and said,

"It appears from what you say that James McAlister has been conducting a relationship with a patient whilst she was still registered with the hospital. Am I right?"

My instincts told me that the timing of events might be a moot point. I therefore replied,

"I can't answer that without knowing at what point she ceased to be a patient. Would it be wrong for him to have done so?"

Mr. Hardcastle explained that medical staff were strictly forbidden to have relationships with patients under their care. I realised it was time to pray under my breath. I must tell the truth yet choose my words with very great care, and trust the outcome to God. This is how I explained it.

"It's difficult to know exactly at what point Mr. McAlister's and Miss Loveless' romance began. When he first brought her to church, he was merely performing a good deed under sufferance. The relationship between them developed into a friendship, then they became increasingly fond of each other, and this has matured into love. But here's the strange thing – I believe we recognised that they'd fallen in love before they did. Unintentionally they'd behaved like a couple in inviting people for coffee when all they meant to do was to share their time together with others who needed encouragement and a listening ear. Only four weeks ago Mr. McAlister was on holiday with his then girlfriend who I believe is one of your hospital doctors. I'm sure he had no intention of dating anyone else."

I took a deep breath. Inside, my heart was thumping with anxiety, hoping against hope that James would not be deemed to have broken his code of conduct. I continued,

"My wife and I believe that Mr. McAlister's and Miss Loveless' relationship blossomed after he returned from that same holiday. I can tell you when it was, because my wife brought her to church in James' absence on Sunday, 13th July, the day of our anniversary."

Mr. Hardcastle studied his notes.

"Well, now, let me see… our hospital records state her discharge date as Monday, 14th July. So if I'm correct, we're saying that Mr. McAlister was on holiday at that point?"

There were nods around the table. I felt as if a huge weight had been lifted from my shoulders.

"So at the point of beginning his relationship with Miss Loveless, she was no longer a patient. That just leaves us to resolve the issue of whether he committed an assault. Reverend McPherson, thank you for your submission, but I have to remind the panel that there isn't such a thing as an excusable assault. What do the policemen have to advise?"

The senior policeman nodded to his younger colleague who stood up and opened his notebook. He had interviewed Deborah earlier that morning. She'd said she couldn't remember Mr. McAlister kissing her, and that it seemed she must have been asleep. But she said she'd be delighted to be kissed by Mr. McAlister, as often as he wanted! The policeman was rather puzzled as to why he was carrying out this investigation.

"Well then," said Mr. Hardcastle, "there doesn't seem a case to answer, does there?"

No-one disagreed. The police said they'd inform The Limes, and Mr. Hardcastle would contact James whom they would expect to return to work the next day, Tuesday.

Chapter 12

You can imagine the sense of relief when Gilbert called me to tell me I'd been exonerated and re-instated! I thanked Gilbert from the bottom of my heart.

It was at 1 p.m. that Mr. Hardcastle called me to officially tell me the news. I had to pretend I was hearing it for the first time. I asked whether The Limes had been informed. He told me that the police had visited the home straight after the meeting to inform them of the decision.

I stood outside The Limes and rang the bell. Penny answered the door, and didn't know what to do. When I asked if I was still barred from seeing Debbie, she hadn't been told otherwise, so I asked her to fetch Nathan. Unlike previously, Nathan took plenty of time to come to the door.

"Good afternoon, Nathan!" I said. "I'm coming to see my girlfriend, the one I intend to marry. I assume that's okay with you?"

He knew I'd ring his head office if he refused. So he simply opened the door and said, "You haven't heard the last of this. We'll be watching you."

Debbie's eyes lit up like sparklers when she saw me. My first words were,

"Darling! I've been cleared of the charge against me! Now nothing can stop us being together."

I looked into her eyes, now gently glowing and softened with fondness, placed my arms around her shoulders and we kissed... and kissed... and kissed for joy. Tears streamed down her face, wetting my cheeks.

After ten wonderfully emotional minutes I turned my head and noticed a half-eaten plate of food on her bedside table. I asked if she hadn't been hungry.

Debbie's face looked sad. "It'sh not that, Jamesh. They shay that now I've got my teeth, I should be able to eat my mealsh in fifteen minutesh, but I can't."

"Who says that?" I asked. I could guess. And the 'rule' had been invented that very day. What a coincidence!

Penny appeared at the door to say the dentist had called. She'd mentioned to him that I was visiting Debbie, at which point he'd said that Joshua had remade Debbie's bottom teeth and that the dentist had a free appointment at half past four. Without any more ado, Penny helped me dress Debbie and we set off.

We arrived at the dentist's just as Joshua was about to leave. He'd just been visiting the surgery to deliver several pieces of work. He had now finished for the day but generously said he'd come in with us to see the results of his efforts. Twenty minutes and several slight adjustments later, I saw Debbie in her complete dentures. The dentist had a mirror which he placed next to her head. She gasped with delight! When I saw her smile, I too had goose bumps all over. I was glad she'd chosen a 'straight' design. It suited her perfectly. The pearl colour of her teeth with a satin sheen looked elegant and tasteful.

"Oh, Jamesh!" she said. "They look sho beautiful, don't they?"

"No, Debbie, that's not what I see," I said. "*You* look delightful. You really are a beauty queen!"

I realised I'd forgotten to explain to Joshua that we were now a couple. He'd guessed!

Never before had the dentist, his technician or Joshua seen a couple celebrating the fitting of a set of dentures as if they'd won the lottery! They all said how much it had made their day.

Back at The Limes I was reminded of Debbie's eating predicament as her incomplete meal was still in her room. I stormed over to Nathan's office only to find he'd gone home. There and then I realised I had to get Debbie out of The Limes as quickly as possible to protect her from any more of his vindictive schemes. And there was only one place she could go. That was my flat.

-o-O-o-

And so, Tuesday morning saw my return to work. Martin, Sister Marion, Grace and my various other colleagues were delighted to see me back. It was good to feel I'd been missed. Martin kindly offered to do the ward rounds so that I could spend time with Mr. Davy.

Mr. Davy had been expecting me. He smiled and sat behind his desk with a large mug in his hand. "Beryl," he called to his secretary. "A coffee for James, please. White, no sugar, is it?" I confirmed this was the case. He told me I'd given him a big scare, nearly losing one of his key team members. But he was puzzled. He knew Olivia and was amazed to hear that I was talking of marrying someone else. I gave him a potted history of my last three months' adventure with Debbie and how it was only this weekend that I'd really understood where my heart lay.

"So," he chuckled, "strictly speaking, she wasn't your girlfriend when you kissed her?" I nodded, with slight embarrassment. "You naughty boy! Anyway, I'm glad you got away with it. But for heaven's sake, James – you've escaped with two near misses lately what with Mr. Glynn and his tooth. Please don't give me any more heart attacks!"

I thanked him for looking after me and especially for lobbying for my key witness, the reverend, to attend the inquiry. Then I explained my current challenge, that of moving Debbie to my flat. Mr. Davy asked how much more annual leave I had due. I explained that I had another seven days and I'd appreciate some time off to arrange for my flat to be adapted. He had made provision for my being covered for a period because he expected me to be suspended for a long time. Therefore he said this would be an ideal week.

"James," he said as I got up to leave, "my son has Downs' Syndrome. He lives in a community home with three other disabled men and women. Having him has changed the way I look on people and what I value about them. I admire what you've done and I wish you every success."

-o-O-o-

With each time I visited Debbie I became aware how urgent it was to move her out of The Limes to my flat. This would mean we'd be living together. Debbie was reluctant. She'd made clear that she wouldn't "run ahead of Jesus" as she put it. She seemed to think she should stay put for a little longer. But I didn't think she fully appreciated how grim Nathan could make life for both of us if she stayed in the home.

On Wednesday morning I visited a store in the High Street that sold a variety of aids such as disabled beds, hoists, and also had a show room containing disabled bathrooms and toilets. They contacted their surveyor who had a free appointment that afternoon. I'd have to let someone else take Debbie back from the coffee shop in order to be at home. Debbie was as excited to see me as ever, and once we reached the café her new teeth were much admired by all our company and by the coffee shop staff. She loved the attention she received, especially from one young man, Terry, who said she was really special. She turned this around and asked him if he was special, too. When he gave a non-committal answer, Debbie told him he was special because God loved him, knew all about him and had a special part for him to play in his world. Would he like to know more? She still couldn't say 'S', so Dethuth was now Jezshuzsh, but otherwise was enjoying not having to contort her mouth and repeat herself to make herself understood, and came across very clearly. It was difficult to say "no" to Debbie. The reverend gave Terry a leaflet showing what was on at church with a warm welcome to Sunday mornings and Mrs. McPherson pulled a card out of her handbag that said,

'For God so loved the world that He sent His only-begotten Son, so that through him the world may be saved.'

This was John's Gospel Chapter 3 verse 16.

Debbie asked him what he'd like God to do for him if He was standing here. Terry was worried about his mother who was sick, so several of us laid a hand on him and claimed Jesus' healing power over his mother.

-o-O-o-

The surveyor carried out his assessment. He reckoned they'd need two days to fit me a disabled toilet and shower. Amazingly they'd had a cancellation that meant the work could begin on Monday. Debbie's birthday was on Thursday and my first thought was how much her boys would enjoy seeing her in a new home with her 'new smile'. Before going any further, I needed to resolve the issues about our living together, and called on the McPhersons the same evening.

The McPhersons appreciated the problem and added that this meant it was important we arranged the wedding as soon as possible. They'd make some phone calls straightaway and come back with proposed dates. Most importantly, the registrar required a statutory 28 days to elapse between giving notice of the wedding and the issuing of a marriage certificate. Gilbert advised me to visit the local Registry Office as soon as possible with Debbie, but also to apply for a waiver from the General Register Office which would cost an additional fee. He said he would write a covering letter to support our application. There was no guarantee of success but he was confident he could present a good case. In the meantime, they encouraged me to move Debbie as soon as I could. They were fully aware of her difficult lot at Nathan's hands. They said that God knew our hearts. He knew that we wanted to honour him at every stage of our life together. I quietly reflected that this was more a reflection of Debbie than me! Living together may have the 'wrong' appearance but in our case it seemed a practical necessity. God knew what we did in the privacy of our home. That was what mattered.

Debbie, whom I saw the next morning, was less easily persuaded. Fortunately, however, Nathan did me an unintended favour by enforcing his refusal to allow more than fifteen minutes to eat her meals and she finally agreed to share my flat. She was beginning to lose weight, not a good sign for a slight person. We arranged for a carer to visit in the morning and afternoon, and settled her dues with The Limes so that all her welfare payments were ours to use. As I wheeled Debbie away in the brand new chair I'd bought, Nathan grinned and said with mock affection,

"Best of luck to you both. Take good care of her, Mr. McAlister!"

And so I began to learn the routine for feeding, bathing and toileting Debbie. We decided her carer would dress her and organise her breakfast but that I'd perform the evening duties.

But the next day was her birthday. I had little time to prepare to celebrate it but was able to buy some tasteful food from Waitrose including a cake, and invited Debbie's boys to the occasion along with Amanda, Penny and Mavis. Amanda came early and washed and blow-dried her hair, then renewed Debbie's lipstick, eye make-up and nail varnish. She was very excited about seeing her boys, and this time they looked at her with delight as they saw their mum looking so pretty. The boys' foster parents followed them in and, in her hospitable way, Debbie invited them to stay but they felt it best to leave us to enjoy this family time. Jonathan and Ethan were delighted to hear that Debbie and I were going to marry. We talked not so much about the boys, but about the coffee shop parties and her new friends, her make-over and her teeth. This may have seemed like self-absorption but she wanted the boys to catch a flavour of the happiness she was now enjoying. She had a favourite game she played with them, 'Who am I?' where you have to work out who the person is thinking about by asking no more than twenty 'Yes' or 'No' questions. I chose Santa Claus for example, which it only took the boys eight questions to guess.

The next evening marked the first day of our normal routine. In total we spent two to three hours together. A pleasant surprise was that Debbie had been right – she did have a degree of control over her bowels and bladder so, by myself or a carer placing her on the loo at strategic times, it kept her 'All-in-One' slip clean and thereby cleared the rash. So after I arrived home for the evening, I'd toilet her then take her for a shower. We both went in; I sat her in a chair and washed her front, then repositioned her to wash her back. I was heartily glad that I'd built up a good deal of bodily strength as a rugby player, coupled with some training at work on ergonomics. This meant I could generally lift and carry her unaided. We both found it lovely to enjoy the physical contact this provided, merely by carrying out basic caring tasks.

Then we'd put on our dressing-gowns and I'd heat up a Waitrose meal. We started with meals that she wouldn't have a challenge to bite and chew. I placed it on one single plate and used one fork. I fed her, in between my own mouthfuls. It took ever so long, but it was a delight. Just to enjoy being in the presence of the woman I loved, felt to me like heaven. Whilst she was eating, she encouraged me to talk to her all about my day at work. She took a keen interest, and very soon it was as if she'd met my patients in person.

Sometimes we had music on in the background.

Then we kissed. Not just kissed, but looked deeply, longingly into each other's eyes. Her eyes seemed to laugh even when she was serious.

Finally, we prayed together, choosing two items each. Debbie's was a confident prayer that often included people I'd talked about at work; or someone at church; or her boys. My prayers were in single sentences but she loved the fact that I joined in, simply but sincerely.

One of our simple joys was reflecting back on what had happened when we'd prayed. Often I felt that when we'd prayed about a difficult case at work, the person the patient encountered the next day was a blend of both of us – my surgical skill and Debbie's way of imparting Jesus' presence. People's eyes shone after I'd seen them. One lady was in terrible pain after corrective jaw surgery. Debbie and I had prayed at home, and Debbie asked me to lay my hand on the lady's head, look deeply into her eyes, and declare her pain gone. As I made my way towards where she lay, there was no-one in a nearby bed or within earshot. I asked the lady's permission to 'speak a word from Jesus' to her pain, and did as Debbie suggested. The lady closed her eyes, whereupon I quickly spoke my 'word' to her and moved on. Later, as I passed by on my way out, she was sleeping peacefully. And for Debbie, I prayed that Jonathan would score a goal in his weekend football game. We now had a brief twice-weekly phone call with the boys so found out straightaway that Jonathan had scored two!

"You'll have to be more ambitious in future, James!" she said.

She was usually ready to sleep by this time. I went into our lounge to watch TV or read until what I called 'bedtime'. Occasionally, if one of her favourite programmes was on, such as Gavin Marlow's impromptu choir rehearsals, Debbie stayed up and we watched together.

One day we were discussing birth control. Debbie said she'd like to be sterilised. I said, "Surely it will be easier for me to have a vasectomy?"

She replied, "No, James. You may need yours someday."

"Why? You're not going anywhere are you?" I asked.

"I haven't any plans, but trust me," and then she repeated, "I just have this sense you may need yours someday…"

We arranged for her to have the procedure and I thought no more about it.

-o-O-o-

Albert confirmed that Debbie did indeed hold a bank account jointly with her partner. She only had a few hundred pounds to her name, but at least the account was still in credit. We arranged for her to withdraw the money and close the account so she would not be liable for any further money he spent. If he ever made contact again, she would pay him half the balance.

And so, like a rapidly assembled jigsaw, the stage was being set for us to begin life as a married couple. But something was missing. One night, after we'd prayed, she seemed preoccupied. When I asked her why, she said,

"James, I don't want to put pressure on you. But I've been asking God to help you find Jesus before our wedding happens. You're very close, I know, but I don't want you to know Him through me. I want us both to know Him for ourselves."

My face fell. "I need to answer a lot of questions first," I said. "I believe God's real because I lost my bet to him. And because I see him in you. But there's all sorts I'm not sure about like creation, like the virgin birth, the resurrection, whether the Bible is all just an ancient myth, why God was so cruel in the Old Testament, why he hates gay people…"

"James!" she interrupted. "Why do you have to try to understand God that way? When you first met me, you thought I was a crazy nuisance. You only understood me when you got to know me. I can't answer your big questions but wouldn't you be better to get to know God, then He may help you understand the answers?"

We finished our evening routine and I tucked Debbie into bed. I kissed her one last time and looked at her face, so trusting, so peaceful and full of love, then switched off the light and left the room. I wanted, for all the world, to know her God, her Lord Jesus. My previous picture had been that Debbie was helpless because of God's cruelty and mismanagement. Now I was beginning to see Him as the One who was present with Debbie. Through her terrible disability, He shone more brightly than ever. Perhaps she was right about my getting to know Him first. I decided that night that I wasn't just going to give God an intellectual grilling. Nor was I just going to surrender myself unreservedly to this deity I found hard to grasp. I was going to do both. I was going to do my homework but I was also going to do what I longed so much to do – to jump into the pool of God's love and splash with joyful abandon just like Debbie.

Sitting in the lounge, I could now trace His hand through the events of the last few months. It seemed as if our relationship had hung by a thread. I wouldn't have seen her again if there'd been a church member to take her the first Sunday... or if I hadn't broken her glasses... or if I'd stuck to my decision and said my final 'goodbye' after she'd got her new pair. The fact that I had changed my mind and seen Debbie again was due to my hearing Gilbert's sermon which only happened because I couldn't escape from the front of church that first Sunday. Then I nearly decided to stop seeing her after my suspension from work. It had seemed like a thread but I now realised it was in fact a strong cord. Debbie's loving God "who will not let me go" had chosen me to be her faithful friend and husband, and I now realised how deeply loved I was, too. In my days as Olivia's partner I couldn't have imagined what it felt like to love someone's very soul in the way I loved Debbie's. Tomorrow it was time to give in.

No! That wouldn't do! I went back to our bedroom, switched on the bedside lamp and woke her up.

"Well, Daimth, thith *ith* a nithe thurpwithe! Tell me wha'th up."

"Debbie, I want to come to know Jesus. Now!" I said.

With her teeth and glasses eventually back in place, she asked me to open John Chapter 14 and I held it so she could read. Verse 23 said,

'Jesus answered and said to him, "If anyone loves Me, he will keep My word; and My Father will love him, and We will come to him and make Our home with him."'

"That's you, James. By wanting to know Him, you're declaring that you love Him. And I know you well enough to be sure that you want to walk His way, to 'keep His word'. So – let's go! Just talk to Him and tell Him you want Him and God the Father to make their home in you. Start by thanking Jesus for dying on the cross for you, and forgiving your sin."

We held hands, and I did exactly as Debbie said. The delight in standing with her as a new member of God's family was one of the most moving experiences of my life. We hugged and kissed each other all over again as our faces were wet with tears. We were now a Christian couple.

-o-O-o-

The following Saturday afternoon after work I arrived back at our apartment block and opened my mailbox. Inside was a brown envelope with solemnly typed letters on the back denoting that it had come from the General Register Office. I took it upstairs, slit it open and, kneeling alongside Debbie's chair, drew out the contents. Imagine our joy when we read the letter inside which said that our application for a waiver had been granted! Provided the remaining checks didn't show any legal reason that we couldn't marry, we'd be able to hold the ceremony the following weekend! We knew we'd nothing to hide. I called Gilbert straightaway. He and Elspeth got to work immediately to put together an order of service for our wedding. They announced it in church the next day, to take place the following Saturday. This was easily the most 'shotgun wedding' the church had ever known! We invited the whole church and other people from the coffee shop fellowship, including Penny and Amanda. I invited Martin from work who unfortunately had to decline as he was on duty, Mr. and Mrs. Davy who accepted, and also Grace and Sister Marion.

I called my parents to tell them the news. There was a long silence. I could hear the mouthpiece being hastily covered by a hand, followed by whispering. Finally, Father spoke,

"Son, this isn't the news we wanted to hear. But you've obviously made up your mind as to what you want. The most important thing is that you're happy. We'll support your decision, but we just hope you don't live to regret it – or not too soon anyway."

Affirmation indeed... I thought of my parents' relationship. They'd always lived as very faithful partners and parents, making sure my sister and I were well provided for and that sensible, safe forward-looking decisions were made to secure our future. I wondered if they had ever really known the depth of passion, of being knitted together with another person's soul that I was only now discovering. Mum and Dad said they'd change their arrangements for next Saturday and that they'd see us at the wedding. My sister was abroad so couldn't join us.

I knew Granddad and Granny McAlister would have understood how I felt. I was sad that Granny said she couldn't come herself, although I knew how hard she'd have found the journey. However, she made it clear how sure she was that ours was a 'marriage made in heaven'. Somehow I must make sure she and Debbie could meet.

We arranged for Debbie's boys to come and we made clear how much we'd like their foster parents to stay for the event.

After Gilbert had announced the wedding on Sunday, Elspeth stood up and explained that there were two special gifts that each church family member could present to us. I noticed that never before had I heard the term 'Church Family'. On my first Sunday at Patterdale this would have seemed a complete contradiction as the church had seemed to have almost no sense of community. But now, five months later, it was indeed beginning to fit the description of a family. Firstly, said Elspeth, your most precious gift is to bring yourself. But secondly, she asked everyone to bring a plate of food. Hands up for sandwiches; hands up for savoury dishes; for cakes; for sweets; and for people to help lay out the room.

Albert was being commandeered as photographer.

Bill, incredibly, volunteered to be chief usher. We couldn't think of a less suitable person but Debbie smiled and said, "Go on, let him show us!"

Gilbert looked at him and said, "Bill, you are appointed!"

Penny and Amanda were delighted when I invited them to be Debbie's dressers, and set out their stall to make her a celebrity. I asked them to enlist the services of a local department store which sent their specialist around to our flat. On being told the date of the wedding, she assumed we were planning for the year ahead. She nearly collapsed on being told we had five days to prepare. Once she'd recovered we found there wasn't a problem, as she had several nice 'off-the-shelf' options to choose from.

The local jeweller said he wasn't used to selling rings off the shelf, but both

Debbie and I were delighted with the choices we made from those he had in stock. He asked how long we'd been engaged. Debbie's reply, with a glint in her eye, was, "It's Wednesday today. Why should we get engaged when we can be married this Saturday?"

The jeweller answered that it was people like us who were putting him out of business! Just then I noticed a lovely engagement ring with a blue sapphire. I asked him to take it out of its case and try it on Debbie. It suited her; she loved its shade and its sparkle, but it didn't quite fit. The jeweller said he could have it altered in a couple of days so it would be ready for Saturday morning first thing. I paid for the three rings. It was nice to have another excuse to kiss each other…

Someone tipped off the Trefoil coffee shop whose manager called me at work and begged for the privilege of providing our cake. It was a gift, provided we could give out leaflets advertising their wares which I said we'd be delighted to do.

And so took place the most hastily planned, spontaneous wedding I'd ever attended. With ten minutes to go before the service, I was standing outside with Bill who was taking his duties very seriously It was lovely to see him in a smart dark suit that he later told us had cost £10 at a charity shop. He'd had a shave and haircut for the occasion, and looked a far cry from the rough-hewn person we'd first met. And then we had two big surprises.

Firstly, ten rugby players arrived, all wearing their shirts but otherwise with matching dark trousers. They gave me bear-hugs and walked noisily through the door. They gave me a very large card and told me to keep tight hold of it as it contained the product of 'a little whip-round'. I suggested to Bill that they might enjoy sitting in the gallery, so he directed them up the stairs to the little-used quarters above, where they were later joined by about a dozen others.

Secondly, just as I looked down the road to see my beloved Debbie coming into view around a corner, two large cars pulled up and about ten young adults poured out onto the street. They saw Debbie appearing and ran to greet her. I could see her face in the distance lighting up with unbridled joy and tearful emotion. These were her Life Group from her church in Hornchester. I heard words like, "We thought we'd lost you," and "We couldn't find you anywhere!" It emerged later that Debbie had been whisked away from her home at a moment's notice to The Limes. She hadn't ever kept a record of her group's contact details which they had often urged her to do, so she hadn't been able to let them know where she was. She said how sorry she was that she hadn't ever done as they'd asked, and they regretted that they hadn't tried harder to find her again. Gilbert had made contact with the senior pastor at the church who had made known the details of the wedding. In this joyful reunion, all was forgiven and the group found themselves seats in church.

Gilbert began the service by explaining, with a certain amount of humour, how we had needed to marry quickly. Then we pitched into his and Elspeth's choices of hymns and readings. We sang, "Love divine, all loves excelling..." and it was marvellous to hear this being toned out with gusto by the lusty sportsmen on the balcony. I recognised a familiar reading in 1 Corinthians 13, which read,

'Love is patient, love is kind. It does not envy, it does not boast, it is not proud. It does not dishonour others, it is not self-seeking, it is not easily angered, it keeps no record of wrongs. Love does not delight in evil but rejoices with the truth. It always protects, always trusts, always hopes, always perseveres.'

I looked at my sweetheart in her wheelchair beside me, dressed in her beautiful cream dress with a blue lining and her veil that made her look like a princess. I could almost have substituted 'Debbie' for 'love' in this passage. But likewise it inspired *me*. I was always going to protect her, to trust in God's goodness towards her, to hope on her behalf whatever diagnosis any doctor declared, and to persevere in making her life as full as possible.

And then we made our vows. I was asked,

"James Arthur, will you take Deborah to be your wife? Will you love her, comfort her, honour and protect her, and, forsaking all others, be faithful to her as long as you both shall live?"

I broke down as I looked into her face, softened to a beautiful pink sheen, and into her lovely tender eyes. I gasped out the words,

"I do! For all the world, I do!"

She was asked the same question, but it had an extra phrase. She had asked for the phrase, "and to obey" to be included. She fixed my gaze, then said,

"I do, too. For all the world, James, I do!"

And, a little later, I promised:-

"I, James, take you, Deborah to be my wife,
to have and to hold from this day forward;
for better, for worse, for richer, for poorer, in sickness and in health,
to love and to cherish, till death us do part;
according to God's holy law.
In the presence of God I make this vow."

I meant *every word*. I felt at that moment that my destiny was to love Debbie passionately, and that I was immensely privileged to belong to her, she to me. It was as if this moment was the focal point of all my life so far.

Finally we 'exchanged' rings, with me guiding Debbie's fingers as we slid mine on. Gilbert declared us man and wife, and then said I could now kiss the bride. I knelt down in front of her chair. I cupped her cheeks into my hands, and planted my lips on hers. I kissed her tenderly and softly. The church exploded in uproar and applause. Then we turned the wheelchair around; I sat alongside Debbie so we could be in full view of the church.

Albert then sang his baritone solo of Debbie's favourite hymn, "O Love that will not let me go." Afterwards, Gilbert told the story of this famous hymn, penned in Edinburgh by preacher George Matheson. As a young man he had been engaged when the doctors told him they couldn't save his sight. His fiancée decided she couldn't marry him. His sister kindly cared for him for many years until she herself fell in love and arranged to marry. On the eve of her wedding night Matheson, reminded of his earlier heartbreak, was faced with the prospect of having no-one to care for him. Suddenly he felt God's love surrounding and inspiring him and, five minutes later, the hymn was written in its entirety.

Gilbert asked Debbie to tell us why she found this hymn so meaningful. She had often found herself humming this hymn during those first dark days at The Limes when it seemed no-one was prepared to fight her corner. I stole a glance at Penny and Amanda, who were now so fond of her, and saw tears running down their cheeks.

Gilbert began his talk by sharing some Bible verses. Firstly he spoke of his admiration for Debbie, that she was such a testimony to the way God didn't let go, and how she inspired and encouraged others' faith. And he complimented me on the way I'd fought for Debbie when others might have left her to wither. He remarked that he'd seen our love grow through the most testing of times, and that we'd overcome many obstacles already. Interestingly, he used the same verse as Granny McAlister – that perfect love drives out fear. At Debbie's suggestion I later wrote out this verse and stuck it above our bed.

Gilbert finished by saying how delighted he and Elspeth would be to no longer call Debbie "Loveless". The name Debbie McAlister had a lovely ring about it, symbolic of the way not only had her name changed, but that God had provided her with a husband to love her and to bring out the beauty in her personality. At this point the entire congregation stood up and applauded.

As the service ended, we sang 'Amazing grace'. This was a signature tune of Debbie's. She often used to say, "This is where it all begins." For her, it did. And, increasingly, for me, too.

The reception did not disappoint. When I'd first seen my rugby mates, I'd worried about how far our bring-and-share meals, mostly prepared by elderly ladies with weeny appetites, would stretch to feeding ten strapping young men. It turned out that they hadn't been expecting to stay, but felt so welcome that they decided to enjoy this unexpected feast. They were very restrained by their normal standards by which they could have polished off a plate of sandwiches apiece! They came up to where we were sitting, and it didn't take long for them to discover Debbie's sense of fun and her famous giggle.

We were moved by the effort that our 'church family' had made. There was every conceivable flavour of sandwich, a sign that someone had coordinated the production process, yet each plate having the distinctiveness of a different person's handiwork. Bill proudly pointed out to me his own egg and cress sandwiches in wholemeal bread cakes which looked as if they'd been cut with a spade. Untidy they may have been but delicious they tasted, all the more so when I remembered how unlikely a chef he was. Mavis had baked buns in the shape of hearts. Half of the buns had blue icing with a letter J on top, half were pink with D on top, and they were laid out in two lines! There was curry, risotto, salad dip, potato salad, a generous cheeseboard, trifle, fruitcake, sponge cakes… Amanda organised a plate of food for Debbie to eat later as, unlike me, she had to make a choice between eating and greeting our guests.

Finally, Terry from the café was asked to cut the cake, and we were all served a slice along with elderflower champagne. Gilbert banged his knife on a bottle and announced that we'd be doing the 'toasts'. There was to be only one speech; mine. Or so I thought. I began by thanking everyone I could think of, including our first class caterers, those who had dressed Debbie, and those who had travelled a distance to be present. These three categories included most of the people present. Then I made a major faux pas. I thanked the rugby team for coming to brighten up our occasion with their tuneful singing. I thanked them very much for resisting the urge to sing rugby songs during the signing of the register. I could see that this had prompted whispering and the making of plans…

I'd decided not to talk about my challenge to 'he-she-it' but had the assembled company in hoots of laughter by describing our coffee shop date with Amanda, sensitively skirting around the reason Debbie prayed for her. They loved my impersonations of her pre-teeth pronunciation. I described the mug and its ignominious descent to the floor where it shattered into a thousand fragments of china and its contents splattered into a million droplets of coffee. I described my imprisonment within a tiny cell bounded by the wheelchair, tables and the staff, that blocked my escape route. And I had our guests in uproar as I recounted my Vesuvius moment followed by Debbie's having the last laugh over Mr. Glynn's molar tooth that I had removed by mistake. Looking back, I was sure that was when I'd started to fall in love with her.

I finished by saying how wrong I'd been about her and about the God she worshipped. Now I was the luckiest man alive to have fallen in love with her, and to have found God for myself.

Debbie's parents had both passed away and she wasn't in contact with her only sibling, a brother. There had been nobody to give her away, hence no 'father of the bride'. To my surprise, Mr. Davy stood up to answer my speech. He amused our guests by taking up the theme of James and his mad moments, firstly alluding to the unfortunate molar, and secondly about my poor record of predicting outcomes on Ward 17, such as Debbie's. Then his tone changed. He mentioned how concerned they'd been at the bleak outlook for this severely disabled lady. He went on to say how he would never have believed she would, only five months later, become the wife of one of his senior surgical team, who now considered himself to have landed a prize catch! On behalf of Ward 17 he wished to give Debbie away, and was delighted for us both.

I hadn't had a Best Man. I'd have asked Martin had he not been on duty. But I lacked a close male friend. Olivia had encouraged me to find a 'man friend' but somehow I'd never 'clicked with' another man whom I felt I could trust. I consoled myself by thinking that I wouldn't have to face the usual embarrassment of incidents from my past being dredged up. To my horror, I saw that the microphone had been passed to Howard, our rugby captain. He said he'd be totally neglecting his duties if he didn't present an honest picture of the bridegroom. He lost no time in remembering my birthday a year or so previously when, in the clubhouse after our match, they'd arranged to get me drunk. I'd somehow lost the button on my trousers and had been dancing on one of the tables with a microphone singing into a Karaoke machine when the unfortunate garment parted company from my waist, leaving me fully exposed!

Everyone grinned at me as my face turned a beetroot colour. But then Howard continued,

"But to be serious, we've sorely missed James since he's been injured. What we like about his way of playing is the way he looks out for the team. You can always count on him to back you up, and to look for the pass, when you've run out of space. When he gets the ball, he's good at judging when to push through himself and when to feed through to another player. We miss you, kid, and we can't wait to see you back when your missus lets you out the door! I know you'll want to take your time over it, what with being newly-wed and all that. Us, we're just really pleased for you and we think you've landed a smashing lass to be your queen. Come on, lads, she needs placing on her throne, don't you think?"

And as a man, they arose. Five of them knelt on one knee to make a couch, whilst the others plucked Debbie from her chair and placed her upon it. They supported her upper body so she looked just as if she were about to open Parliament. Oh, how she lapped it all up! Then they came for me. I realised it was useless to resist and let them place me next to her on my team-mates' knees. There was only one thing I could do next. I turned to Debbie, placed my arms around her neck, and enjoyed one more passionate kiss to the deafening cheers of our guests. I felt I'd been stripped psychologically naked in a way I'd have hated up until recently but I felt supported, affirmed, deeply cared for in a way that I could never previously have imagined.

Albert hurriedly retrieved his camera. His shots of us on the rugby players' knees were among the best of the entire wedding.

With the formalities over, the occasion drew gradually towards its ending. Our various groups of guests began to leave, coming up to congratulate us one by one. Among the first to go were my parents, who had a long journey. They quietly said to me,

"James, we understand now. We never realised..."

Half the guests had left. Debbie was tired and hungry, so as I said goodbye to our remaining guests, Elspeth wheeled her into a quiet corner to belatedly eat her share of the feast. Not long after she'd eaten, she fell fast asleep. Elspeth fondly covered her over with her own soft coat. You could see happiness written all over her face as her head lay back onto the padded support on her chair. What a brilliant wedding it had been! Gilbert and Elspeth said they had never before presided over such a beautiful, joyful marriage ceremony. It was as if the building itself had been blessed as it hosted a heavenly occasion.

So, another milestone had passed. And… now we could consummate our relationship!

-o-O-o-

I couldn't wait until after breakfast the next morning. We looked fondly into each other's eyes, started with a deep, deep kiss, and then…

…and every day that followed…

Debbie was still adjusting to her teeth. I had fun laughing at her attempts to say 'S'. She could either talk with a lisp, in a less exaggerated way than her toothless pronunciation, or she'd hiss slightly. She thought it funny, too, and in the end settled for the hiss. I thought it sweet! Sometimes I'd ask her to read sentences such as,

"Jesus sends salvation for sins," which she pronounced,

"Jeshushshenshshavlash… shshsh shomething…!" then we both burst into giggles.

Humour like this put us in the mood. You would have thought that making love with someone whose only external organ to express herself was her mouth, would have been a dim shadow of the experience I had had with skilful, able-bodied ladies like Olivia who had been my sixth such partner. But with Debbie, I adored the person inside in a way totally new to me. Her joy was slightly muted because her internal organs had lost some of their ability to respond. But she still managed to express the passion she felt, which more than made up for her limitations because I could sense her radiance all through her body. It was like I'd told her; her body may have been severely disabled but her spirit soared like a bird.

-o-O-o-

Now that Debbie lived in a welcoming place, she began to have more visitors particularly amongst the ladies at church. She couldn't hold a Bible herself to read it although we always read a short passage as part of our morning routine. She enjoyed doing studies with her visitors. Previously she'd memorised a lot of passages and verses and these had kept her going since she'd been deserted by her ex-partner, but she now welcomed some fresh input.

One afternoon I arrived home to find her talking gibberish! It was as if she was speaking an African language, and her face was a picture of ecstasy. I felt scared. Was this what Nathan had heard when she moved to The Limes?

She realised I was looking at her, stopped, and smiled deeply into my eyes. She looked very happy, and welcomed me home. She realised I was nonplussed, and said,

"Don't worry, darling. I'm only praising God in tongues. Look up 1 Corinthians chapters 12 to 14 and you'll see what I'm doing." I did so, and found several references to speaking in a tongue during a church meeting; but that didn't tell me what it was. Then Debbie remembered that in Acts Chapter 2 it describes the first time tongues were used, on the day of Pentecost when the church was born. We looked it up in her Bible, now 'our' Bible. Verses 2 to 4 read:-

'And suddenly there came a sound from heaven, as of a rushing mighty wind, and it filled the whole house where they were sitting. Then there appeared to them divided tongues, as of fire, and one sat upon each of them. And they were all filled with the Holy Spirit and began to speak with other tongues, as the Spirit gave them utterance.'

Debbie explained that on this special occasion, the disciples were given languages to praise God, each of which was a language that could be understood by one of the groups within the crowd who came from all over the Mediterranean. Her own tongue was probably a known language but she'd no idea where it was from. "It's my love language to praise God and Jesus," she said.

I'd noticed in 1 Corinthians that it talked about some things that didn't happen in the modern day Church, or not to my knowledge. Miracles, gifts of healing, prophecy. If these were important, where had they gone? Debbie said that they had happened in her previous church in Hornchester.

"So, do these things happen in other churches in our town here?" I asked.

"Maybe they do," said Debbie, "but I believe God's planted us where we are. Patterdale Road is our family. But," (and I could see Debbie's familiar mischievous glint) "that's because we've got a part to play in making things happen!"

I loved her for being so full of life and so positive.

"Could I speak in tongues, Debbie?" I asked.

She explained that I could, but that I'd need to be filled with the Holy Spirit, just like those early disciples. Before I could ask more, we were interrupted by a couple of phone calls and by a visitor who'd called in with a cake for us. The evening was drawing towards its conclusion when Debbie asked, "So, James, do you still want to speak in tongues?" I didn't need to reply. I held her by her shoulders as she looked into my eyes with a huge grin, and said, "Holy Spirit, come and fill James now. *In His name, James, Jesus baptises you with His Holy Spirit!*"

She started speaking her own foreign language then said, "Now, James, think about Jesus. Don't think about what's going on – just enjoy Him. Launch out and talk to Him. Here, pull me close as if we were kissing." And she stuck her tongue out so it tickled mine. Then she said, "Go!" and continued to speak in her tongue. I opened my mouth but nothing happened. "Come on, James!" she said. "Dive in; just start speaking, any old sound!"

So I did.

I thought of the Jesus who had become so much part of my life through Debbie, and who had recently become my Lord too. I looked at Debbie, so full of fun and joy. And I opened my mouth and started to make sounds. Next thing I knew I was babbling away, in what sounded a mixture of baby talk and a proper language. My whole face relaxed and I was soon aware that, just like Debbie, I'd been totally absorbed by the experience. I forgot my inhibitions, I laughed uncontrollably, and I almost forgot I was holding Debbie who had to shout, "James! Put me back on my pillow!" My words here just cannot explain what I was experiencing adequately to do any justice to the sense of well-being I felt. My joy was a double one. Not only did I now know Jesus and had been able to speak in tongues, but I now was one with Debbie in a new way. There was nothing more I wanted, alongside her, than to serve and follow God and His son Jesus, whom I now knew as the source of life, laughter and love.

Eventually, just as in an afterglow, our emotions settled down. Debbie closed her eyes. I joined my beautiful wife in bed, held her limp hand and we both drifted off together into a deep sleep.

What an unbelievable feeling greeted me as I awoke next morning! As I woke Debbie, her whole face was aglow with the joy of my new discovery. I couldn't wait for our short morning reading, and followed it by a heartfelt "Thank you, thank you, Jesus!" which she echoed. I'd have kissed her for ever if time had allowed, but work beckoned.

As I took my usual shortcut across the corner of the park, the leaves on the trees were now adorned with the first tints of autumn. I remembered how they'd appeared to me the day after Debbie – then described as "The toad" or "The Euthanasia Lady" – had prayed for my knee back in April. Somehow that day I had noticed the play of the light on the infant leaves like never before as, unbeknown to me, God's grace had begun to burst in upon my life. How grateful I was that my knee hadn't been instantly healed, that I'd been available – against my wishes – to take Debbie to church! And now, once again, the leaves spoke to me symbolically. Up until now, they had been different shades, shapes and sizes of green. Now they were about to become yellow, orange, deep red and brown. In that moment I knew little of what awaited me in days to come but I could see my life opening up to a far more beautiful kaleidoscope of rich, joyful colour. In that moment my heart swelled with gratitude that I was joined to such a wonderful woman as Debbie, the precious gift whom God had allowed me the privilege of discovering.

Sister Marion and Grace were on the ward. Their initial astonishment about me and Debbie had turned to amusement and much ribbing accompanied by reminders of some of my earlier unkind remarks about her. But this had soon given way to delight as they saw how 'loved up' I'd become, and to joy as they shared our wedding day. They'd noticed how much more I gave my patients my full attention and empathised with their fears, their symptoms and their pain. I'd found it had taken me a long time to face the more drastic types of surgery after my traumatic experiences in Darfur. I coped by completely separating James the surgeon from James the feeling person. Patients, to me, had to be considered like units of production in a factory otherwise I couldn't treat them. Since I'd been with Debbie this barrier had begun to be dismantled.

Today we had a particularly challenging new case on the ward. Gerald, aged 55, had cancer in his mouth and was facing a mandibular resection, a complicated operation in which we had to remove and reconstruct part of his jaw. Nowadays we aimed to complete the whole procedure under one anaesthetic. We'd met and I'd explained the procedure during his consultation a fortnight previously.

Together Debbie and I had prayed about this operation. I was to lead the surgical team although Mr. Davy would be present to 'mentor' me throughout the procedure. As I walked into Ward 17 my eyes met Gerald's, and as I looked at him sitting anxiously awaiting his pre-med, I saw the rising panic in his eyes. I decided to risk being politically incorrect. I went over to him, sat with him and asked if I could pray for him. As if pleading, he whispered, "Yes please!" whereupon I drew the curtains around his bed for privacy, and placed my arm around his shoulder. I prayed for him as discreetly as I could, and then continued gently speaking in my new prayer language. Gerald's face softened and relaxed. I knew that comfort and reassurance were being channelled through me from God to him. There was a Gideon Bible in his cupboard which I opened at Psalm 23, King David's 'Good Shepherd' psalm which was a favourite of Debbie's, and invited him to read it.

Once in the theatre I became thoroughly absorbed with the technical challenge of performing his long operation. I completed the procedure with no snags or complications, earning myself an encouraging pat on the shoulder from Mr. Davy.

-o-O-o-

The next day was Wednesday, our 'town' day. Debbie looked forward to shopping with me. It sounds so funny, but she particularly loved my wheeling her around Marks and Spencer so she could help me improve my dress sense! We laughed about her 'buying me' a more fashionable cardigan, pullover, or whatever it was. She chose masculine perfume for me. And together, we enjoyed buying matching hats, scarves and gloves. Usually I arranged for the items to be delivered to our flat.

We always made sure there was plenty of energy left for coffee shop time. This particular Wednesday the terrace was full. The manager said to us on the way in,

"James and Debbie, we love having you all, but we simply haven't room for any more customers!" The shop had pointed out that about half a dozen of those who sat with us were their own customers rather than church members;

they just enjoyed being a part of us. It was a nice problem to have. Debbie soon grabbed a few people's attention by telling them that James had been taking foreign language classes. Of course, I had to tell them why, and they were all intrigued to know about my new prayer language. Penny's and Amanda's eyes popped wide open, as they remembered that first evening when Debbie entered The Limes, when they'd rushed in a panic into Nathan's office after hearing her "speaking nonsense" in her room! This led to the inevitable fits of giggles, but there were some who quietly asked us if they, too, could experience what I had. Debbie and I both felt a sense of restraint, noticing that the McPhersons were at a table out of earshot. Without communicating we both wanted to honour this couple who'd helped us so much on our journey. We didn't want to act outside of their authority.

We decided to stay and chat to them afterwards. I told them my new story, which I noticed Elspeth welcomed more than Gilbert. But we also explored how we were going to move forward with the coffee shop. The McPhersons had heard comments from some church members that they were missing out because they were at work. We decided we'd split the group, with half remaining in the coffee shop and half moving to the church at 7:30 p.m.. The shop had been so kind to us that we decided we'd buy a selection of their cakes to enjoy in the evening with coffee made by ourselves. The evening meeting would give the opportunity for socialising to be mixed with teaching. Elspeth looked at Gilbert and said,

"I wouldn't mind listening to what Debbie has to teach us about the way the Holy Spirit works!"

Gilbert said it made sense although I could tell he wasn't as thrilled.

Debbie and I thought it would be a shame to no longer come to this pleasant gathering on the terrace but we knew we had to move on to where we seemed to be needed.

We didn't know that our Wednesday pattern was about to change for another reason; that of work. If you had told me when I first met Debbie that she'd soon be a hospital employee I would have thought it more likely the moon would sprout legs and dance on top of the sun.

Chapter 13

Mr. Davy was to be away one day and asked me to sit on a panel he attended in which surgeons who performed operations on patients' faces and mouths met with a small group of local dentists to discuss matters of mutual interest. On the agenda was a report on a study into the outcomes for people whom we'd treated. We all shared a concern that this group of patients were often deeply self-conscious about their appearance. Some left hospital with deep scars across their faces. The dentists added their concern that some people who lost their teeth felt a sense of shame, of embarrassment, of part of their personality being taken away. It was bad enough having to learn to talk and to eat differently, and many people never recovered their enjoyment of food. It was difficult to look people confidently in the eye and smile.

As the meeting drifted on, I thought of Debbie. I had come to know her during that difficult initial period when she looked almost sub-human, when only her deep sense of God's love for her had given her a sense of dignity and inner strength. I had witnessed the way she laughed and giggled at her own disabilities. And as I had fallen in love with her, I had longed to see her beautified, and had seen her transformed both by working on her appearance and through our romance. Together we were continuing to face the challenges of her condition, scoring little victories that built up her confidence and drew us ever closer together.

For example, we'd gradually refined our choice of menu so we could both enjoy our food whilst she found it palatable. Meat was difficult unless it was very tender and free of gristle. We were limited in which sorts of bread we could buy. But fruits and vegetables gave us huge scope. Our favourite food of all was to eat thin sticks of celery and carrots coated with cream cheese. I loved to hear Debbie biting and crunching them noisily, savouring the tastes released as she chewed. I'd always tended towards being a vegetarian so I was pleased to embrace our choices. I refused to have 'his menu and her menu'. We ate from the same plate.

Sometimes I had witnessed the way Debbie interacted with her visitors. On a typical afternoon, Debbie encouraged her visitors to come around 2 to 3 p.m. so they could leave in time for her to have a sleep at around five. Sometimes, however, her visitors were still with her when I arrived, usually because they'd been unburdening themselves of some challenge in their lives. I unintentionally caught the tail end of many a conversation, and was impressed by Debbie's humour, empathy and her perceptiveness in encouraging her guests to look for solutions and exercise faith.

I realised I was daydreaming rather than concentrating on the meeting. As we moved through the agenda, the suggestion of a self-help group kept surfacing. When the chairman announced "Any Other Business", I said I knew the ideal person to facilitate it. The dentists reacted immediately with enthusiasm and I agreed to approach Debbie to work for three hours on a Wednesday, 3.30 till 6.30 p.m. The earlier half would be for appointments, the latter half for group work so it could include working people. I knew her well enough to say that three hours was the maximum she could manage.

-o-O-o-

The same evening I arrived home and found Debbie with two late middle-aged ladies one of whom had been Mavis' gossiping companion that afternoon at The Limes. They'd stayed because the conversation had become rather animated. Debbie couldn't easily raise her voice but she was talking with passion, saying,

"But don't we believe in a supernatural God? Why are we talking about this as if we just belonged to any other club in Somershire? If we can't trust Him, then why do we come to church to worship Him?"

Debbie introduced me to Margaret and to Hilary, whose husband was the church treasurer. Hilary was upset because her husband Ron had received a request for a payment to the Baptist Union that the church could ill afford. The church's building inspector had recently examined the roof after a patch of damp had appeared in the ceiling and, as a result, they'd called in a reputable local builder. He'd estimated the immediate repair would cost £18,000, almost equal to the church's entire reserves. However, worse was to come. The stylish Victorian building would eventually need entirely re-roofing, at a cost likely to stretch into six figures. On the back of this, a payment of £37,000 to the Union was adding insult to injury. Ron had been furious with Gilbert McPherson when he suggested it was important to honour God by paying our share. Hilary reported on a heated conversation she'd overheard.

"But, Gilbert," so Ron had said, "where's the money going to come from? It isn't just going to fall out of the sky, is it? There are only two ways to deal with this. The first is to get more money in, and with a load of ageing people in the congregation there's little chance of that. The second is to reduce your expenditure. So if you want to pay the Union you'll have to find other ways to save money. I'll leave it to you to decide how!"

I could see Debbie was tired, yet was completely engaged. As her husband I knew I had to step in. I suggested they call a halt, and then invited Hilary to call around with Ron on the following Sunday afternoon. Maybe as two couples we could explore the matter together.

By the time we'd showered, Debbie was ready for a sleep. I woke her up an hour later for our meal. I wondered if she'd be up for any more conversation after her busy afternoon. She still wanted to hear about my day at work. Then, as we dressed for bed, she said,

"James, I'm still tired. But nothing's going to stop me giving myself to you now. Come on, let's enjoy the very best part of our day together!"

Half an hour later she prayed for me, then dropped asleep with her head in my arms as I prayed for her. Oh, how I loved her, body, mind and soul!

-o-O-o-

It was with very great pride that I placed my request for a lanyard to be made for:-

Mrs. Debbie McAlister
Group Facilitator, Patient Support
Oral and Maxillofacial Surgery

-o-O-o-

"Debbie," I said one evening, "what d'you think the church should do about its debts? I mean, if they haven't got the money, how can they pay the Baptist Union?"

"James," she replied, "it's no different to what I had to do when I first went into The Limes. I hadn't any friends, and I couldn't see how I could find anybody to share my faith with. But I praised God, and I trusted Him to provide. And look who came along!"

How I loved the way that, even in the middle of a serious discussion, we could have a giggle!

"We trusted Him together over Mr. Glynn's tooth. We trusted Him over you keeping your job, and over setting up our home together. And look what He gave us – a dream wedding! He loves us, James, and He loves the church. He really wants us to believe it. And He wants us to love Him in return. That means we've got to trust Him to look after us when we pay up what He asks. He's not poor, is He? He knows how He's going to provide what we need. But we can't run the church just like a business. It's God's business; He's got His own sort of economics."

"But that doesn't help the treasurer pay up," I protested. "He's got the invoice on his desk, and his cheque book in front of him. What does he do?"

"James," said my wife through her shining eyes, "it's an adventure!"

We talked on into the evening before ending it in our usual style, praying too about the church's dilemma, for Ron the treasurer and for ourselves and the part we could play.

-o-O-o-

At church that Sunday morning, Hilary introduced Debbie and me to Ron whom up until then we had only known by sight. Ron's greeting was lukewarm to say the least.

"So, are you financial people? I mean, I presume, you must have some experience in dealing with money matters?" he asked.

I explained that we weren't experts but that we, or particularly Debbie, felt we had some insights to share about God's economics. I noticed furrows appearing on Ron's brow, particularly on either side of the top of his nose, behind his prominent black glasses. I simply said that Debbie and I had been talking about our faith and about the way she had seen God meet her needs in many different areas of her life.

"Oh, it's one of *those* conversations, is it then?" he replied tersely.

I noticed that Gilbert had moved back into church after saying his doorstep goodbyes, and thought it wise to brief him about our afternoon visit. He smiled a knowing smile and said he was pleased someone else was taking up the challenge. He had last preached about generosity five years ago and had been criticised for 'soliciting people for money'. He was aware of the church's precarious situation but in the Baptist Union, the minister isn't directly responsible for the financial health of the church. But he couldn't just stand by and ignore the church's money matters. He knew it mattered to God.

Then he drew a Bible from a pew and found some scriptures for us. Debbie was delighted; she had vague memories of the passages but wouldn't have known where to find them. Gilbert assured us that he and Elspeth would be praying about our 'encounter' with Ron and that they'd be interested to know the outcome.

I read out the passages as Debbie and I were having lunch, and we chewed them over along with our food. At 3:30 p.m. prompt, our doorbell chimed below at the entrance to the flats. Ron, Hilary and another well-groomed middle-aged gentleman with neat grey hair entered the lounge.

We had a comfortable settee and two upright chairs, and I motioned to our guests to have the settee. The two men declined, saying they preferred to keep their backs straight. I offered coffee or tea but they assured me they'd just nicely eaten lunch. I sat next to Debbie's chair at one end of the settee with Hilary at the other, and saw immediately that the men's heads were a full 9 inches higher than mine. They knew a bit of psychology!

"So, what's this about then?" began Ron.

Unlike me, Debbie was unaffected by the men's show of strength. She explained how she could understand what a difficult position Ron was in. It wasn't an easy job being the treasurer and she thanked him for doing this job behind the scenes so that the church could run smoothly. She could imagine it must not have been pleasant to receive the Baptist Union's letter just as he was wondering how the church could pay for its roofing. But she'd felt challenged after Hilary had explained the situation. She believed there was a different way to look at the Union's letter. Surely we worshipped a wonderful, great, loving, supernatural God who had created everything we see around us. Why did we see ourselves as being a poor church?

"I think this is all a bit pointless," said Ron quietly to his friend Giles. "I can't see where this is going to lead or how it's going to help us."

It was my turn. I approached discussions differently, and as never before I appreciated how Debbie and I complemented each other so richly.

"Our church's situation has some interesting parallels in both the Old and the New Testaments," I said. "Let me read you what the prophet Malachi said to the Jews who were struggling to find money to build their temple." And I read Chapter 3, verses 9 and 10,

"'You are under a curse—your whole nation—because you are robbing me. Bring the whole tithe into the storehouse, that there may be food in my house'.

"There's no other way of putting it," I continued, "if we withhold money that should go to support our parent organisation, we're robbing God. If the church owes money to the Baptist Union, surely that has to come first?"

I could see impatience rising on the two men's faces as Ron said, "Look, I'm not here to be accused or insulted by two people who know nothing whatsoever of church finances. Quite simply, young man, if the money isn't in the bank, it isn't in the bank. End of..."

"But it isn't the 'end of'," I said. "Listen to what follows." And I read on...

"'Test me in this, says the LORD Almighty, and see if I will not throw open the floodgates of heaven and pour out so much blessing that there will not be room enough to store it. I will prevent pests from devouring your crops, and the vines in your fields will not drop their fruit before it is ripe, says the LORD Almighty. Then all the nations will call you blessed, for yours will be a delightful land, says the LORD Almighty'."

Seizing her cue, Debbie continued, "You see, God wants to bless us, to lead us out on an adventure of faith. He wants our church to overflow with wealth. There'll be so much that there's lots to give away to others. Look at the way the church overflowed with love and generosity the day we were married. Ron, you're the treasurer. You're in a wonderful position because you're right in the middle of this adventure."

The two men got up to leave, but Hilary was reluctant. "James," she said, "did you have another passage to read to us?"

I opened our Bible to 2 Corinthians Chapter 9, verses 6 to 11, where the apostle Paul was talking about a collection. He was encouraging them to support the church in Jerusalem which had run out of funds. Hilary made a note, and then followed her husband and his friend out of the door.

Debbie and I held hands, kissed, spoke in tongues for several minutes then undressed and celebrated the way God had joined us together and was still doing so ever more completely.

-o-O-o-

It was Wednesday. At 3 p.m. promptly I wheeled Debbie to hospital and we made our way to a comfortable conference room on the fourth floor. Would she have any appointments for her individual or group sessions? Yes, indeed! I asked if I could stay to watch the first one. Linda was a lady in her late thirties who had needed a jaw reconstruction and had a prominent scar across the right side of her face. We'd worked hard to preserve her muscles so she was gradually regaining the ability to eat, talk, and smile. But had she anything to smile about? She'd clearly been traumatised by her operation. She was married but her husband's attitude fell a long way short of being fully supportive.

After listening to Linda pour out her story, Debbie explained a little of her own ordeal, then smiled her usual deep smile. We'd bought her a smart blue jacket so she'd look the part, and with her rather striking glasses she looked every bit a healthcare professional! Then she asked Linda to hold up a mirror to her face and practice smiling to herself. Debbie giggled at her, teasing her about her half-hearted efforts until she began to let all her facial muscles join in so that she beamed at herself. It was a lop-sided beam but in its peculiar way Linda had an attractive smile that transcended her ugly gash. Then they talked a little about how Linda saw herself, and – as I knew she would – Debbie told her about God's wonderful love 'that will not let me go'. She shared a little of how she and I 'found each other' before movingly asking if she could pray for Linda. I prayed under my breath in my new tongue. I could see the lady's face warming as she received a huge draught of love that had been so lacking. Four o'clock arrived but she said she'd cancel her taxi so she could stay for the group session. I, however, felt I should bow out and leave Debbie to her task.

I returned at 6:30 to find Debbie utterly spent but deeply fulfilled and contented. I watched four people file out of the room where they'd met. On each face was a serenity and a sense of having been in a very special place during the last hour and a half. Debbie slept all the way home, and it wasn't until an hour later that I woke her up to begin our evening.

-o-O-o-

We decided a good division of our Wednesday group would be to leave a nucleus at the café that consisted of Albert the baritone soloist and his wife Sarah with Bill, Mavis and also Penny and Amanda. Albert and Sarah were known in the church as a faithful couple who had served for many years as stewards, children's workers, choir members, and were known to be hospitable and caring. They'd recently offered Bill the spare room in their house for "what he could afford". Once away from the hostel, it was easier for Bill to keep himself tidy and smart, just as at our wedding. He'd landed a much better job delivering plants for a nursery just out of town. It was a regular, full time job and required someone who was personable and able to communicate with the customer. There was no doubt that the Wednesday coffee afternoons had brought Bill out of himself a great deal. He proudly insisted to Albert and Sarah that, as soon as his first pay cheque arrived, he would pay them a more realistic rent for his room.

Mavis was always lively and chatty. She was welcoming, and she was growing in faith and in confidence. Amanda and Penny from the home were "still exploring" as they put it, but had been greatly impacted firstly by Debbie and me, and more recently by our wedding.

In view of Debbie's job being on Wednesday we decided to hold the evening meeting on a different day. Tuesday seemed best. The first week, the McPhersons came to introduce the group. Elspeth was keen to get going but Gilbert retired after about half an hour. I was concerned, followed him out and we walked home to the manse. He made a pot of tea, and then he sat at the kitchen table and opened up to me.

He explained that what we'd talked about, the Holy Spirit and the gifts such as healing, prophecy, tongues, miracles, had been part of his college life. I recalled how earlier they'd told me about their week "living by faith". Unfortunately events had got out of hand when students started to hold their own meetings rather than attend their lectures and the college had clamped down heavy-handedly. This had left many students with their fingers burnt.

Despite this, Gilbert left college with a passion to share Jesus. In his earlier years as a minister Gilbert had been full of fire, and hadn't been content to merely preach in church. He and Elspeth preached in the marketplace, singing in duet whilst he accompanied on his piano accordion. He remembered the day when five teenage lads came in tears to them after they'd sung and preached, saying, "What do we have to do to get right with God?" There and then, they took the step I'd just taken, of asking Jesus and God the Father to make their home in their lives. One of them went on to become a minister, another, a youth worker.

They'd brought up their family and enjoyed an influx of other families which swelled the Sunday school and the youth group. Life had seemed good. However, as they settled into middle age, Gilbert became aware that he was increasingly going through the motions. Only occasionally now did they bring someone to know Jesus, and church life became a predictable affair of delivering well-crafted, nice-sounding sermons which impressed but never changed people. He was a professional minister. Words like self-sacrifice, passion, heart for the lost, and Fire of the Holy Spirit were ones he avoided.

At Patterdale Road, Gilbert's ministry went a stage further downhill. Aware of rifts within his congregation, Gilbert had decided his main focus was now simply to keep out of trouble.

Seven years to retirement, he'd thought. He had the skills never to rock boats, to see political manoeuvring for what it was and avoid being to blame.

Then Debbie arrived, with me dragged along in tow like an angry toddler.

The coffee shop fellowship began.

And then Gilbert and Elspeth were drawn into the battle to save my job and were instrumental in joining us together. This had given them both a new lease of life. But whereas to Elspeth the thought of introducing the Holy Spirit's gifts was exciting, to him it brought back too many painful memories.

At this stage in the conversation I felt amazed and humbled that this man, to whom I owed a great deal, had trusted me with the secrets of his heart. That was when I discovered something new about the Holy Spirit's role of speaking wisdom into my life. I felt these words being burnt into my mind:-

"Your role is to encourage this servant of Mine by letting him help you understand Me."

I shared with Gilbert how I had essentially parked my intellectual objections to come to faith, but that I now needed to discover why I believed what I did. He said he'd do his utmost to help me. He urged me to make a start by reading Luke's Gospel then went to his study and found a book with notes on each of the chapters. I had started my own first term at Bible College!

-o-O-o-

I never expected to be involved in healing relationships. I shouldn't have been surprised; as Debbie's husband, new adventures came with the territory. Matthew was a slightly built young man who'd seen her in a Wednesday afternoon one-to-one session. He'd been set upon by thugs who had broken his jaw. Our oral and maxillofacial surgery team had repaired it but, as well as cutting open his jaw, had had to extract half his teeth. He was expecting to become a father in about six months' time, and his schoolteacher girlfriend Melissa was becoming impatient. It was time Matthew pulled himself together, she said, and found a proper job. Paid work, for him, had meant casual jobs in cafes and bars. His dream was to earn his living by running a music studio, an idea at which he'd already had one attempt. This had ended in him having to sell his gear because he couldn't make it pay.

Debbie explained to me that Matthew had admitted he'd lost his confidence. It seemed the experience of being beaten up, losing his teeth and adjusting to dentures had traumatised and emasculated him. He said Melissa always seemed critical of him.

At this point Debbie felt she was being steered into uncharted waters. She had no training as a counsellor, and even had she done so, this wasn't a challenge for a lady on her own. She wisely stopped the session and agreed to find out where to refer the couple for the help they needed. But meanwhile she suggested they, and we, could meet at our flat where we could pray for them.

And so, on Friday evening, the doorbell rang at 7 p.m. and a rather interesting-looking couple walked in the door. Melissa was taller and more muscular than Matthew, wore rings in her ears and eyebrows, and wore heavy flat boots with enormous laces. Matthew was dressed in a dapper pink shirt with a silky red neckerchief; his delicate gentle features such a contrast to those of his dominatrix. They accepted my offer of coffee and Waitrose's best cookies.

We began by asking Matthew, then Melissa, to express how they felt about their situation. Matthew's feelings of hopelessness, and Melissa's of impatient frustration came through clearly. They started to talk about their previous history but Debbie and I had agreed we'd ask them to leave this to discuss with the professionals. To us, they were a man and a woman expecting a family.

Debbie and I shared our own story with them. I never failed to be moved by Debbie's, and as usual I learnt something new. I'd always known her as a woman of confident, unwavering faith. This time I learnt that this may only have been recent; she'd made a special commitment to God the day she was wheeled into The Limes. She determined then that she would prove God to be faithful, to believe His promises whatever happened to her. I also learnt that, the moment she first met me, she felt the Holy Spirit saying, "I'm going to bless that surgeon through you," and that this encouraged her to pray for me in Ward 17. For my part I had our guests and Debbie in stitches as I recounted my first impressions of her, mimicked her words and remembered the various nicknames by which I referred to her. But by the time I explained how God had met my challenge, their mouths gaped open and their eyes widened with amazement.

Debbie and I were holding hands; I squeezed Debbie's fingers and felt her glowing all through her body.

She shared how she could do absolutely nothing for herself, but that my tender, intimate care of her as I toileted, showered, dressed, fed her and – particularly – cleaned her teeth, made us both feel very romantic. She asked Melissa if she could exploit Matthew's vulnerabilities in a similar way. Debbie's eyes had a mischievous glint as she went into a little detail about our private life… and had us all giggling…

We challenged both to leave the past behind and commit to being parents. We urged Matthew to 'be a man', to take courage and believe he was capable of being a good father and a supportive, competent partner. We challenged Melissa to accept and encourage Matthew to be himself, to build his confidence. It was clear he was looking forward to caring for a young child much more than she, and once her maternity leave had finished it would make sense for him to stay at home as a dad than to be forced out to work at a job he disliked.

Finally, we asked if we could pray for them both. Melissa said,

"If you'd asked me that before we'd met you, I'd have said absolutely no way. But I can't deny something very special's happened in your lives. P'haps things could change for us, too. You've given me some hope that they can."

We prayed that God would heal Matthew's memory and the humiliation of his beating, and that he'd eventually be able to forgive his assailants. We blessed them in Jesus' name, declaring His blessing on their union, their baby, Melissa's school, their home and their understanding of Him. Somehow we both felt a special compassion towards this couple despite their having different backgrounds to us and, as yet, no faith.

Debbie did make enquiries about specialist counselling for them as a couple, but it didn't prove necessary. By the time arrangements had been made they'd already begun to rediscover the joy of their physical relationship, and from what we could work out they seemed increasingly happy together.

Chapter 14

It all came as a most unpleasant surprise. I was late leaving for work, couldn't find my keys or my phone, and snapped at Debbie. I yelled at the top of my voice,

"It's alright for you, isn't it? All you have to do is b****y-well sit there like a queen on your throne, whilst I go out and earn our bread and butter! It's James this, James that, James the other, and I have to come running from wherever the hell I happen to be. You have top priority all the time. Sometimes I wish *I* could be disabled!"

I thumped the dining table then slammed the door and walked out into the street. It wasn't long before my tears started to flow. I loved Debbie with all my heart. Ours had been a beautiful, pure relationship in which we were uncompromisingly open-hearted towards each other. What had gone wrong?

I was distracted during my morning rounds and found it a huge effort to concentrate on my patients. As it happened, Mr. Davy had asked me and Martin to join him for a chat before surgery began. Both of them noticed straightaway that I was distraught. I blurted out that I'd snapped at Debbie. I hadn't expected their reaction, which was that they weren't surprised.

"Can you call her now?" asked Mr. Davy. Looking at my watch, I realised that her morning carer would still be with her. "Go on, James," he said, "speak to her."

The carer placed her phone to Debbie's ear, and I said, "Darling, I'm so, so sorry. I'm just heartbroken that I spoke to you so horribly."

"Don't worry, James," she said, "I forgive you. I know you love me. We'll work out what's wrong. I think I know already."

We ended the call soon afterwards. I shook my head. "She's such a wonderful woman!" I said.

"Yes, she is," said Mr. Davy, "but you too have needs, James, and they aren't being met." He shrugged in a way that said he'd have liked to continue but couldn't at present. "Now, we've a full list today. Can you cope with yours?"

Having apologised to Debbie, I decided I was okay to launch into surgery. It was nearly 6 o'clock before I finally hung up my surgical clothes and prepared to head home. Martin was just finishing at the same time. He commented that he really missed our games of squash on a Thursday evening. He asked what sort of exercise I was getting. The answer was - very little.

-o-O-o-

On the way home I reflected that even my Wednesdays were now taken up with Debbie, Debbie, Debbie. After our morning in town, she had her sleep before I dressed her for work and we headed out to hospital. Then, at 6:30, I would pick her up to return home. I did this because I loved to see her fulfilled, and she never failed to let me know how grateful she was. But my being her 'perfect husband' had taken its toll on me.

Debbie was having a hard time physically. She never moaned, but she continued to be troubled by the occasional flaring up of her U.T.I. (Urinary Tract Infection). I made sure we kept a stock of effective medicines and that we used them immediately she began to have a problem, but it was a war of attrition that sometimes sent us scurrying to her GP's surgery for fresh antibiotics. Then, being confined to a wheelchair and unable to move, she developed pressure sores. We worked together to devise coping strategies so that her carers and visitors could change her position regularly to keep these to a minimum.

She never complained about her teeth, but sometimes her gums developed tender patches which needed treatment. On a number of occasions we had to include a visit to the dentist on our Wednesday schedule for denture adjustments. Typically of her, she always looked forward to seeing the staff and enjoying a giggle. Occasionally she had trouble with seeds lodging in her gums, and on one occasion I spent twenty minutes with a torch and a toothpick freeing a raspberry seed from where it was sitting obstinately. She faced this with courage and, as ever, lots of juicy kisses when I finally succeeded.

Monthly periods weren't fun either. Debbie had to wear an extra liner inside her 'All-in-One' slip. It wasn't a problem provided there was only one sort of discharge... but rather more ominously, a lump was growing which, had she not been sterilised, could have been mistaken for a pregnancy. Her carers and I took turns in wheeling her for various appointments and she was eventually diagnosed with a uterine fibroid. She'd need a hysterectomy which would at least relieve her of her periods. I attended the latest of these appointments as we needed to discuss the special challenges that her disability would present during her treatment and recovery.

The trouble was that whilst most of the time it was a delight to meet Debbie's needs, I hadn't any choice. I knew she bore a lot of discomfort with good grace, but there wasn't any way I could say, "Not now, love. I need a rest." And sometimes I just wanted a break. Increasingly a part of me wanted to scream out, "Just leave me alone!" Then I felt guilty for not being a loving husband to my needy wife.

Now I was beginning to understand the McPhersons' warnings. But I determined there and then that we were going to find a way through. I thought of our wedding ceremony and the way God's presence had graced the whole occasion from start to finish. No way were we going to let the poison of resentment foul up our marriage.

I arrived home to find her just as pleased to see me as ever. We talked that night about what had gone wrong. She said,

"James, you know I'm happily married beyond my wildest dreams. But I know how hard it must be for you. I've noticed you've got a lot more irritable lately, just in little ways. I know you've been sacrificing yourself for me, but it's like you're feeling you can't ever please yourself. I don't want you to feel like that. D'you remember what Howard your rugby captain said on our wedding day? He said how much he wanted you to play for them again, as soon as Missus – that's me - let you out of the door. James, I'd be very happy if you went to play rugby again. It's a wonderful game, 'cos that was how you got injured. That's why I could pray for you. And it was 'cos you got injured that you could take me to church!"

"You mischievous little imp!" I giggled.

"James," she said, "we've got plenty of money to pay for more care if you're going to be out on a Sunday afternoon or an evening. I love it when you come home at teatime, but I want it to be a happy 'you' not a 'you' that feels he's got no choice except to be here for me. Oh, and sometimes when you play rugby, I'm going to come and cheer you on the touchline!

"And another thing. I know it gets to you if I'm always asking you to come at my beck and call. I know I can't do a thing to help myself but often I bother

~ 132 ~

you when I don't really need to. I'm sorry; I know I could have made life easier for you. Oh, by the way, d'you remember how once before you told me off for saying Daimth this, Daimth that and Daimth the other?"

We giggled. This was so, so like Debbie…

At the conclusion of our talk she was, unusually, completely spent. However, I felt more deeply cared for, appreciated and amazed than ever before by the incredible woman whom God had placed alongside me as a beautiful gift.

-o-O-o-

We arranged that on Wednesday afternoons, I'd hand over to a carer who would take Debbie to hospital for her 'patient support' sessions. This allowed me to start physiotherapy to regain the full use of my injured leg in preparation for rugby. After four sessions I felt well enough to resume my games of squash with Martin which we arranged on Wednesday evenings after he'd finished surgery.

For the sake of confidentiality, Debbie had to be careful what she told me about her sessions but from all the feedback I received, patients said how helpful they'd found her to be. I wasn't surprised.

One afternoon we had a short list of patients and I finished early. I arrived home to find Matthew with Debbie. By Matthew's side was a guitar. They'd been singing. I was rather startled by this. Debbie seemed perfectly happy and was enjoying his company. She always told me who'd been to see her, and we held no secrets from each other. Matthew was rather embarrassed and made to put on his coat, but Debbie urged him to take his time.

"Would you like to hear what we've been doing, James?" she asked.

Rather nonchalantly, I said "Okay." Matthew started finger-picking his guitar, very skilfully, and launched into,

"Are you going to Scarborough Fair, Parsley, Sage, Rosemary and Thyme?"

This was of course a folk song made famous in the sixties by Paul Simon and Art Garfunkel. What I hadn't expected was that in the second verse, Debbie chimed in with the beautiful descant that spans the melody between each line. I'd noticed at church that she had a sweet voice, although had to pause for breath where there were long, sustained phrases.

Sometimes we'd talked about our past lives. Debbie had enjoyed dancing and, as a teenager, had featured several times in shows where her exhibitionist qualities shone. I could imagine her, free and easy, making beautiful flowing movements and captivating audiences with her sparkling eyes. One day I'd said so, and she'd replied, with a giggle,

"And then I charmed Mr. James McAlister who was enchanted by my beauty in my bog-eyed specs and the ease with which I shuffled about on my bed…"

I'd added, truthfully, "That was when Mr. James McAlister saw what's in your soul."

Debbie had also told me that she used to belong to a folk club where she'd met Scott, the father of her children. Sometimes they'd 'do a turn' together and this was where she'd learnt to sing descants. She had a gentle, natural voice although her illness now prevented her from raising the volume.

Matthew made his way out. I expected Debbie would want to take a nap, but she seemed wide awake. It was me who needed a bit of space, so I made myself a cup of tea before we began our evening routine. I was slightly put out if I was honest. She enjoyed having visitors but usually they were female and talked about knitting, cookery and grandchildren. Debbie always set out to encourage their faith but by 5 p.m. they'd tired her out so that she took a nap before I arrived. This time she seemed energised. Wasn't it *my* role to make her feel like that?

An hour and a half later we lay together in bed where I began to cuddle her. She could tell I wasn't my usual self.

"Come on, James, relax and enjoy yourself!" she said, as she used her sparkling eyes, her beautifully painted lips and her soft tongue to tempt me into action. As she succeeded in overcoming my grumpy resistance, I felt her emotions towards me were more intense than ever before. Many times previously I had needed to admit Debbie had insights that I didn't possess. In a moment of acceptance, I let go and simply enjoyed loving and being loved by my fired-up wife.

-o-O-o-

A part of our routine was to see Jonathan and Ethan who now looked forward to visiting once a fortnight on a Sunday afternoon. They had tea with us, purchased from Waitrose who packaged the items ready for me collect. Their foster parents had remarked how much brighter the boys seemed now that they knew their mum was happy, too. Debbie was able to laugh effusively with them and encouraged them to hug her, kiss her, and place her limp arms around them. I grew fond of them and we enjoyed playing board games together. Debbie and I enjoyed buying gifts for them on Wednesdays in town whenever she decided to take a break from her mission of smartening up her man. We always prayed for them as they finished their visit, and blessed them. On one occasion the time crept up on us, the doorbell rang and the boys' foster parents arrived to take them home. There are no prizes for guessing that Debbie insisted on blessing them, too. They were private people and initially they agreed only because my wheelchair-bound wife was so hard to refuse. As Debbie blessed them I saw how their faces softened. I believed the Holy Spirit was urging me to bless this couple's own family who had grown up and flown the nest. As I did so in very simple words, I noticed a few tears trickling down their cheeks.

One Saturday I was able to take a holiday from work so that we could take the train to the town where they lived. Jonathan was playing in a cup final game. I loved shouting encouragement from the touchline and Debbie did her utmost with her quiet voice. The team lost but we were impressed by how well Jonathan played. The coach said he'd had an extra spring in his step that afternoon because we'd been on the touchline.

-o-O-o-

We both looked forward to Tuesday evenings. By the end of the year, around twenty people were regularly coming along to enjoy 'Food and Faith' in the church hall. The menu featured coffee, cakes and fellowship, followed by a 'Faith Spot' in which Elspeth and Debbie shared Bible passages about the Holy Spirit. I missed this part because I was spending time with Gilbert. They talked about how the Spirit makes a difference in our lives, and how enjoying His presence lights up the whole process of living. I continued to notice that, once people came to know Debbie, they no longer saw her as a tragically disabled person. She epitomised everything she spoke about.

She and Elspeth talked, too, about the remarkable things that can happen when the Holy Spirit enables us to do what Jesus did. They read short clips from Heidi Baker's 'Always Enough', telling of how she and her husband Rolland asked God to send them to the most hopeless country on earth so that they could prove Him. I'd read the book, and it rang bells for me, with my challenge to he-she-it! They ended up in Mozambique where they saw, and are still seeing, remarkable miracles of healing and of God's supernatural provision. And this was where Debbie's condition became a problem. More than once, her friends asked if they could pray for her to be raised up out of her wheelchair.

She encouraged her friends to pray about her minor medical problems, but felt we should leave praying for her MS until our faith as a church had grown. I agreed with her. It was clear, too, that Jesus shone more brightly than ever through Debbie because of the way she faced her disability. She was always quick to add that Jesus shone through both of us because of the way He had placed us alongside each other as an unlikely but delighted husband and wife team.

As time went on, another feature of Tuesday evenings was 'My Story Time'. An increasing number of group members told their stories of how God was changing them. Someone may have had a remarkable sense of God's presence in a difficult situation. Another may have been able to pray for a friend who was in trouble or sick. An elderly man, Harold, laid his hands on his son's painful shoulders and within a few hours he was almost pain free and able to return to work after a week's absence. Someone else may have had a special flash of knowledge about, or insight into a situation. Mavis woke in the night thinking about her daughter. She called her daughter and said she had one word on her mind:- bullying. Unbeknown to her, her grandson had been very cheeky the previous evening and his parents were wondering what sort of punishment to mete out. It emerged that the lad was indeed having a hard time at school, and that his behaviour at home was a reaction.

Meanwhile I was enjoying my personal theology course. Every week I arrived with fresh questions for Gilbert who relished the challenge. I read about the virgin birth in Luke Chapter 1. I declared that this was medically impossible. Yes, said Gilbert, but if God had created the laws of nature, why couldn't He act over and above them when He needed to? After all, hadn't He responded to my Euthanasia Person challenge? This may not have involved a physical miracle but had you told me that the helpless, pathetic, toad-faced, boggle-eyed, supposedly deluded creature I had first met would become my wife, I'd have quite categorically declared it impossible.

Others of my questions arose from areas exploited by the New Atheists. I asked Gilbert whether it bothered him that science is gradually explaining away all the gaps in our knowledge in a way that leaves little room for God.

"Oh, really?" he asked. "Tell me, James, what do you feel when you're operating on one of your patients' mouths? You can explain how it all works but do you seriously think it could have created itself randomly without any knowledge of its own design plan?"

I had to admit that I was feeling increasingly angry that I'd been taken in by the New Atheist mantra that says, "The world looks as if it's been designed, but in fact it hasn't." Gilbert lent me another book, 'Fearfully and wonderfully made' which was written by Dr. Paul Brand, a British missionary and surgeon who pioneered limb-saving leprosy treatments in India before settling in the USA where he continued his work. The book was co-authored by theologian Dr. Philip Yancey. I was impressed not only by Dr. Brand's medical expertise in which he described the incredible synergy between body parts, but by his compassion for his many individual patients and for the whole world population of leprosy victims. He posed the question as to whether he believed in evolution but left it dangling temptingly in the air... but he left us in no doubt that he believed our bodies were built according to God's design. I felt a great deal in common with Dr. Brand especially as I now looked to the Holy Spirit to bless my patients as I operated on them.

-o-O-o-

My consternation about Debbie and Matthew finally came to a head one afternoon when yet again I found him at home on my return from work. As before, Debbie seemed energised, even sparkling, and she and he were enjoying a good giggle. I was decidedly cool towards him and saw him hastily out of the door. Debbie was upset with me. I looked her straight in the eye and said,

"Look, I've invested so much in our marriage. I haven't done this so you can entertain boyfriends while I'm at work!"

Debbie's face puckered up and tears began to form.

"James! How could you ever think *that?* You're my husband and nothing's changed at all between us. But Matthew's like a brother to me. He brings out a special part of me that likes to create. Darling, you and I can't meet all of each other's needs. Both of us need other friends. It just happens that he's a man, but there's no way I want to take him away from Melissa. Don't you understand? I feel I love you even more after I've spent time with Matthew. And I bet you'll feel the same about me after you've been out playing rugby."

I *didn't* understand, but my trust in Debbie was absolute. She was as good as her word. That night she felt even more close, passionate and loveable than ever.

She made sure I knew where to find Matthew's number on her phone, and then I settled her in bed. Then I called him to apologise for being short with him.

The great day arrived when my physio declared me fit for rugby. I called Howard and we agreed that I'd be available for home games and for away matches at other grounds within the city, but that for the present I'd miss those where we played further afield. I now loved to be with Debbie at church which I'd hate to miss, and I wanted to be at home on some Sunday afternoons to see the boys.

We agreed that on my first game I'd stay on 'the bench' until midway through the second half, to give me a gentle introduction and plenty of time to warm up. I took Debbie home after church; we'd arranged for a carer to spend time with her and to give her lunch. I grabbed a quick bite, kissed her goodbye and left with my kitbag.

It felt odd but also exhilarating to be back in the clubhouse. I hadn't played rugby since the Sunday after I met Debbie. The lads were delighted to see me. They were about six weeks into the season and doing okay, but they were looking forward to having me play on the wing again. I donned my tracksuit and a weatherproof jacket to keep out the late autumn dampness, and followed my team mates out onto the pitch. There were only a handful of spectators one of whom was our coach, who held a battery operated megaphone through which he shouted instructions and called players on and off the pitch.

It was a tightly fought game. The lead swung one way, then the other. The opposition had the better goal kicker so, despite our having the best of the open play, we ended up seven points behind with twenty minutes to go. On I went glad to gain a slice of the action as the drizzle became heavier. It took five minutes to 'play myself in', but then my animal instincts engaged and I began to thirst for the ball. From a throw-in on the other side of the field, the ball was passed along the line. I could see that my opposite number was anticipating the pass that would find me. I made a run towards Greg, the player with the ball, received it cleanly, then changed direction and darted towards the touchline. With a sudden swerve I burst inside and made towards the goal line, straight ahead of me. Then I heard a familiar but faint voice. It was unmistakeably Debbie's.

"Go for it, James! Keep running! You're nearly there!"

Inspired by this I found a burst of speed out of nowhere and surged past the waiting fullback. As Debbie kept calling, I ran to within 5 yards of the line, but found my way blocked by another player who had scurried back to cover. Then, to my right, I saw Greg who had almost kept up with my run. At the last possible moment I slipped the ball back to him, whereupon he dived over the line just inside the corner flag. Five points.

Ken, our full back, placed the ball to attempt to kick the conversion. I looked to the touchline and saw a heavily clad Debbie in her chair along with Matthew and Melissa who must have called during the afternoon and brought her to see the game. What I couldn't work out was how on earth she'd been able to make herself heard. She couldn't normally raise her voice.

It's a tall order to find the gap between the posts from a try scored in the corner and it proved too much for Ken. We still trailed by two points. There were only five more minutes. From the restart we caught the ball and passed it up and down our three-quarter line. After what seemed an eternity we decided there was no way through so finally we passed to Ken who booted the ball up field and into touch. The opposition fed the ball into the line-out but the player who handled it didn't feed the slippery wet ball back cleanly and it was dropped. Scrum down. We were aware that this was likely to be the final 'play'. Our scrum did its work well, and the ball was once again fed from scrum half to stand-off, then along the line of three quarters to me. Our pattern of play was all too predictable to trouble our opponents and I knew I had to do something special. This time I motioned to Greg to send me a long pass. I gathered it, and then turned inside towards the crowd of opposition players. Ken anticipated my thoughts perfectly. He ran across me so that he was positioned outside me in open space. He knew what I'd do. Just before my path was blocked, I swivelled around and sent him a long pass. He gathered it sweetly and raced for the line. He side-stepped the opposing full back and ran for all he was worth.

My rugby instincts were by now fully attuned and I raced to keep up with him. Then I clearly heard, much louder than before, "Daimth! Daimth! Come on, gep doethe kneeth up an' thcore me a tzwy!"

Ken could see that he was going to make the line but that I was hot on his heels. At the last moment, he generously slipped the ball to me so I could have my moment of glory.

Get those knees up, indeed – how dare she?

It was indeed the last 'play'. Even though the try wasn't converted, we'd run out winners by three points. I ran over to Debbie who had charmed our coach into letting her use the megaphone and had had Matthew hold it to her mouth. Melissa was replacing her teeth which she'd asked them to remove so she could place the device deeper into her mouth to get more volume! What a rascal she was…

I picked up my giggling wife and carried her into the centre circle where our coach was about to begin our post-match debrief.

"Here she is," I said. "This mischievous lady's to blame. It's all her fault we won!"

Debbie's face glowed with the enjoyment of her moment of admiration. I think she also knew that her shouts urging me towards the goal line had directly influenced the scoring of Greg's try and therefore changed the outcome of the game. What a headline – Medics' Rugby Team Acquires Secret Wheelchair Weapon!

"Too right it's her fault, James," said Howard, "it's great to have you back! Both of you!"

It took about ten minutes to clean up Debbie's wheelchair from all the mud it had accumulated. Then, back home, I filled the washing machine to its maximum capacity with my filthy kit and Debbie's wet covers.

Debbie felt very warm and close that evening. As we talked about the game, I tickled her and she burst into giggles of joy.

I never again complained about Matthew's visits.

-o-O-o-

I could fill this book twice over with cameos from the months that followed. Christmas with Debbie was very special, as she insisted on my dressing her as an elf which utterly suited her personality. She'd had her ears pierced which gave me the opportunity to buy her some sparkly earrings with silver balls, and a delightful necklace with a reindeer jumping over a moon. I loved the fact that she could be so 'deep' and yet at other times behave so like a little girl, totally oblivious to the reality of living in a wheelchair with a serious progressive disease. We spent a whole day with Jonathan and Ethan, playing games then lavishing on them a few carefully chosen presents which ranged from construction sets, puzzles, through to football scarves. We'd bought these on our Wednesday expeditions to town during which I had secretly been relieved to have a break from Debbie's attempts to augment my wardrobe... I noticed that Ethan had begun to giggle in a similar way to Debbie. Both he and Jonathan were so different now from the sad, anxious boys I had first met.

My parents came to share Boxing Day with us. Mum had cooked a Christmas dinner which she'd cleverly packed so we could heat it up. At first they appeared very concerned to make sure their son was alright. I'd warned them how long it took for Debbie to eat her meals but even so I could see the consternation on their faces as they observed her slow progress. They realised this was our daily pattern and I could read their thoughts, as to what a burden this must be for me. However, they could see how much I enjoyed feeding her and Debbie's gratitude for every mouthful. Mum took over for a while so I could chat with Dad.

In the weak afternoon sunshine we walked around the park. Debbie and I wore our matching hats, gloves and scarves. She looked so bonny and so content. I reflected how content I felt, too.

Later in the afternoon, Debbie had been taking a nap in her chair in a quiet corner. Mum, Dad and I were talking about retirement. Dad had almost reached his pensionable date but wanted to hang on to his role as partner at a solicitors' firm. Mum would have liked him to work part time and for them to take a long holiday. "After all," she said, "you aren't just a solicitor, are you? You're my husband, you're a family man, you're a gardener, you're a bridge player..."

Mum had put her finger on Dad's problem. His work was his identity. All of a sudden, Debbie's quiet voice sounded across the room. I brought her closer. Her words were,

"Dad, I know what it feels like when you lose a part of your life. I used to be a very busy person. I was an occupational therapist before I had Jonathan and Ethan. When I was a teenager I used to dance and perform in shows. I was really looking forward to my boys getting old enough so we could take part in shows together. Then I developed MS, and all my dreams were stripped away from me. Fortunately I'd found Jesus, or rather He'd found me. It came to the point where the only thing I could cling onto was being God's child. I had nothing else going for me. That was when God began to restore me and I met your wonderful son, James. Now I feel so amazingly fulfilled, just being myself and enjoying the people God places across my path. I've never, ever felt so happy in all my life!"

She paused, then continued,

"So, Dad, do you know Jesus, and the difference He can make? If you go into retirement with Him it'll make it a new beginning rather than an end."

Dad squirmed. He let out a cough and a splutter... Somehow I could guess that Granny had long prayed for the day someone would ask her son such a forthright question.

The subject was hastily changed, and it wasn't very long before the time came for my parents to head home. But I could see they were beginning to feel fond of their daughter-in-law, to respect her, and to understand a little more why their son had married her.

-o-O-o-

It was as well that I'd decided not to complain about Matthew. He became a frequent visitor, often accompanied by Melissa who was gradually filling out as her 'due date' approached. I could tell something was in the air. One afternoon in spring, I found both of them with Debbie who announced to me that they were going to sing 'her' song which they'd been composing over several weeks. It was based on Chapter 54 of the book of Isaiah, and she said the words summed up her story very well.

Isaiah was one of the ancient Jews' most remarkable prophets. He lived at a time when the people had forsaken God and worshipped idols instead. God had been very patient, but over the years He'd become exasperated with them and had declared that they were going to lose everything they held dear. They would be going into exile. They would see themselves as a childless woman whose husband had abandoned her. I knew from my reading of Luke's Gospel that childlessness was almost the ultimate disgrace for a Jewish woman. John the Baptist's elderly parents, Zechariah and Elizabeth, had had no children and felt this very deeply. This made it all the more marvellous when God miraculously intervened.

But the Jews' story wasn't going to end there. God was going to restore them to a glory and a fruitfulness that they'd never known before, and change their hearts so that they loved Him. The chapter had been a favourite of Debbie's pastor in Hornchester. He often used to ask people who felt their lives were barren, to come forward for prayer. As Debbie handed me the words, I had to admit they looked most appropriate.

Debbie's Song – Isaiah 54

V1   *Sing, O barren woman, you who have not borne,*
      Break forth into melody, be no more forlorn,
      Look around and see (the host of) your new family.
      (You shall have…)
      Fruitfulness, joyful abundance,
      Greater than all the blessings of the married wife

V1A *I felt rejected, scorned and refused,*
      Ashamed, forsaken and confused,
      "Oh why, my God, must I walk this way,
      Afflicted, with no comfort in dismay?"

V2   *Sing, O barren woman, you who have not borne,*
      Break forth into melody, be no more forlorn,
      Many shall appear (and ask) to make their dwelling here.
      (They shall find)
      Homeliness, welcoming kindliness,
      Blessing, security and grace upon their life.

V2A *The Lord in anger hid His face from you*
      He punished you to teach you to be true,
      But never will His kindness now depart,
      His covenant is written on your heart,

V3   *Sing, O barren woman, you who have not borne,*
      Break forth into melody, be no more forlorn,
      Dazzling, precious stones (adorn your) pinnacles like thrones.
      (You shall know)
      Loveliness, beauty of godliness,
      Become the fountain of the Spirit of the Lord.

      Repeat V1 (not V1A) to finish.

"Would you like us to sing it to you?" asked Matthew.
I couldn't refuse.

Matthew was a marvellous classical guitarist with a well-honed finger picking technique. The song began with a few bars featuring him alone, and then the girls came in. Melissa had been in on the act and sang along with Debbie, but added the words in brackets that bridged the phrases in the third line of each verse. This allowed Debbie to catch her breath. Melissa's voice was deeper than Debbie's with a greater range, so she sang a lower harmony part in Verse 3.

I was utterly moved to tears as I reflected on the way God had taken a woman who had lost her children, and given her a new family which began with me, but also included a large part of the Patterdale Road Baptist Church members and the various others who formed her widening circle of friends. Verse 1A, sung alone in Debbie's quiet voice, summed up her despair as she was imprisoned in The Limes. It was one of life's greatest ironies that God used her operation to remove her teeth as a means to bring her out of that place to meet me!

As I looked at her, nicely made up and proudly wearing earrings and the necklace I'd bought for her, Verse 3 stood out with its reference to the woman's new beauty. I loved the way she looked after herself, mustering the help of her carers and female visitors alike to keep her looking her best. That was how she felt inside, and when I commented one day she told me she always wanted me to enjoy looking at her when I came home. And I did. She always had such a sparkle in her eyes for me, whether she was waking up from a sleep or had a visitor with her. But it wasn't just that. I knew that an increasing circle of people including a team of rugby players now saw the inner beauty that had so captivated me.

"Now, James, we have to find a part for you!" said Debbie. I had let slip that, as a boy, I'd learnt the piano to Grade 6 so I could read music. I'd packed it in when I was 13 and doubted that I could pick it up again. Matthew had the answer. In the corner of the room was a bass guitar with a small amplifier. He'd brought this in a taxi for me! He had also brought some very basic recording equipment. Before my arrival the three of them had produced a recording which Matthew played back to me. He plugged in the bass guitar and expertly played an accompaniment to show me what he had in mind.

"You'll be able to learn this, James, no problem," he assured me.

He handed me the instrument and re-played the recording. I'd a rough idea how the bass' fingering worked and the three of them were most encouraging about my first, faltering efforts.

Matthew and Melissa left us to enjoy our evening. I stayed up for a while after saying goodnight to Debbie who was tired after an exciting, but full day. Then I had another go at my new assignment. I really enjoyed this new hobby especially as I was adding to my wife's special creation. She and Matthew had composed it jointly although the lyrics were mostly her work, the music mostly his.

Two weeks later we made another recording with all four of us taking part. This was timely. Our creative pursuits had to be placed on hold. Their next visit, three weeks afterwards, was to introduce us to baby Edward.

Chapter 15

Debbie never ceased to surprise me. It was now mid-April and my birthday, which was on a Wednesday, had arrived. Only once, several months ago, had I told her the date. Tuesday was our evening in church, and Terry from the coffee shop had arrived bearing two beautifully iced Victoria sandwich cakes. One bore candles, which he lit and I blew out to the inevitable accompaniment of 'Happy Birthday'. Then both were shared out among the twenty-five or so people present, placing half of one cake in a box for us to take home.

The following morning, Debbie asked me to look in the wardrobe in our spare room. Neatly concealed there was a box containing several packages, all parcelled up in 'rugby ball' wrapping paper. Inside were a new pair of bedroom slippers with a Mickey Mouse on the toes of each; four bottles of real ale; a smart wallet to replace mine that was frayed at the edges; a pair of leather gloves; and a personalised mug with 'Daimth' in elegant red lettering on a background depicting the Scottish flag. And last but not least, a bar of my favourite chocolate. She'd obviously enlisted the help of a sales assistant at M&S last time we visited, when I'd gone to the loo; then organised various carers and friends to put these together over the previous fortnight. The birthday card said,

To the husband I'd always dreamed about
From the luckiest wife that could possibly be,
Happy Birthday, My Darling.

The handwriting, which I didn't recognise, simply said, 'James, you are such a wonderful gift from God to me. I enjoy you more every day we're together.'

She watched me open the packages with the ever-present glint in her eyes, and then asked me if I remembered what had happened the same day a year ago. With a little prompting she reminded me it was the day she'd prayed for me in Ward 17. Of course! I'd forgotten it was on my birthday. I kissed her, looked deeply and fondly into her eyes, and added that this had been by far the best year of my life. She knew it had, but it never harmed to repeat that it had been the year Debbie and I found each other, and when Jesus found me.

-o-O-o-

A few weeks later marked an eventful Monday evening. Patterdale Baptist was holding its AGM in church. In what proved an act of foresight I suggested to Gilbert that we set up a microphone. Somehow I had an idea that we would be listening to a quiet female voice that needed amplification.

As we entered the building, we were given a copy of the Agenda and The Treasurer's Report. The AGM wasn't run by the minister although he had an input. He'd asked that this year, we set the tone of the meeting with a hymn followed by prayer. Then business began. As various people reported on their areas of interest, you really would have thought we were a rowing club or a bridge club. The God we worshipped seemed not to have been invited.

Gilbert had asked for an extra item to be included this year. He called it Spiritual Growth. Firstly, Albert and Sarah talked about their Wednesday afternoons in the Trefoil Coffee Shop. Whilst Albert could be serious, he enjoyed being light-hearted as he talked about the good humour of the occasions and the various table-shuffling manoeuvres that the staff so willingly made for them. Suddenly the Treasurer Ron's friend, Giles' voice piped up,

"Excuse me, what's this got to do with church business?"

This took all the wind out of Albert's sails. He wasn't used to being unnerved like that. Then to our amazement two unlikely people walked up to the front. Bill took the microphone first.

"For me, it was when James and Debbie invited me for coffee that I first began to believe I mattered to God," he said. That was all. Mavis followed by saying,

"I'd been coming to church all these years but I'd never ever understood what it means to know Jesus as a friend. It was when I started going for coffee with Debbie and James that I experienced Jesus' friendship through them. Now I know I'm forgiven for my sins and I know how much He loves me.

Nowadays when I go to the coffee shop, I share Jesus' love with other people. Surely, that's church business?"

The meeting had become electrically charged. Half those present were deeply moved and agreed with Albert, Bill and Mavis. Half sat in stony silence, fuming at the way they believed a business meeting had been trivialised.

The polarisation became stronger still as Elspeth spoke about the Tuesday evening sessions on the Holy Spirit. She spoke boldly about the way the group was growing in numbers but also in discovering afresh what it was to have a New Testament faith following in the footsteps of the disciples in the Book of Acts. You could have cut the atmosphere with a knife. Even more so when the next item was announced: the Treasurer's report.

Ron strode majestically to the front. He adjusted his spectacles, cleared his throat and arranged his notes. He referred us to his report and began to go through the figures. They did indeed make sober reading. Based on last year's £31,000 contribution to the Baptist Union, the church would have broken even during the year, with its expenditure going purely on the business of paying its bills. That was without allowing for the £18,000 cost of repairing the roof, for which we would need an appeal to various trust funds he had in mind. Otherwise this would blow almost our entire reserves. I could sense the reassurance of his tone, saying, 'Trust me, I can pull a few tricks out of the bag when I need to.'

Then came the body blow, the request for £37,000 from the Baptist Union, £6,000 up from the previous year. Ron read out the letter which said that the regional council had prayed carefully about the decline in membership in our region. They believed the time had come to appoint two new members of staff to spearhead an initiative to bring the Good News into the inner city areas with their many social problems. They asked each church to join with them in sharing the cost.

"You can clearly see that we can't afford to pay the Union to run their fancy schemes," he said. "If the meeting agrees, we'll pay them the same as last year."

I couldn't sit still any longer. I stood up and asked,

"So, what do you believe happened when the council prayed about it? Are you saying they didn't hear God rightly?"

Ron combed back his hair with the palm of his hand, and adjusted his glasses again.

"Quite simply," he said in his best 'look-here-young-man' voice, "we're being financially reckless if we exceed our budget. God says we shouldn't steal. As far as I am concerned, that's what you seem to be suggesting we do."

I could feel the vibes from my left. I knew it was time. I pushed the wheelchair up to the front and asked Ron to pass me the microphone, which I placed next to Debbie's lips. She started her speech.

"I come here because I love and worship a wonderful, great God. He isn't short of money, and He never wrings his hands in despair because He can't pay a bill. The challenge for us is to learn to believe and trust that he can provide what we need here on earth. If he couldn't meet our needs, I wouldn't come here. You all know how wonderfully He's provided for me over the last year and you were a part of that when you provided our fabulous wedding. But trust comes with our obedience. James, can you read out the passage from Malachi please?"

I read out the verses I'd previously shared with Ron, Hilary and Giles. Then Debbie continued,

"Now, it talks about bringing the full tithes into the storehouse. I know Gilbert's spoken about this before. How many of us give God 10% of our income? What would happen if we all did this as a church?"

At this point I interjected, "I've just done a quick calculation based on what we all give. If we're all giving 10%, it means our average income is just £12,000 per year. I know some of you are just drawing the basic state pension, but I know there are a lot of us, including me, who earn much, much more. Folks, I'm speaking for myself here – let's bring the whole tithe into the storehouse!"

As I spoke, people's voices began to murmur. I had to grasp the microphone to finish my last sentence. Some were calling out, "Here, here." Others tutted. Yet others were turning around and gesticulating to others in the rows behind them. Debbie's eyes flashed at me. She wanted another 'go'. With every ounce of effort she spoke again.

"Church Family," she said, as the buzz subsided, "don't you want your faith to be an adventure? Isn't God so precious that it's worth us giving our lives to serve Him? After all, didn't He give everything He had, even His son Jesus, for us? He really, really loves us and He's got wonderful plans for our church! We've got another passage ready to read that talks about how much He loves a cheerful giver. It's fun giving generously to see His kingdom grow!"

But by this time, Debbie's voice was completely drowned out. The meeting was in uproar! Finally, Ron asked for the microphone, raised his voice, and made one final statement.

"If this church does not accept my motion that we pay only last year's contribution to the Union, then I shall resign!"

Gilbert stepped in quickly. No, making a decision on the basis of an immediate vote was not the way to resolve the question. He grasped the nettle and proposed the AGM was suspended, to be reconvened the following week at the same time.

-o-O-o-

The McPhersons had cancelled the Tuesday evening group because they had wanted to encourage the whole church to be at Monday's AGM. The following morning, just before surgery began, I noticed a missed call from them on my phone. I decided to return the call as I knew breaks would be very brief once we'd started on our list. Gilbert answered. He said he and Elspeth would like to talk to Debbie and me. He asked if we'd like to come for our evening meal that night with them. I thanked them but suggested that at short notice it would be more practical if they came to ours instead. My mum had left us some delicious shepherds' pie meals to warm up from the freezer, and we enjoyed having visitors. Elspeth said she'd make a pavlova for us. This sounded a good idea as Debbie would find this very easy to swallow.

Debbie was very happy about the change of plan. She'd been secretly disappointed that there was no Tuesday group although she thought in hindsight that it was a good decision as the atmosphere would have been affected by the inconclusive AGM.

Once dinner was on the table and we'd said grace, Gilbert and Elspeth lost no time in explaining the reason for their visit. They wanted to 'go on the attack' as Gilbert put it, rather interesting language for a minister whose main motive had been to keep out of trouble! He had slept very little the previous night. As the first light of day had begun to appear, he felt in his spirit that God was giving him a choice. Either he must quell the debate and urge the church to agree with Ron's proposal, and then settle for a quiet life. After all, it wasn't he who'd have to argue with the Baptist Union. Up until recently that would have been his choice. Or, he must launch the church on a new path where we, as a body, chose to defy the cold logic of accountancy and embark on a journey of faith. If we chose the latter, we must commit ourselves to growing the church.

There and then, wide awake in his bed, Gilbert said yes to the choice that he perceived God was hoping he'd make. He settled down on his pillow and the next thing he knew, it was 7:30 a.m. Elspeth was shaking him to wake up and drink his early morning tea. He explained to her about his unsettled night and how he'd said yes to a bold challenge. His wife was delighted, and together they started to talk about a Guest Service which would take place on a Sunday evening.

"So, James and Debbie, we've wanted to talk to you because we'd like you to play a key part in this service. We believe your story is so powerful that we'd like to build around it. It's such a wonderful example of God's grace in action."

Debbie and I were sitting holding hands. We looked at each other, smiled, and immediately said, "We'd *love to* do this! And, Gilbert, we're so pleased you've chosen the difficult, not the easy way."

Following some discussion, it seemed a good idea to plan the service two months hence, around the time of Debbie's birthday which came just before our anniversary. We told them about Debbie's Song and that we'd need to invite our friends Matthew and Melissa to perform it with us. They weren't believers – yet. That final word prompted the appearance of that all-familiar glint in Debbie's eye. She'd been unusually reluctant to press the young couple on coming to faith, saying 'it'll just happen to them'. I could sense she was already experiencing joys to come. We played a recording of the song to Gilbert and Elspeth, whose eyes filled with tears.

Towards 9 o'clock, the McPhersons noticed that Debbie had begun to yawn and said they must leave shortly. But first, they asked if we could pray together. We spoke to God about the AGM, the Guest Service, about Ron and the decision over the Baptist Union letter, and about this Sunday's service in which Gilbert was planning to challenge the church to have the courage to exercise its faith. We and Elspeth laid our hands on Gilbert and prayed that God would give him a special boldness and a clear message. As each of us prayed, the others spoke in tongues. That night a passion was born and a confidence that the Holy Spirit was now taking His rightful place as leader of our church.

-o-O-o-

Wednesday dawned, a beautiful June morning. Our regular carer was on holiday so I set out to perform the personal tasks that she normally carried out for Debbie, who always made a point of looking her best for our shopping expedition. Today she said she'd like to wear her open-toed sandals. It was normally finger and toenail day, so she suggested these were left for tomorrow's carer. I fancied having a go myself, and forty-five hilarious minutes later held up Debbie's manicured, glossy peach-coloured fingernails to her eyes with great satisfaction. Debbie wondered why I'd never thought of being a beautician rather than a surgeon. Then I washed her face, brushed her hair, cleaned her teeth and applied her lipstick. We both loved every minute of my grooming her, she so helpless, trusting and appreciative, I so conscious of her delicate beauty.

Her teeth looked especially pretty. Someone in her self-help group had ventured that, surely, she'd have liked her ivory ones back again if they were healthy. She said not, because her dentures had been her husband's gift to her and that now she felt they were part of her personality, expressing the showy yet delicate and vulnerable person she felt she was inside.

There wasn't anything particular we needed from M&S so we headed out to the park. I decided to bring our camera, just in case our trip out provided photo-opportunities. And who should we meet but Matthew and Melissa with baby Edward in his pram. Matthew carefully unstrapped him to reveal a bright orange baby suit, and then handed him to me as I sat on a bench. I felt a thrill as the tiny human being wriggled in my arms. I remembered that until recently this was the sort of feeling I had dismissed as needing to be fought against, nature's trick to ensure the procreation of our race. Nowadays I was much more prepared to soak up the experience. It was the second time that day that I'd enjoyed a beautiful, intimate human cameo of warmth. Then we sat Debbie up in her wheelchair and arranged things strategically so that Edward could lie in her lap with her arms around him. She looked into his eyes and spoke to him gently. I heard her speaking words of faith.

"Would you have liked one like that?" said Debbie to me.

"Yes, in another life," I replied, "but my choice has been to care for you, and I've absolutely no regrets whatsoever. And," I continued, "I'm looking forward to enjoying a lot more of this little fellow as he grows up."

There was a lot to talk about. As usual the ladies started to explore the fine detail of breast and bottle feeding, nappies and sleep patterns whilst I asked Matthew all about his own angle as a dad. Matthew was enjoying himself despite the broken nights and hard labour. He had a patient, caring manner which complemented Melissa's matter-of-fact approach. He said we must come round and see the mobile that he'd created out of a bicycle brake cable, cardboard covered with silver foil, and various transfers. With his help I then took a series of photos of us as a group, then separately, holding Edward. I took several of Debbie. I loved looking at her when she wasn't posing; aware of her beautiful face that expressed such love to everyone she met.

Eventually we went our separate ways. Our path led us towards a children's playground. I was suddenly aware of how much I enjoyed watching the boys and girls scampering about, climbing up and then tumbling down the slides with no inhibitions. Debbie enjoyed the experience too, because it reminded her of Jonathan and Ethan whom she'd taken to similar parks before she fell ill. Even with our different histories, both of us felt faint stirrings of wistfulness that children were not to be a part of our wonderful marriage. But then we looked into each other's eyes. Neither of us could have believed we could be so happy and we weren't going to let our joy be tarnished by what was not to be our portion in life.

-o-O-o-

On Sunday morning we arrived at church early. After breakfast, we'd prayed for Gilbert knowing that today would represent a watershed in his ministry at Patterdale Road Baptist Church. It was crunch time. He had asked me to read the New Testament lesson, which happened about twenty minutes into the service. I read 2 Corinthians Chapter 9 verses 6 to 15. In reading it beforehand I had been deeply moved by the middle section:-

'Remember this: Whoever sows sparingly will also reap sparingly, and whoever sows generously will also reap generously. Each of you should give what you have decided in your heart to give, not reluctantly or under compulsion, for God loves a cheerful giver. And God is able to bless you abundantly, so that in all things at all times, having all that you need, you will abound in every good work. As it is written:
"They have freely scattered their gifts to the poor;
their righteousness endures forever."
Now he who supplies seed to the sower and bread for food will also supply and increase your store of seed and will enlarge the harvest of your righteousness. You will be enriched in every way so that you can be generous

on every occasion, and through us your generosity will result in thanksgiving to God.'

Albert and Sarah led the prayers. They covered the usual topics such as the wars in the Middle East, people known to us who were sick, the forthcoming local elections, but then Albert spoke out a heartfelt prayer about the resolution of our financial challenge, asking that God would show us *His* solution. Sarah followed with an equally heartfelt prayer about the many in the community who needed to hear God's Good News, praying that we would offer ourselves as instruments to help the church grow. Amen!

One hymn later, Gilbert walked to the lectern. You could hear a pin drop.

"Church," he began, "today we have to decide who we will serve." He told us honestly of the choice which he believed God had confronted him with that night in bed. Were we here to serve ourselves; to make safe choices, to accept society's verdict that God either didn't exist or was impotent, and that the Church was irrelevant? Or, were we here to play our part in the advance of His Kingdom upon earth, following in the steps of the apostles? He contrasted the two mind sets.

In the first, we accepted that God no longer worked supernaturally. All our financial decisions were made using the same criteria as in the secular world. We accepted, too, that society was changing and that nowadays people didn't believe in a supernatural God. They might attend a church if they felt like it but they saw no reason to make a whole life commitment to a community of believers. We accepted that in a few years' time, Patterdale Road would have to be amalgamated with a larger church in the city centre.

In the second, we saw ourselves as committed to serving a supernatural God who loved us deeply and had a passion for the people of Somershire. He enjoyed our worship; He was thrilled when we set our heart to know Him more deeply. And He loved to surprise us as we embraced the challenges of our own lives and of the Church. This applied to our finances too. We shared His concern for the people round about us and saw them, as He did, as 'sheep without a shepherd', needing to hear the Good News.

Then he unpacked the reading. Giving generously isn't just good for the recipient, he explained – it's good for you, too! Who wouldn't want God to 'bless you abundantly, so you will abound in every good work'? He referred back to his and Elspeth's days at Bible College, where they had a sense of God overflowing out of their hearts as they rounded up their last pennies to buy meals for needy people on the streets out of their tiny allowances. He unpacked how it felt to live a lifestyle of generosity, to feel as if you had a constantly replenished bag of seed, and a 'harvest of righteousness' as you began to see how others were being blessed.

We had never heard Gilbert speak with such conviction. It was a delight to hear his voice broaden into Scottish tones as he drew to a close.

There was obvious tension in the church hall afterwards. There was a sense that certain cliques of church members were closing ranks, casting nuanced glances, whispering furtively. Those whom we described as our friends carried on as normal, seeking people to share with, to encourage, to listen to, to pray with.

Later that day, Debbie and I talked about our own financial position. Finances weren't something we often discussed, but with her allowances, my surgeon's salary and our comparatively frugal lifestyle, we both agreed it was time to take seriously our giving to church.

-o-O-o-

Delays in the operating theatre are unwelcome at the best of times. Murphy's Law states that they'll happen at the most inconvenient moments. I was the lead surgeon for an operation to remove a cancer patient's lymph glands in his neck. On my list, this was our final procedure and we expected to have it wrapped up by 5 p.m. All was going well until the patient suffered a bleed. Stemming and then repairing it proved more complicated than expected and by 5:30 it had become obvious that we would need to continue into the evening. I asked a nurse to pick up my phone which was laid on a nearby trolley along with my other personal belongings, and to find Penny's number. The nurse knew me well enough to explain to her that I needed to ask a big favour. Penny held a key to our flat and was one of the few people who could feed and dress Debbie then get her to church by 7:30 p.m. Penny agreed, realising that it wasn't something I'd have asked lightly.

By 7:15 all was finished and the patient was placed back on his trolley. I cleaned myself up, changed clothes and made my way as quickly as possible to church, arriving at about 7:45 p.m.

The meeting was in full swing. I sat alongside Debbie, and motioned to Penny to thank her very much for her help, indicating that she should feel free to go. Penny was our friend but neither a church member nor a believer. Strangely, she didn't move.

Ron was at the front reiterating his proposal that we held our Baptist Union contribution at £31,000. Gilbert now nailed his colours to the mast. He wanted us to honour the prayerful request of our denominational council and believed that by doing so, we would lay ourselves open to God providing for us, "as I preached about yesterday morning." At this point I went to the front and said,

"From today, Debbie and I are committed to 'bringing the full tithe into the storehouse'. She told you last week how we have been blessed. We've made our choice. We're going to honour God with our money, starting with 10% of our entire income. We want to live a generous lifestyle. And we want an adventure in faith!"

The church started to hum with rival opinions being expressed. Giles stood up and said that the church was no place to play irresponsible games with money. We could be liable for legal action if we gave away our resources and left the building in a state of decline. Was that what God would want? Albert, who had regained his nerve following his put-down the previous week, said he supported me. He said that if God was who we believed He was, then surely His economics didn't just consist of sanctified accountancy. Finally, the matter was put to the vote, and by 32 votes to 23 the church passed the motion that we would pay the Union in full, £37,000.

Ron walked to the front, announced his resignation, and strutted imperiously in a slow, dignified manner out of the building. Giles followed close behind.

Gilbert and Elspeth were not to be denied. They thanked the church for making what they called a landmark decision, but thanked those who had voted with Ron for taking part in the debate. They encouraged them to stay with the church and see what happened. Then they called Debbie and me to the front and announced the Guest Service, hoping that everyone would join in by taking part, welcoming people and inviting friends, family and colleagues. You could sense that at least half the people present were inwardly cheering.

-o-O-o-

Albert, who had taken over as Church Treasurer, received a steady stream of people who wanted Standing Order forms to commit to the regular giving of 10% of their income. This was a wonderful new beginning although it didn't address the mountain we as a church would have to climb to restore the roof.

Plans for the Guest Service began to take shape. A small group of us met for twenty minutes each week after the service, with regular informal get-togethers in between. Publicising the event was an important challenge. Albert and Sarah's daughter Mary had been trained as a graphic designer and worked in a print shop on the High Street. Mary only came to church occasionally but, when asked by Sarah, warmed to the challenge of producing posters and flyers for us. Sarah herself volunteered to take overall charge of publicity and I agreed to support her. And, Matthew and Melissa were delighted to be asked to sing Debbie's Song with us.

Debbie and I had never had a honeymoon. During the summer we took a four day trip to Edinburgh, travelling by train after making careful preparations to make sure there was provision for her wheelchair. I'd toyed with us hiring a Motability car with a hoist to lift her wheelchair inside, but the rail journey proved a relaxing way to travel and meant we could sit together soaking up the scenery. We enjoyed staying at a comfortable guest house in the city centre. A particular highlight was our visit to Edinburgh Castle with such splendid views from its steep walls.

The real purpose of staying in Edinburgh was to go to Curriehill to see Granny. As she answered the door, I noticed how much more frail she'd become in the year since I'd seen her. However, once she and Debbie had set eyes on each other, it was as if each received a sudden burst of energy. It was love at first sight! Here were two women who had totally set out their stall to follow Jesus and who served Him with every ounce of their being through frail bodies. And they both loved *me!* I couldn't get a word in edgeways so, after making drinks and laying out a display of biscuits, I sat down and listened. I heated up the lunch that Granny had provided, and talked to Granny myself as I fed Debbie, filling her in on some of the fine details of what had happened since my last remarkable visit. Occasional grunts from Debbie indicated that she wanted to add something as soon as she'd swallowed her current mouthful!

Both ladies sat back in their chairs for a nap after lunch and I ventured out for a walk. I crossed the valley and strode through a gate, taking a path that led up into the Pentland Hills. Here the path led into a ravine with increasingly steep sides. The sun shone most of the time, giving the ravine a warm, friendly feel. But occasionally a dark cloud would obscure it, leaving the ravine feeling forbidding and hostile. It was exhilarating to feel the wildness of this place, a new vista opening up to my eyes at every turn of the path. I felt in my spirit a gentle whisper that said,

"I'm going to take you to wild places you never expect. But I'll *always* be with you."

On my return two hours later, both Mrs. McAlisters were awake and had resumed their chatter. I made a drink for us all then once again listened in. Debbie was feasting on Granny's many stories of God's faithfulness particularly in the early years of her married life when she and Granddad lived hand-to-mouth with very little money. They'd saved up a deposit to buy their first home when a missionary from Ethiopia visited their church to talk about an orphanage that she'd founded, which desperately needed funds. With Granny three months pregnant with my dad, she and Granddad needed their own home urgently. When they arrived home to her parents' where they were living, both of them told each other that they felt compelled to give their entire deposit to the orphanage! As they joyfully handed over the money, they received news that Granddad's maiden aunt had died, leaving in her will a request that her picturesque home would be passed to another family member. The family graciously invited them to live there. It needed a lot of work over a period of time but, once modernised, provided a lovely place for them to raise their family until they moved to the bungalow where Granny still lived, a few years before Granddad retired.

As we parted company, Granny blessed us both, looked into my eyes and said,

"James, I could never have wished you a better wife!"

I thanked her for helping me at such a critical point in my journey the previous year.

-o-O-o-

The long summer days gave us the chance twice to take out Jonathan and Ethan. They came over the evening before our trips and slept in our spare room. The first time, we made an early start and travelled by train to the seaside. One of Debbie's younger carers, Joanne, was keen to earn some extra money by accompanying us, which freed me to spend time with the boys playing crazy golf, having a dip in the sea, building sandcastles and going in a paddle boat on a lake. Debbie watched her sons and husband enjoying themselves, feasting on the boys' laughter and on the way I was letting my hair down. As we sat on the beach munching sandwiches I asked her how it felt to have to watch us from her wheelchair. She smiled warmly and said,

"James, I'm blissfully content. I love seeing you all being happy, and I thank God for the way He's restored my life through you." This may have been true but I had the sense that I'd kick-started a train of thought.

It was a warm day, and we'd taken off her outer layer of clothes leaving a thin blouse along with shorts. Because of her fair complexion we'd doused her in sunscreen lotion and I'd bought a sombrero hat to guard her face and neck from the sun's glare. As we'd all nearly finished our sandwiches I felt a craving for an ice cream. Behind me on the promenade was a van which was doing a roaring trade from people like us. I jumped up, grabbed my bum bag and announced that I'd be back very shortly with something they'd enjoy.

The queue proved to be longer than I'd expected, and it was a full ten minutes before I set off back, hands full with five Magnums – large chocolate ice creams with a stick that come in wrapping paper. As I turned towards the beach, I looked and saw the wheelchair with no-one in it. On the sand was Debbie's sombrero but no Debbie! In a panic I walked as quickly as I could without spilling my load. As I drew closer the mystery was revealed. Debbie was indeed behind the sombrero, her body – such as was visible - lying away from me so it had been obscured by the hat. She was submersed in the sand and the boys were busy pouring bucket-loads over the remaining humps where her skin poked through! She was lying in a neatly shaped hole, a small mound supporting her head.

I had always stressed that I didn't want people to take risks lifting Debbie who was a 'dead weight'. I knew some special techniques but stressed that untrained people would risk damaging their backs and could easily drop Debbie if they made a mistake. She wasn't as safety-conscious as I, which occasionally made me irritated.

"Who on earth's idea was *this?*" I blazed. Then I looked at Joanne and the boys. "And how did you get Mum safely out of her wheelchair?" I demanded.

Joanne pointed towards a muscular man sitting nearby with his family. He had a shovel, and she explained that he'd just been passing where they were sitting,

"...and I asked him to dig me a hole in the sand so I could be buried. I asked them to watch the expression on your face when you couldn't see where I was!" said Debbie. I looked at her, so contented in her mischief. "He offered to help lift me, so I asked him to hold my top half whilst the rest of them grabbed my legs. And here I am!"

"Ooooh, wait till I speak to him!" I said, shaking with rage. To the protests of Debbie and the boys I marched off towards the man with the shovel. On the way, I suddenly thought,

"Okay, calm it, James. Why *shouldn't* they have had a bit of fun?"

In that moment my anger melted away, and transformed into an overwhelming appreciation of the extraordinary spirit of the woman I loved, who delighted in teasing me when I took myself too seriously. In so many ways she had released me to enjoy being myself, to laugh at myself and to love myself.

I did speak to the man, but only to ask to borrow his implement. I quickly dug a similar hole alongside Debbie and lay down beside her. I asked Joanne to return the shovel and told the boys to hurry and eat their ice creams so they could cover me up, too! Quickly I ate my own, and then placed my arm tenderly around Debbie's neck so I could hold hers next to her mouth. As she was eating it, the boys covered me up until both of us were left with only our heads, my arm and the remains of Debbie's ice cream not submersed. The boys loved photographing us on their phones, then we asked a passer-by to photograph us *en famille* with the boys and Joanne sitting behind our heads. As Debbie licked away her final mouthful, I buried my cheek into hers and then we turned our heads and kissed, to the cheers of Jonathan and Ethan who lost no time in grabbing one last snap apiece.

The other day wasn't as successful. This time we went ahead, hired a Motability car and drove to a theme park. We made the best of the day but it was disappointing to spend such a long time in queues waiting for our turn on the various rides. And, in the afternoon, there was heavy rain, sending us scurrying for cover. Debbie was hoping to watch us riding the roller-coasters but there was little for her to see, so she busied herself making friends more deeply with Joanne. For the boys' last two rides I released Joanne to join them and sat quietly holding Debbie's hand. On the way home, no-one complained. Being a family meant experiencing the good, the bad and the indifferent times together.

-o-O-o-

The Guest Service was drawing steadily nearer. Gilbert and Elspeth had finalised the order of service. After some discussion, we had decided to call the event, 'A Change of Name'. This particularly referred to Debbie's previous surname which would feature in her story. But it also referred to one of her favourite worship songs, 'I will change your name'. This was composed in America and sung by a church called The Vineyard. She was to sing this song which suited her gentle voice accompanied by Matthew's finger-picking.

We four musicians had somehow managed to practice Debbie's Song during two half hour rehearsals snatched during Edward's nap times after he'd been fed.

Mavis was busy organising refreshments and had planned to have elegant tablecloths laid out in the hall. Mary's publicity material looked pitch perfect; I had made a plan of places to display our posters and had bundled the flyers for our church family to take and distribute. Mine would be given to colleagues in hospital where I would need to be discreet. I also planned to invite Howard and Ken from the rugby team.

We prayed together for the event on Tuesday evenings, before church on Sunday, and whenever people met in each other's homes, in coffee bars and in the park. A great sense of anticipation grew.

It proved more difficult than I'd expected to distribute my flyers at work. We'd agreed that we would always invite people personally then place the flyers in their hands rather than just hand them a leaflet which would immediately end up in a bin, so I needed to catch my colleagues when they were alone and not too busy to give me their attention. Eventually I covered everyone on my list, which included Marion, Grace, Martin and even Mr. Davy. Also included was Rosemary, a junior house doctor who was spending six weeks with our team. Rosemary had a fresh, open-minded approach to her work and a pleasant, positive attitude. She wasn't a believer but said she'd come, and would ask a couple of her doctor friends.

During the week before the event, several people went out into the precincts nearby to distribute flyers and to invite shoppers to come. We ourselves took a turn at this. It was hard when four out of five people waved us away as I held out a flyer, but amongst those who didn't were several folks with whom we had interesting conversations. We had an advantage, people noticing the poignancy of a wheelchair user who expressed so much joy. Altogether the church distributed six hundred flyers and put up twenty posters to advertise the event.

We prayed that fifty guests would turn up, and Mavis catered accordingly. The couple who cleaned our church spruced up the gallery which had been unused for about eight years with the exception of our wedding. On the day of the service we held a short morning service at which the prayer time was extended in anticipation of the evening.

Rugby wasn't due to begin after the summer break for another fortnight, and we'd kept the day clear of other commitments. Debbie took a long rest in the afternoon, and then we dressed early and made our way to church where I'd earlier stored the bass guitar. I wore my best leather jacket, whilst Debbie looked at her prettiest wearing a gorgeous pink blouse partially covered by a cream-coloured cardigan, setting off her Christmas jewellery. Her hair shone and was beautifully styled with waves, adorned with a pink bow. By half past five, the church was a-buzz. Matthew and Melissa arrived to set up our simple equipment, and we had a very quick rehearsal of 'Debbie's Song' which was much admired by the others around us. Mavis' army of caterers was busy making sure our guests would lack for nothing. Bill, who had surprised us by his competent stewarding at our wedding, stood outside with orders of service ready to welcome all comers.

Ten to six. Around thirty of the church family had arrived. In came our first guests in the form of Penny and her husband. They had come with Amanda, who six months ago had committed herself to follow Jesus although couldn't come on Sundays as we had no provision for children as yet.

Five to six. We hadn't filled half the bottom pews, never mind the gallery. Three more guests arrived. First came Joshua from the dental lab, whom we'd seen during the week when we'd visited the surgery to ask for a denture adjustment. It had become obvious that his frequent appearances there had much to do with his attraction to one of the dental nurses. He simply couldn't say 'no' to Debbie's giggling invitation. Behind him came Terry from the coffee shop, for whom Albert and Sarah had been especially praying. Terry was pushing Hilda his sick mother in her wheelchair, and we invited her to use the space where Debbie normally sat. We'd repeatedly prayed for Hilda but with no evidence of healing so far. She had now been diagnosed with cancer.

Two minutes to six and the pews were about three quarters full, but with no more guests. As 6 o'clock chimed, Gilbert stood up and began his welcome. After all that effort to pull in the people of Somershire, all we'd seen were a tiny handful of guests. Mavis' army would be hard pushed finding customers for all their cake, tea and biscuits, the one silver lining being that people like me could enjoy a second slice. Just then we heard youthful voices at the door. Rosemary and her two friends burst in and sat down near the front. Gilbert smiled warmly and introduced our first item, the traditional hymn, 'Jesus, the name high over all'.

Elspeth followed by talking about modern people's uncertainty over what to believe and their search for a framework to live their lives. I was impressed that she and Gilbert had been out and about talking to people in the precinct, and that she quoted replies that they'd been given to basic questions about the point of life.

Albert read the story of the Prodigal Son from Luke's Gospel Chapter 15 stopping, as had been arranged, at the point where the younger 'prodigal' son is welcomed back into the family. Then a strange thing happened. Gilbert asked him to read on, to cover the story of the older son who had resented his father's welcome of his brother following the young man's ignominious return.

Then came Debbie's Song. Into the microphone chimed Debbie's voice as she introduced it, describing her bleak situation at the time I met her. She described the way she'd felt abandoned, was in pain from her 'waterworks' and her teeth, and couldn't see how she would ever be reunited with her sons. She movingly talked about her pledge to trust that God wouldn't forsake her. Then we performed the song. The church was in complete silence.

I stood up and described my frivolous challenge to the god I didn't believe in. I had my listeners in hoots of laughter as I described my first impressions of Debbie with her skew-whiff glasses; then the way I injured myself the next day in a rugby tackle and was left hobbling with a crutch. I spoke of my six month ordeal in Darfur and how I'd been traumatised by the needless suffering I'd witnessed and the awful state of the victims of war and hunger that I'd had to treat. I explained how I couldn't possibly believe in a God of love. That was, until I met the very person whom I saw as being the epitome of despair and the result of God's callous neglect. I amused my listeners further by describing Debbie's prayer for me in the ward and my impatient embarrassment.

After their titters had died down, I turned and looked directly at my listeners. Whoever could have believed that God would use that very person to love my soul back to life, so that it altered the whole way I saw the world and especially drew me back to feeling compassion for my patients? Whoever would have guessed that I would become the answer to my own challenge and become the means of making Debbie happier than she'd ever been before?

Debbie took the microphone and explained that she'd previously been Debbie Loveless which summed up perfectly how her situation appeared. But God had other ideas.

Then she sang, to Matthew's accompaniment,

"I will change your name
You shall no longer be called
Wounded, outcast, lonely or afraid

I will change your name
Your new name shall be
Confidence, joyfulness, overcoming one
Faithfulness, friend of God
One who seeks My face."

As Debbie's sweet but gentle voice sounded over the intricate guitar sounds, every eye began to fill with tears. Matthew mesmerised us with several bars of musical magic before they sang and played the song a second time. Some of us, including myself, choked with emotion.

Gilbert stood up. He spoke about the prodigal son and how he had assumed several 'names' during the story. He began as the joint Son and Heir to his father's estate. Then he became the Rich Kid on the Block. As his money ran out he became the Swineherd, The Fugitive, and then the Prodigal. Finally, he became once more the Son! Never before had I heard Gilbert speak with such passion about the Father's love. As a father and grandfather himself, he could understand how deeply the father's heart must have been wounded that day when he bid his cocky, ungrateful son goodbye, leaving home with his vast inheritance. But as he described the son's return from the father's point of view, we could feel Gilbert had entered into the feelings of the father in the story in a very special way. He made God's love sound utterly irresistible.

Then he departed from his original script and spoke about the older son. His names were Dutiful, Right Living, Entitled, and Angry. He had no sense of warmth towards his father let alone his brother. He needed to realise that he, too, needed love and forgiveness just like his brother, and to accept his father's invitation to be with him and to enjoy his presence.

Gilbert summed up by asking if there was anyone here present who wanted to accept God the Father's invitation to be forgiven through Jesus and take their place as His son or daughter. He asked, too, if anyone present saw themselves as the older son, having lived a 'good life' but needing for the first time to come into a genuine loving relationship with God the Father. We all closed our eyes and Gilbert asked if anyone would like to raise their hands to respond. Then came our last hymn,

'How great the Father's love for us, how vast beyond all measure,
That He should send His only son to make a wretch His treasure.'

As he announced this, Gilbert invited anyone who'd placed their hand up to walk out to the front if they were happy to do so.

Penny and her husband went forward.

Terry and his mum went forward.

Rosemary and one of her two friends, a young man, went forward.

And, to our amazement, Hilary the former treasurer's wife and her friend Margaret went forward. Hilary hadn't been in church since the fateful AGM. We later found out that they felt Gilbert's description of the Older Son in the story described them precisely.

Gilbert had organised me, Albert, Sarah, and Elspeth to be available to take contact details, pray with, and introduce a simple Gospel booklet to anyone who had responded, whilst Matthew and Debbie once again performed, *'I will change your name'*. I had the thrill of praying with Terry and Hilda. Hilda movingly told me that if she died, she would be very sad indeed to leave her family behind. But now, if the worst happened, she could look forward to dying happy knowing she belonged to Jesus. Terry said he'd look forward to coming on Tuesday evening, with Hilda if she was well enough, to enjoy the cakes his shop had provided!

Mavis' catering show was in full swing as we belatedly made our way into the hall. Every table had a tiny but tasteful bouquet of flowers that depicted the welcome we intended. Of course it had to be the sponge cake for Debbie who had earned every mouthful. It was an evening to savour, even though the numbers weren't as we'd hoped.

But the best part was yet to come. Just as the hall was emptying, Bill appeared and, true to form, launched himself at a plate of uneaten cakes that Mavis had just lovingly covered in foil. He'd returned from taking Matthew and Melissa home with their equipment, using Albert's car. Matthew and Melissa had felt they couldn't stay for refreshments; his parents had kindly babysat for Edward but he and Melissa didn't want to leave them to cope alone for too long.

Matthew had said to Bill,

"*We* want to accept the invitation that the reverend talked about. Please tell James and Debbie that we'll be round to see them tomorrow evening."

-o-O-o-

I had never seen Debbie cry so much before with tears of utter joy. I had never seen her so tired, either, as we arrived home shortly before 9 p.m. But she insisted I let her rest for an hour then wake her up.

And that night something very special happened that set the seal on a truly wonderful evening. Whether it happened because Debbie was so fulfilled, or whether it was a special gift from the Holy Spirit, will remain an open question. As we came together she experienced a full release of her physical emotions in a way that we'd come to believe was medically impossible.

Chapter 16

The days that followed were full of late summer glory. I felt that my Tuesday evening sessions with Gilbert had achieved their purpose and that he'd done a very workmanlike job in grounding me in my faith. I now believed God was good – all the time. I had confidence to believe the Bible was God's 'Word' and could be trusted to represent His thoughts and feelings, if correctly interpreted. And I accepted that He was the creator of the cosmos, and of our wonderful planet that teems with life. I'd reserved judgment on the creation versus evolution debate, for now.

God had given us ten new believers to care for, and it was time for me to share my own faith with them. After some thought, we and the McPhersons decided to use the Alpha Course and hold it on Tuesday evenings. With the need for catering, for a prayer group and for others to support the course as group leaders, our whole Tuesday evening fellowship could be put to work. We agreed that Elspeth and Debbie would continue their teaching about the Holy Spirit for the caterers and prayer team during the latter part of the evening.

The Alpha Course begins with an introductory week then launches into the basics of living the Christian life using a very practical approach. All eight people who'd responded in the Guest Service came along. And right from the start, they proved eager to learn and to grow in their new faith. Rosemary had done SCUBA diving and said she felt as if she'd discovered a casket of gold on a sunken galleon. This was too good not to share! By Week 3 there were not two but four young medics on the course.

Matthew and Melissa joined us 'by extension'. They had indeed put their trust in Jesus, Melissa grudgingly admitting that if you'd have told her a year ago she wouldn't have believed she could possibly ever become a Christian. They felt the babysitting challenge was too great to come on Tuesday evening, so Albert and Sarah visited them at home to do a potted version of the course. And for further input, there was always plenty to discuss when they visited Debbie on weekday afternoons.

One afternoon I arrived home to find not just them with baby Edward, but also Rosemary visiting Debbie. It was the two songs that Debbie sang more than anything else that had moved Rosemary to the point of wanting to come to faith during the Guest Service. She herself played the cello and was fascinated by the idea of playing music to worship God.

A cloud that often crossed our golden sky was Debbie's UTI which recurred occasionally but with dogged persistence. I hated to admit the truth that it was becoming harder to treat. Sometimes, when I returned from the hospital, her pleasant face showed the signs of acute discomfort. I hated to see her in pain.

One day early in October I arrived home to find a brown envelope addressed to Debbie. Her hysterectomy was to take place later that month. She was asked to arrive early on a Monday morning. At church the previous day we were invited to the front where around ten people laid hands on us both, praying especially for Debbie and her safe-keeping through the operation. Elspeth prayed that angels would surround her in the theatre. Over coffee afterwards, almost everyone came up to express their wishes to her, some simply squeezing her hand, others kissing her forehead. The church family saw her as a trailblazer in the same way Manchester United would see their star goal scorer.

It turned out that Hilda was due in hospital a week after Debbie for the removal of a tumour on her liver.

At 7:30 a.m. we arrived at Ward 9, which was designated, 'Female Surgical'. I was not at all impressed. Ward 17 was always kept neat, tidy and meticulously clean thanks to the influence of Sister Marion and her colleagues. They used to refer to 'caring the old-fashioned way' and disinfectant could always be smelt in the air. I had often been appalled at the way some of the other wards were maintained and Ward 9 was typical. As we entered, I reached out for antiseptic gel from the dispenser but alas, found it empty. The four nurses on duty were sitting idly chatting as we walked in. One of them took me to what was to be Debbie's bed. I felt uneasy that this ward didn't have the same cosy feel that I was used to. Something told me to look down below the bed. There was debris on the floor and amongst it was a cast-off syringe. I looked further and, hidden behind the cabinet for her belongings, were two soiled cotton wool pads. I drew the curtains and, keeping my voice down, shook my head and said to the nurse,

"This ward isn't in a healthy condition for sick patients."

The charge nurse had heard me getting upset and stepped inside the curtains whereupon I produced my identity badge.

"I am not leaving my wife on this ward unless you straightaway clean this area up!" I said.

The nurses pointed out that cleaning wasn't their responsibility and that it wasn't their fault that cleaning hours had been halved in the last five years as the service had been contracted out 'to make it more efficient'.

"Okay then, I will go to Ward 17 and find some overalls," I said. "Now I insist that you get me a brush and shovel, a mop and bucket, and some bleach. Let's forget the rules about whose job it isn't, and get on with the business of saving lives!"

The nurses felt sufficiently shamed to supply me with overalls from their own cupboard and the three of us worked for half an hour to restore the area around Debbie's bed, then the five others within her bay, to basic respectability. Noticing that half past eight was approaching I kissed Debbie, ran my hand fondly through her golden locks one final time, gazed deeply into her eyes and blessed her. She insisted in blessing me, too. She made me promise not to worry.

My own ward rounds and surgical list seemed to take forever, although we finished slightly early at 5:45. Straightaway I made my way to Ward 9. A nurse called Janet escorted me to the bed where Debbie laid unconscious with a tube set up to dose her with morphine. The surgeons had reported that her two hour operation had been straightforward and they expected her to regain consciousness some time during the late evening. I introduced myself to Janet and to the other staff on the afternoon shift. I made sure they understood Debbie's vulnerable situation; about how, as she began to recover, she'd need feeding, changing, and her position in bed adjusting. They seemed more motivated than the lethargic morning shift. I sat with her for half an hour; I read scripture verses, prayed a blessing on her and spoke words of fondness. I wondered if I'd detected a faint smile but it was probably coincidental.

Albert and Sarah had invited me for supper. I appreciated unwinding in the comfort of their generously proportioned Victorian terrace with its high ceilings, large back garden and tasteful conservatory.

On Tuesday morning I arrived at Ward 9 promptly at 7:30 a.m. I noticed the whole ward was in much better condition. After the previous day's set-to, the nurses didn't argue with me for coming outside visiting hours. Debbie was only faintly conscious but her eyes opened and her face flickered in a spark of recognition. It was so lovely to see her again, drugged as she was, and she gave me a faint smile whispering,

"Daim, I yove you…"

after which she closed her eyes and dozed off. I kissed her, blessed her, spoke over her and sat holding her hand for fifteen minutes. Then I wished her "sweet dreams, my darling" and said a final goodbye. On the way out I saw a lady dressed in dark blue whose lanyard said she was the Nursing Manager. I made clear my feelings on the state of the ward the previous morning. She explained that the cleaning was done on a rota in which Ward 9 was done on a Monday. If I wasn't happy, then someone would have to find extra funds from another budget to fund further cleaning staff… I saw I was getting nowhere so asked if her mother was alive. She was. I asked,

"Would you be happy for your mother to be admitted to Ward 9?" I got no answer.

Surgery finished at 6:15 whereupon I made my way promptly back to the ward where Janet said a bright hello. I was comforted to know that Matthew had called to see her, as had Rosemary after her time in the theatre that afternoon. About six Get Well cards sat on her bedside table and the number was growing. Debbie was awake with her head deep in her pillow. Despite still being drugged she smiled, gazed at me and pursed her lips for a kiss. She asked me how my day had been. True to form, she'd begun to make friends with Janet and was praying for the other ladies in her ward. Some things never changed.

On the way out, Janet asked how long we'd been married. When I told her it was only just over a year, she gasped and said,

"So, you married her just as she is now, unable to help herself?"

That's when I explained how lucky I was to have Debbie as my wife.

I wasn't surprised to hear that Debbie had been giggling, nor that she'd asked Janet to help her look her best for James when he arrived…

Wednesday was my day off but I visited Debbie in the morning as was now my habit. This was the happiest of my visits to her whilst in hospital. She'd begun to introduce herself to the other patients although was only able to converse with Sally in the adjacent bed, another hysterectomy patient. As I arrived, Sally was sitting in the visitors' chair and they were exchanging stories. I encouraged her to stay put, fetched another chair, and listened along with Debbie as Sally explained to us her family story which took up ages... until I noticed a look in Debbie's eye that said, it's time...

I looked across at Sally and said, "Sally, if Jesus were to break into your family story, what would you want him to change?" And together, we prayed into Sally's painful situation and shared with her the love of Jesus that had become the centre of our lives.

I left the afternoon free for other visitors and went home to tackle a pile of long-overdue paperwork. I joined the coffee shop group in the afternoon.

It was on Wednesday evening that I began to be more concerned. Debbie wasn't as relaxed as I'd previously seen her. Her wound wasn't healing as quickly as I'd have expected. And, I wondered if she was becoming feverish. She'd had more than enough visits from nurses wanting blood samples and also from her consultant. Janet said no-one had expressed any undue concern, but she could see what I meant. Was this to be expected? The charge nurse, who didn't know I was a surgeon, assured me that she was in good hands. That night I had a sense of foreboding. I tried to read, or to watch films, to quell my unease. I received a reassuring text from Gilbert and Elspeth who'd visited her in the afternoon, as had Mavis and Hilary. They assured me that they were praying for us regularly and that I should feel free to call round any time I wished.

On Thursday morning I burst into Ward 9 to find Debbie's fever was worse. A horrible possibility struck me. I'd seen it only once before – the onset of an MRSA superbug infection. Nothing would have surprised me in such a filthy environment. I alerted the nurses and explained that I'd like to speak to whichever doctor was first on the scene.

In the middle of my rounds, Marion called me to the nurses' station. The doctor on Ward 9 had seen Debbie, noticed her feverishness, and could understand my concerns. He said he'd assess the situation. They'd take swabs and run tests. Routinely the results would take three days but they'd speed up the process for Debbie. I pressed him to try to get the results the same day.

During the day the fever became worse. I joined her after work and sat at her bedside mopping her brow. She was beginning to find breathing difficult. Janet agreed they'd keep a close eye on her and be ready to administer oxygen if it was needed.

On Friday the news came through that Debbie had indeed been infected with a superbug and they were transferring her to the Intensive Care Unit. It seemed to be a virulent strain, perhaps made more problematic because she had been treated so regularly with antibiotics to fight her UTI. At 6 p.m. prompt I made my way over to see her and found her in a small room on her own, with various tubes attached and breathing through an oxygen mask. I talked to the staff and they removed the mask so Debbie could talk.

"James, I'm not afraid," she said. "Are you okay?"

"No, Debbie, I'm not. I feel very, very frightened because I love you so very much and I'm scared I might lose you."

I fed her the oxygen mask again for a minute, and then she asked me to hold her close. "James," she said, "nothing can separate us from the love of God. *Nothing!* Can you read Romans Chapter 8 to me?"

As I read from my smartphone, it seemed as if the script appeared in three dimensions so that various portions stood out about an inch from the screen. They didn't of course; it just seemed that way.

"'And if the Spirit of him who raised Jesus from the dead is living in you, he who raised Christ from the dead will also give life to your mortal bodies because of his Spirit who lives in you.

"'I consider that our present sufferings are not worth comparing with the glory that will be revealed in us... we ourselves, who have the first fruits of the Spirit, groan inwardly as we wait eagerly for our adoption to sonship, the redemption of our bodies'."

I stopped. "Debbie, are you expecting to die or something? This passage seems spooky. It's all about giving life to mortal bodies that die, and about bodies being redeemed. I'm here because I want you back!"

"James, I can be happy either way," she said. "Jesus is with me both here and in heaven. Go on, you haven't finished yet." And I read on. This time more verses stood out:-

"'Who shall separate us from the love of Christ? For I am convinced that neither death nor life, neither angels nor demons, neither the present nor the future, nor any powers, neither height nor depth, nor anything else in all creation, will be able to separate us from the love of God that is in Christ Jesus our Lord'."

I burst into tears and sobbed uncontrollably. I sobbed because I was moved by my wife's unshakeable faith that boldly stared death in the face without an ounce of fear. I sobbed because I was terribly afraid I might lose her. And I sobbed because I loved her so much and hated to see her helpless and in so much suffering.

That evening I accepted the McPhersons' invitation and continued my sobbing in their sitting room. They phoned several members of our Tuesday group and asked them to cascade the message so that people could pray. And they said they'd organise a special group to visit the hospital the next day, Saturday. Only a limited number would be able to enter the Intensive Care Unit at one time so they'd pray outside the ward. We agreed I needed to let the boys know, so I called their foster parents and explained the situation. When I arrived home I spoke to Jonathan and Ethan. It helped that I could manufacture a professional way of telling them their mum was ill. Otherwise I wouldn't have managed it.

The following morning I arrived early and again made my way to the Intensive Care Unit. I learnt that the overnight team had started to administer a different antibiotic that they hoped would quell the disease. Debbie had been mildly sedated although I could see she was in discomfort and asked the nurse to do all she could to help. I was in distress myself as I arrived in Ward 17 to begin my rounds. Marion stopped me and pointed into the ward where Martin had already busied himself. He'd come in specially to take my place. Everyone who knew us wanted to do whatever was possible to support us at this difficult time of our lives.

I was very glad they'd done so. Ward 17 and the theatre were no place for a worried, sleep-deprived surgeon.

In the afternoon as I approached the Intensive Care Unit, I heard a beautiful sound echoing along the corridor. Melissa and two others were singing gentle worship songs outside the ward accompanied by Matthew's guitar and Rosemary's cello. Gilbert and Elspeth were at Debbie's bedside. Bill, Albert and Sarah were in the corridor holding hands, praying. I joined them, aware that both Debbie and I needed the strength that others brought into our lives at this critical point. Eventually the McPhersons emerged, carrying a small bottle of oil that they'd used to 'anoint' Debbie. I went in to see her alone. I had the strangest feeling, as if the room was a theatre with many people watching a drama being played out, an audience whose sympathy and care brought light, life and laughter to a place of sorrow. Debbie was conscious but faintly so.

"Oh, my darling, I do so want you back!" I said, and withdrew her mask.

"James," she gasped, "let me go. My work's done." Gasp.

I looked at her, pleading, and wrung my hands trying to deny what I saw. "Debbie! You can't leave me! I love you so much!" But she continued, fighting back her drowsiness between pauses for oxygen,

"God's purpose for you has only just begun." Gasp…

"I wouldn't have missed the last eighteen months for *anything*…

"I could never have dreamt I'd find such a wonderful husband…

"God's going to provide a special comforter for you…

"And I've another word for you from God.

"You'll know when it happens…"

But she never explained. She drifted off and lost consciousness. I replaced the mask but she didn't resurface.

Those were our last words to each other. Some patients have an extraordinary fighting spirit that marshals every drop of resistance their body can offer. Debbie embraced death willingly. Only on reflection did I understand. The daily suffering that she had made light of wasn't going to diminish over time. She faced the prospect of a further slow decline which she'd have tackled with all her humour, grace and faith. But it would have been agonising to see it unfold.

-o-O-o-

Three days later, at 5:30 a.m. on Wednesday morning, she died. She wasn't conscious; I was at her bedside holding her hand. I left the staff to do their work and retired to find some decent coffee and a muffin. Sitting in an empty canteen, I fell fast asleep and awoke just before 8 a.m. Then I returned to the Intensive Care Unit where two doctors were completing Debbie's death certificate. One of them I recognised from the Female Surgical unit; the other was based in Intensive Care. They were debating the principal cause of death, and I overheard the former say,

"…but surely, wasn't the MRSA secondary? I mean, with her overall condition there was always going to be a high chance of contracting septicaemia of some sort. I'd place Multiple Sclerosis with all its attendant complications as the primary cause."

Death from a superbug infection is a serious event for a hospital to admit, so it was little wonder that the doctor wanted it registered as a subsidiary cause.

I wasn't having that!

When I identified myself as Debbie's husband who was also a surgeon at the Infirmary, I took both doctors off guard. I pointed out that on the previous Wednesday morning, a day and a half after Debbie's operation, she had appeared to be making a good recovery. As far as anyone could tell, her surgery had been successful. Then I explained my serious dissatisfaction with the state of Ward 9 and related to them how I myself had needed to be involved in cleaning it up. There was no way of knowing for certain where Debbie's infection had come from but what I'd witnessed had led me to suspect that practices in the ward were, to put it professionally, not of a consistent standard in a number of areas.

Eventually they agreed to record the cause of death as:-

- o   1a MRSA septicaemia
- o   1b Hysterectomy
- o   2 Multiple Sclerosis

I hated with a passion the 'No Win No Fee' posters that were displayed throughout our hospital. Such lawyers are, in my view, amongst the worst parasites of our society. But I wasn't letting the hospital get away with what I'd seen. They were going to pay, not because I wanted the money but because I saw no other way of making them clean up their act. I'd ask a reputable solicitor to take up a compensation case.

I cut an exhausted, haggard, lonely figure as I slowly made my way home.

-o-O-o-

I just felt totally, utterly numb. It seemed as if I was the victim of a cruel cosmic joke. Firstly God had played the most magnificent trick on me in answer to my arrogant challenge, and I had embraced Him as a loving Father. But finally the lady whom I had designated Miss Euthanasia had actually had her life ended! I looked around our lounge at the empty hospital bed on which Debbie had spent much of her days, and at her wheelchair. I looked at the featureless, off-white ceiling of our room. I felt as if I was being mocked. Someone had given us a beautiful glass vase as a wedding present. I picked it up and hurled it onto the tiled floor. I spent the rest of the morning with a brush and shovel picking up the debris. It gave me something to do.

Cards began to arrive in the post. I simply placed the envelopes in a pile, and refused to open them.

Texts appeared on my phone. I didn't reply.

I caught the train out into the countryside and went for a long, long walk. That helped.

Finally I drummed up the resolve to go back to the Infirmary to visit the mortuary where Debbie's lifeless body lay. In my concern to challenge the wording on the death certificate I'd forgotten to collect a little bag of her belongings that the nurses had put aside for me. Amongst these were her glasses and dentures, both of which I'd bought her in those early days when we had courted each other without realising, and her jewellery, bought for her when our love had blossomed. I asked to see her body. It was as if the corpse spoke to me, saying,

"Come on, James. It's time to stop now. I need a funeral. You need to move on."

And so it was that I dragged myself to the McPhersons and allowed them to welcome me. Gilbert recommended a funeral director whom he rang on my behalf, and we arranged the service a week hence.

Taking this step energised me to get busy and to organise myself. I opened and arranged my cards. I replied to my texts. I worked with Gilbert to plan the service and to make sure we invited everyone who knew Debbie. Amongst these were Amanda and Penny. I slipped another envelope inside Penny's, addressed 'Mr. Nathan Cooper'. Had time allowed, I'd have made a complaint against him after Debbie had left The Limes, but life had been too busy to pursue it. Oh well… he might as well have the chance to say one last goodbye to her. He had certainly had an influence on her life!

With a heavy heart I rang Granny. She wasn't downhearted. "Och, James," she said, "she was such a sweet wee lassie. But it isn't how long you were together that counts. It's the depth of your love." And she insisted I hold the phone whilst she fumbled with her Bible, to find Psalm 116 verse 15:-

'Precious in the sight of the LORD
is the death of his faithful servants.'

"James, don't shut God out now," she said. "He'll be doing something very special through Debbie's funeral. Let Him change you through it."

I wouldn't have been able to accept those words from anyone else. And it was as well that I heeded her. Five weeks later I attended Granny's funeral.

There was another reason I was glad I'd heeded her. The day before

Debbie's funeral my phone buzzed into life and I saw that Rosemary was calling me. She was at work.

"James, have you heard about Hilda?" she asked. Oh no, thought I. Not another one biting the dust, surely?

"Did you know she was in the same room that Debbie had occupied in the Intensive Care Unit? Well, the surgical team had decided her cancer was terminal so they didn't remove her tumour. They transferred her to Intensive Care to stabilise her before she went back to her ward. Anyway, the same group of us went to the Unit yesterday evening to pray for her. Gilbert anointed her with oil just like he'd done for Debbie. And today she's back in the ward but sitting up in bed, smiling! She says she feels so well that she wants to go home. They've arranged an MRI scan for her this afternoon but it looks really encouraging."

I couldn't sing and shout for joy but this news lifted my spirits enough for me to face the next day.

The Intensive Care Unit staff later said that for several weeks afterwards, that same little room had a very special feel about it. Patients in that room thrived in unexpected ways.

-o-O-o-

The day of the funeral dawned, misty and grey. Outside on the pavement the wind was chasing fallen leaves around like a sheepdog, piling them in huge mounds at the side of the road. I remembered how, this time the previous year, I'd been thrilled to notice the colours of autumn as I'd first experienced God's Holy Spirit filling me until I almost burst with joy. The autumn colours had come again, but with them a terrible sadness. After breakfast I pulled out my photographs of Debbie. On the funeral service sheet was a picture of her wearing her sombrero on the beach, her face expressing the fullness of life, sweetness, joy and laughter that so defined her.

I decided I'd set about to arrange them in albums. Yes, it was time to pull myself together, to face the task of disposing of her equipment and belongings. It was time to gather up all our mementos, parcelling some out to Jonathan and Ethan, then to begin life all over again. Looking into the future, all I could see was greyness.

The funeral was at 1 p.m. At 12:30 I was halfway through my photos and decided I must drag myself off to the church. Just as I was about to walk in, I saw the four people I was dreading meeting: Jonathan and Ethan with their foster parents. Somehow it was as if I saw Granny's face looking at me. I reached out, placed my arms around the boys' shoulders, and said,

"Boys, this is hard for us all. But we're your mum's family and somehow we'll get through – together."

Tears ran down the boys' cheeks. For the very first time since Debbie's death, I too began to cry. It was a relief. We sat down at the front, in the same pew.

At first I felt as if the whole occasion was happening around me, as if I was there but not participating. The hymns and readings were intensely beautiful but at first they didn't touch me. We started with the same hymn with which we'd finished the Guest Service,

'How great the Father's love for us, how vast beyond all measure,
That He should send His only son to make a wretch His treasure.'

Then Albert sang, *"Oh love that will not let me go..."*

Hilary read a passage from 1 Corinthians 15 about perishable seeds and corruptible bodies... I couldn't concentrate. Corruptible bodies? I thought of recent headlines about the South Birkenshire Police Force...

Debbie's Song was rendered beautifully by Melissa to Matthew's accompaniment, with Rosemary's cello filling in the bass part that I had originally played. I noticed many a tear in people's eyes as the strains of Melissa's voice sang the final verse. Matthew and Rosemary continued playing for two more minutes, extemporising in a beautiful way that recreated the atmosphere of Debbie's room in Intensive Care. At last the service began to touch me.

I noticed Rosemary's shining chocolate-coloured shoulder length hair as it waved to and fro, her fingers moving with increasing emotion to create a rich vibrato. Somehow this combined perfectly with Matthew's delicate finger work to create a musical picture of my beloved Debbie. Rosemary's dark brown eyes were moistened with tears as she poured herself into the music.

Gilbert had invited members of the church family to share special cameos about Debbie, and had chosen four out of the fifteen people who had wanted to contribute.

Matthew told us about the way she'd come to my first rugby match and urged me on through the megaphone, then enjoyed being held aloft by her James to receive her honours after the game.

Amanda told us about that afternoon when she'd gone to Debbie's room after work to share her sorrows, and how Debbie had wept alongside her. This was followed by our prayer together in the coffee shop, after which she found the strength to deal with her situation.

Terry told us how much the coffee shop staff looked forward to Wednesday afternoons. It had been especially hilarious when Debbie and I used to be there with all the logistical challenges of accommodating her wheelchair. But they all loved watching her drink through her straw when her eyes sparkled with pleasure. She had set a new standard in the art of gratitude.

Finally, Hilary humbly told us how she had been totally changed inside. It all began after Debbie and I had challenged her critical attitudes. At the Guest Service she admitted she had never known God as her Father. She wanted what Debbie so obviously had. Now that she'd accepted Jesus for herself, she'd known a joy she could never have imagined.

Gilbert's talk was based upon the 'seed and corruptible' passage. He explained that, just as a seed has to die in the earth to become a tree or a plant, our bodies must die so that they can be raised up glorious and beautiful. In our case, we shall receive a body like Jesus' after his resurrection that doesn't grow old. Debbie's poor disabled body was no more and she was to be raised to a glorious new life, lived in the presence of the Jesus that she so obviously adored. He spoke with a quiver in his voice about her courage and indomitable spirit, her mischievous giggle that we'd all miss, and the way her vulnerable openness drew people to Jesus and to each other. Finally, he declared from verses 54 to 57,

"Death has been swallowed up in victory.
'Where, O death, is your victory?
Where, O death, is your sting?'
The sting of death is sin, and the power of sin is the law.
But thanks be to God!
He gives us the victory through our Lord Jesus Christ."

We finished by singing John Newton's hymn, "Amazing grace, how sweet the sound that saved a wretch like me..." which Debbie had always said was 'where it all began'.

As the service finished I stood up and looked around. The building was packed. I saw Howard from the rugby team; Joshua; people from Debbie's self-help group; café staff and customers; a kaleidoscope of local people. Bill had been ushering, and had sent some folk up to the gallery. In the corner of my eye I noticed a figure disappear quickly out of the building, and had a sense of deja vu.

-o-O-o-

Things were all a blur as many people came up to shake my hand or place an arm around my shoulder. Again I began to feel numb. It was almost a relief to be ushered into the undertaker's car to go to the Crem. Just a few faithful friends joined Gilbert and myself; namely Albert and Sarah, Bill and Hilary. It was a swift, formal end that had to take place and we were relieved to return to church for refreshments.

With a great effort I joined Jonathan, Ethan and their foster parents. The boys' sadness was so plainly written on their faces, and the older couple just didn't know how to help. What comfort could they possibly bring?

Just then a lady in her late 50's walked into the room. I hardly recognised Hilda whom I'd always seen in a wheelchair. She knelt down at our table until I offered her my chair. Smiling all over her face, she took the boys' hands.

"I've just come here straight out of hospital. Your mum wants you to know she's fine," said Hilda. "You'll never guess how I know. I was very, very poorly and I was lying in the same bed that your mum lay in when she died. The Reverend Gilbert and his wife prayed for me to be healed. As I was lying in bed, I saw your mum sitting in the visitors' seat opposite me."

"Wasn't she in her wheelchair?" asked Jonathan.

"No, she wasn't," said Hilda, "and as she spoke to me she moved her arms and legs. She said to me, 'I'm passing on my mantle to you. As I've prayed blessings on people, now you must do the same'. And then I looked again, and your mum had gone."

"Was she a ghost?" asked Ethan.

"No, certainly not!" said Hilda. "I don't know how to describe it, but she looked much more real and solid than ever before. She looked very pretty and she wasn't wearing glasses."

It occurred to me that Hilda must have only just arrived and had missed Gilbert's talk about incorruptible bodies.

Then Hilda blessed the boys. As she did so, the huge dark cloud of sadness began to lift visibly from their faces.

-o-O-o-

I had declined the many offers of company from kind church family members. My parents had sympathetically invited me to stay with them in Durham for a few days. But now I just wanted to be alone for the evening along with Debbie's photos.

The funeral, Hilda's remarkable revelation, the kindness of so many people and their outpouring of love, all helped a lot. But in my heart was a huge, gaping hole. I had loved as intensely and passionately as it was ever possible to love. No-one could understand how that felt. I thought back to Debbie's final words about God sending me a comforter. I couldn't possibly conceive of anyone who could come alongside me now.

At 6:30 p.m. there was a ring at the doorbell.

The Best Man

Six years later, Maputo International Airport, Mozambique

Hello, I'm completing this novel on behalf of my best friend James. We're waiting to catch a flight home after our visit. I'm here with Angela my wife and our adopted sons Jonathan, 17, and Ethan, 14 who were, of course, James' step sons. I'm not sure whether 'are' or 'were' is correct but it doesn't matter. We regard ourselves as a part of the same family.

James and Rosemary are doing a remarkable job at the mission hospital where they work. Initially they came out for a six month stint with their delightful, cute little girl Ruth, now four years old. They returned home to prepare for their second child, and Rosemary gave birth to their son, a bonny young man who has just celebrated his second birthday. He is named after me. Now they're here permanently. It's a challenging place to work with very limited supplies of equipment and medicine. There are problems with an interruptible power supply, a generator that breaks down all too often and a water supply pipe that blocks up occasionally. More than once they have performed operations under candlelight.

You can tell that both James and Rosemary love being here. James explained to me that he and Rosemary have different specialist skills. As the principal doctor, Rosemary is an expert in general medicine and in the work of setting up clinics and organising field staff to run them. However, James' specialist skills are based around oral and maxillofacial surgery. This has proved very useful when they've tackled complicated surgical cases. She is busier, so James spends more time with the children. They both explained to me that they need all their medical and dental training and experience and a fair bit of improvisation. They've needed to be wise in understanding the local people and bringing the best out of them, and they've needed compassion by the bucketful. During their first stint they had to relearn how not to overreach themselves. They learnt how to pray together about their work and to pray over their patients. They had to remind themselves to exercise the gifts of the Holy Spirit alongside practising medicine. James says he often remembers what Debbie would have said about speaking over patients using tongues.

Little Ruth enjoys the freedom to run around and play with African children. There's a sense that every adult regards themselves as 'in loco parentis' so James and Rosemary are happy to take the risk of letting her 'roam' around the village and hospital grounds.

You might not have thought James could have fallen in love so passionately all over again with somebody so very different from Debbie. But he did. He says it helped a great deal that Rosemary knew Debbie and had come to appreciate her deeply. James is a 'culture vulture' and enjoys theatre, classical music and travel, tastes which Rosemary shares. Yet just like Debbie she's grateful for what life has given her, and has a thankful, positive approach to its challenges. Right from the day she came to faith at Debbie's birthday service, she knew that Jesus and his Gospel were good news. She couldn't keep it to herself, and she wanted to exercise her faith wherever possible.

They married about eighteen months after Debbie died. It took about six months for James' heart to heal, after which he and Rosemary became drawn to each other and soon became inseparable. They and I were a part of Patterdale Road's first baptismal class since the McPhersons arrived. The baptism service was a moving occasion which both James' and Rosemary's parents attended, so they met each other on the very day when James 'asked Rosemary out'. One of the most moving duties that I had to perform in my role as his best man came the day before the wedding when Matthew presented me with a card. He'd made it on his computer according to a set of instructions which he said were from Debbie before she died. It showed a path through a forest. At the side of the path was a cross tied to a tree. The path continued, and showed a man and a woman walking hand in hand towards the sun. Inside it read,

James,
If I have heard God clearly, you will receive this on your wedding day.
Congratulations to you, James and Rosemary.
God has joined you together and I am absolutely delighted for you both!
Have a wonderful life,
Debbie xxxxx

How could I know if it was genuine? I knew Matthew and thought it was unlikely that he'd make up a prophecy. I decided to share it with James, who looked puzzled. Then his face lit up in a spark of recognition.

"Ah, so *that's* what she meant!" he said. "Her last words to me were that she had another word from God, and I'd know when it happened. Well, it just *is* doing!"

What a wonderful comfort this was to James, knowing that his beloved Debbie was so happy with his new choice of life partner!

-o-O-o-

Angela and I had had a struggle to persuade the adoption agency that we'd be suitable parents for our boys. It had taken Rev. and Mrs. McPherson's best efforts, along with those of James, to persuade them. Ten years previously, Angela had suffered a miscarriage. The next year she was expecting again only for the baby to die in her womb after five months of pregnancy. It seemed like life was playing a cruel joke on us when she had to go through the process of giving birth to a dead foetus, then later she was told she wouldn't be able to have children. The adoption agency challenged us about our motives. Our own children, if they'd been born, would have been around the age of the children we were adopting. Were we just trying to plug a gap left by our own grief, or were we really prepared to offer a loving home to two boys?

Eventually we persuaded them. We reassured them that behind us was our church family which included adults who had parented teenage children. Also, their step father James, who hadn't felt he could take on the role of a single parent after Debbie died, was our close friend. He'd be involved in their upbringing.

And it has worked well! We're still in contact with Mr. and Mrs. Graham, the middle-aged couple who so kindly fostered the boys through those difficult months when they first went into care, then later when they lost their mother. They had held the fort well for two-and-a-half years. Once the boys came to live with us, they opened up completely new windows in our own lives. Suddenly our days were filled with seaside holidays, theme parks, junior football, cubs and scouts, maths homework, model making, foreign exchange visits, cycle rides, hiking in the Lakes… Oh, it has been so much fun! Our neat garden with flower beds, a manicured lawn and a vegetable patch was soon messed up by goalposts, volleyball nets and, in the summer, a water slide. The boys wanted a puppy which finished off anything that had survived them... but we love Millie dearly, and she has made our lives very much richer.

Sometimes James and Rosemary have joined us, especially at birthday times. James especially enjoys Ethan's giggle because it reminds him so much of Debbie's.

Both boys have sometimes been bullied, and one term Jonathan refused to do his homework. We've always brought these issues to God, praying as a family about our challenges whenever we can. We've found Albert and Sarah to be towers of strength and wisdom here, as we did the McPhersons until they left.

Gilbert McPherson retired three years ago after forty-four years in the ministry. His leaving service was a highly emotional occasion and he told his packed church that his final four years had been by far the best that he and Elspeth had experienced. By then the church had a small core of student nurses and young doctors as well as a growing children's work. A thriving youth ministry grew out of two remarkable acts of courage by Matthew, another story that will one day be told. Our new minister and his wife are young parents and have attracted several growing families, and have carried on building up the young medics' group. We have sent out two couples as missionaries, one being James and Rosemary. The balcony is now full on Sunday mornings and next year we shall begin regular evening services.

The church has a brand new roof and there's talk about an extension. Albert told me confidentially that the income of our church members today is less than the income of seven years ago but that our overall 'giving' has doubled. He is pretty sure that some of those who left the church in protest over our 'financial recklessness' could have written a cheque straight from their bank accounts to pay for the entire new roof if they'd wished...

James pursued his medical negligence case against his own hospital, settling out of court for a figure lower than he'd have won from a 'No Win No Fee' company. A condition was that he would meet the managers from the hospital to insist they draw up an action plan to rid Royal Somershire Infirmary of the most common causes of MRSA. With Albert to help him, he worked out the cost to the hospital of treating MRSA and paying out compensation claims. He showed it was about the same as the money they'd 'saved' by slashing the cleaning budget. That didn't allow for the suffering and human cost of the disease. Half the money awarded to him went into a trust fund for Jonathan and Ethan. Half went towards the Church Roof fund, on which it made a sizeable impression. James is very happy that since the time that Debbie died, there've been fewer MRSA deaths in Great Britain because cleanliness standards have been raised, awareness of the risks has increased, and hospital wards are inspected regularly.

-o-O-o-

I felt so privileged to be James' Best Man. Like him, I'd never had a close male companion before, but just as God had joined our souls together in grief, he joined them in happiness. I had walked with James through the days when he'd first woken up to Rosemary and was thrilled for him when they began to date. I wasn't at his previous wedding but everyone told me how special it was because of its simplicity. Rosemary's parents were quite well-heeled and took great pride in providing a generous reception at a hotel 2 miles out of town in a wooded glade. The music at the wedding was provided by a group of eight including Matthew and Melissa, using both rock and classical instruments. There was beautiful poetry including a verse specially composed for the service.

-o-O-o-

It was the last hymn at Debbie's funeral that broke me. I slunk out of the service and found a wall to sit on, then thought about these words,

'...that saved a wretch like me.'

I was certainly a prize wretch, and what was more, I needed saving. I sat in misery, oblivious to the passers-by and the traffic, for half an hour. I called work and told them I couldn't come back that afternoon. I went home and wrote a speech, then made a list. On the left was a list of all the mean, nasty things I'd done. On the right was what I intended to do differently. Then I made a simple meal for myself and Angela. It was a nice surprise for her when she arrived home at five from her admin management job.

We talked over tea and agreed that I would visit James that evening. After two phone calls I found out the address of his flat, and set out ready with my list and my speech. It was around 6:30 when I rang the doorbell. He was in. With a quiver in my voice I announced myself, and it was a great relief when the outer door clicked open and he asked me to come up. The door of his flat was wide open. I took a deep breath, ready to begin my speech.

I never got that far.

James threw his arms around me, and I responded in kind. For half an hour we both wept, wept and wept. His tears were tears of grief; mine were what I now know as tears of repentance. Then we sat together looking at James' photos of Debbie. I could immediately tell how blissfully happy they'd been during their brief marriage, and how Debbie's love of life had soaked itself into every little corner of their life together. Finally the moment came for me to show James my list.

James looked at it carefully and, for the first time that evening, gently laughed. He took a pair of scissors and separated the left from the right, then gave me back the list of actions. He picked up a wooden cross from his mantelpiece, a skewer from his cutlery drawer and some matches. He knew I was about to go home and said he'd come outside with me, and then put on his coat. Then he told me a story about Debbie and a lady called Mavis, who I now know. Mavis had thought God kept lists of our good versus our bad deeds so he could 'weigh us in the balance' at the end of our lives. It was only when she came to know Debbie that she realised that Jesus had died to forgive her sins. What a relief! All she had to do was to accept His offer of forgiveness and to place her trust in Him.

Together, we crossed the road into the park. James tore my 'bad list' into pieces and stuck them on the skewer which he planted in the soil next to his cross. Then he lit the bottom scrap of paper. Within a minute, all that was left was a few charred remains.

Somehow I felt I didn't need to say sorry to James for my meanness to him. I knew I was forgiven.

We met every day throughout the week that followed. James took me to Debbie's favourite park bench and we walked around the paths where they'd so often travelled with her wheelchair. On Saturday we spent two hours at the Trefoil Coffee shop, this time with Angela. We listened, fascinated, as James remembered the many conversations that Debbie had enjoyed there. I was particularly fascinated by the first coffee date they'd had with Amanda when James knocked over Debbie's drink... I couldn't help noticing the staff's affection for James as they, too, had fond memories of her. Of course we all ate sponge cake! And, as James used our time together to remember all that had gone on with Debbie, I came to know her too.

Angela and I joined James at church on Sunday. We had many questions but they were for later. We just soaked up the atmosphere.

Angela's abortive pregnancies and the news that we would never have children had been a bitter pill to swallow. We had thrown our energies into making our home comfortable and tasteful. I bought a greenhouse and we wised up on all things horticultural. We went on cruise holidays. Both of us were promoted at work to positions of reasonable seniority and went on management training. But it didn't fill the aching, yawning gaps in our lives. Angela suffered bouts of depression which she mostly coped with using medicine, along with the occasional fortnight off sick from work. I grew a shell around me that hid the grief and bitterness inside that I couldn't express outwardly. In particular I blamed God. I said he couldn't possibly exist but in a way I hoped he did, because I wanted for all the world to stand in front of his throne and scream one word at the top of my voice.

"Why?"

One afternoon a lady called Deborah Loveless arrived at The Limes in her wheelchair. As I introduced myself to her, I listened to the story of why she'd been sent to our home. I said, rather cynically,

"Oh good grief, God help you now!"

She looked at me and said, "Whatever happens to me, I believe God loves me deeply and every day I'm here I'm going to trust Him with every ounce of my being."

From that moment on, I hated her. I hated her with a passion. I hated it when she kept asking the staff to take her to her room so she could choose radio stations that she enjoyed, or play CD's on her machine. I hated it when she began to have visitors. It wound me up 'big time' when people began to come to take her out, especially when my staff had to get her ready. Why couldn't she just occupy a chair in the lounge and become a zombie like so many other residents? Why couldn't she be happy to eventually lose her marbles and become a witness to what I believed was the case, that life is meaningless? Instead, she began to 'get a life' which I thought she didn't deserve. I felt that what I'd most wanted had been snatched away from me. Why should *she* be given special treatment?

I was delighted when Penny came anxiously to my office one day to report that she'd heard Deborah speaking gobbledegook in her room. From then, I told people that she 'wasn't all there'. Clearly she must be going mad! Only later did I realise what she was doing. I myself now speak words out loud that I can't understand, as I enjoy communicating in my love language to God.

Of course I saw James as my arch-enemy because he spoke up for Debbie. I hated him for the way he had given her back her dignity and especially that he'd made her look beautiful. One of the meanest things I ever did was to discredit him when I saw him kiss Debbie. I couldn't believe the way that, four days later, I was completely outmanoeuvred. James later explained that my allegation against him was the best thing that could ever have happened. It forced him to declare his love for Debbie and commit to marrying her! I never needed to apologise verbally to James. A lot of unspoken communication happened between us.

At Debbie's funeral my hard shell cracked wide open as I witnessed the amazing outpouring of gratitude for her beautiful life. She'd had an impact on so many people and it was as if her vulnerability, her helplessness had acted as a magnet for needy souls. People witnessed to the way her giggle had so often channelled God's grace into hopeless situations. She wasn't a woman of many words but those she spoke were full of kindness, yet truthful and frank. Many people said she had a way of speaking God's words straight to their hearts. Her prayers were simple, direct and powerful. And here was I – I who had set out my stall to destroy her!

Over the week I spent with James, he gradually explained the Christian Good News. After dinner one night at our home, Angela and I took our first steps of faith and asked Jesus to be the Lord of our lives. We joined the next Alpha Course which we soaked up like blotting paper. Right from the start we set out our stall to follow Jesus as wholeheartedly as James, Albert, Sarah, Mavis and the other Christians who had now become our examples. James carried on spending a lot of time with us both, and with me alone. Amongst the other newcomers at the course was a young dental technician, Joshua, with his fiancée, a dental nurse. He had never enjoyed making dentures for any patient as much as for Debbie, and like me he'd been deeply affected by her funeral.

One Saturday afternoon James took a day off from work to see Jonathan play football. We offered to drive there with him, and found ourselves entering into the game much more than we'd ever have expected. Jonathan was at the centre of a dispute after he scored a disallowed goal. This led to him being very upset afterwards and disappointed that his team had narrowly lost. Most of us agreed that his goal was 'good' and that if it had been awarded it would have changed the course of the game.

Angela and I found ourselves sharing the way Jonathan felt, whilst we did our best to distract him so he didn't dwell on what had happened. We all agreed to go for a meal in a New York Italian restaurant to cheer him up. In a small way, Jonathan's disappointment seemed like a mirror of ours with the babies we lost several years ago. That day, a bond began to form as we felt drawn to the boys and they began to trust us. About a week later, James and I were walking in the countryside. He began to talk about how he wasn't happy to leave his step sons permanently in foster care. Yet he wasn't ready to have them home to live with him. At that moment I had a bold idea, and later on I floated it past Angela. The next morning both of us looked at each other and grinned.

"Let's adopt Jonathan and Ethan as our sons!"

James was delighted.

-o-O-o-

For a while, Angela and I considered changing our jobs for a more vocational type of work. However, we decided to stay and grow in the soil in which we had been planted. Our church has become increasingly lively; our jobs leave us free in the evenings and at weekends so we can spend time with the boys. They are flourishing, and Jonathan now helps at the church's children's club. However, I needed to make changes.

As I grew in faith, I found my attitudes towards both the staff and the residents at The Limes being challenged. There were things I couldn't easily influence such as the budgets and our staff's dismal rates of hourly pay. However, it cost nothing to thank my staff for walking the extra mile with residents and their families. It cost nothing to encourage them for good performance. And it cost very little to provide them with chances to gain qualifications whilst they were working. I enjoyed taking an interest in them as people and was delighted when Amanda told me she was going to be re-married, to Bill from church. We made sure they had an enormous box of biscuits amongst their wedding presents...

I began, too, to see the residents as Jesus sees them. Behind many of our elderly or disabled people's outward appearance is a story of how they've fought brave battles in their younger lives. I like to encourage them to feel valued again. We've started a scheme in which we invite friends and relatives who visit our residents to offer to lead an activity, give a talk or perform for us.

The church is included in this, and we've started a very simple Bible Study group that meets weekly. We try to find ways that our residents can contribute towards running the home and welcoming people, which also makes visiting a more pleasant experience. This is yet another example of how Debbie's influence has spread out like ripples in a pool.

-o-O-o-

So I want to finish by quoting from Debbie's favourite hymn, which is also mine.

'Amazing grace, how sweet the sound
That saved a wretch like me,
I once was lost but now am found,
Was blind, but now I see.

T'was grace that taught my heart to fear,
And grace my fears relieved,
How precious did that grace appear
The hour I first believed.'

I could say a hearty 'Amen' to every word, based on the first week following Debbie's funeral. But looking to our future in Heaven:-

'When we've been there ten thousand years
Bright shining as the sun,
We've no less years to sing God's praise
Than when we've first begun.'

I so look forward to setting eyes on Debbie again in Heaven where I shall see her in her glorious resurrection body. I know she won't hold a thing against me. She will simply be delighted that I am there, to know that I, yes even I, am an unlikely part of her wonderful legacy.

Nathan (meaning 'The Lord has given')

THE END

Acknowledgments

Writing this book has been a journey for me, its author, as I have experienced a complete range of emotions within the lives of James, Debbie and its other characters.

I'm particularly grateful to several people who have read the book and advised on its contents. These include my wife Jane and my friends Richard Brassington and Lindsey Buster. Dr. James Gerrard and Dr. Clare Donnellan have provided insight into the medical and hospital-related aspects of the story. I am hugely grateful to Professor Jonathan Shepherd, a distinguished oral and maxillofacial surgeon, for his encouragement but also his input and correction of my various misapprehensions.

I've appreciated the enthusiasm of our vicar, Rev. Marion Russell who also made several detailed suggestions that have enhanced my appreciation of Debbie's condition and her feelings.

I've tried to make the final version as authentic as possible but I wouldn't wish my 'advisory team' to be held responsible for any inaccuracies in the details. They won't have read the final version in full. This is, after all, a novel and not a textbook.

Enormous thanks go to Pam Dimbleby, musical director at St. John's Church, Rastrick, for composing the music to Debbie's Song and laying it all out as a manuscript with words.

Two ideas woven into the book originate from a moving radio broadcast by Rev. Dr. James Dainty in October 2016, entitled 'Compelling Love'. I listened to this shortly before starting to write. The recording can still be heard on Jim's website - just search Google for "Rev Jim Dainty resources." I'm grateful to the editorial team at Mirador Publishers. Sarah, you have continually encouraged me along the way, and inspired me to keep going after an initial setback.

There are three very special people who inspired this book, to whom I wish to dedicate it.

Firstly, to Ian Nundy, Senior Pastor of Vision Church, Leeds. Ian, it was you who identified that I could write, and encouraged me to take it up. Without your encouragement, I'd never have dared to compose this novel. Thank you so much for 'seeing' that I could be a writer and for helping me believe I could develop my skills as a way of sharing Jesus.

Secondly, to our friend Celia. You gave me the inspiration to create 'Debbie'. She's very different from you but it has been your love for God, your refusal to blame Him for your condition, your listening ear and your compassion, plus your patience in suffering that gave me the idea for this book. Unlike her, you continue to face the future with no foresight of what it will hold other than the knowledge that God will 'never leave you nor forsake you'. My prayer for you is that you'll read this and glimpse how much your faithfulness brings joy to God's heart and – as I believe – to the community of Heaven, just as Job did in ancient times.

Thirdly, to Jesus Christ and His people. Often I feel humbled and immensely privileged to have found such treasure and such love. It's too good not to share.

Maybe you, the reader, have wondered where some of the fanciful ideas in this book have come from. Almost all of the incidents I've created here are based on actual or similar experiences of Christian people and I believe the whole story _could_ have happened.

I hope you've enjoyed this novel and I thank you for reading it.

John Hearson, Brighouse, 2017

About The Author

John Hearson has lived and worked for over 40 years in Yorkshire. He is married with three children and a grandson. He believes that family life provides a rich treasure store with which to explore the glorious complexity of relationships. This, his first novel, is inspired by the life of a courageous friend.

Debbie's Song
Isaiah 54

John Hearson

Pam Dimbleby
& John Hearson

2

bund ance,_____ great-er than all the bless-ings of the mar-ried wife.

I felt re-ject-ed, scorned and re-fused, a-shamed, for-sak-en and__ con-
The Lord in an-ger hid His face from you. He pun-ished you to teach you to be

fused, "Oh why, my God, must I walk this way, af - flic-ted, with no com-fort in dis-
true, but nev - er will His kind-ness now de-part, His cov-en-ant is writ-ten on your

may?" Sing,_____ O bar-ren wo man, you_____ who have not
heart. Sing,_____ O bar-ren wo man, you_____ who have not

Lightning Source UK Ltd.
Milton Keynes UK
UKOW04f1609100118

315901UK00001B/18/P